YEAR OF THE CRACKMOM

"A novel so **chilling, brutal and honest**...we almost didn't publish it."

-C. Washington, V.P, The Cartel Publications

a novel by

V.J. GOTASTORY

PUBLISHER'S NOTE:
This book is a work of fiction. Names, characters, businesses, Organizations, places, events and incidents are the product of the Author's imagination or are used fictionally. Any resemblance of Actual persons, living or dead, events, or locales are entirely coincidental.

Library of Congress Control Number: 2009938646
ISBN: 0-9823913-1-5
ISBN 13: 978-0-9823913-1-0
Cover Design: Davida Baldwin www.oddballdsgn.com
Editor: Advanced Editorial Services
Graphics: Davida Baldwin
www.thecartelpublications.com
First Edition

Printed in the United States of America

Dedication

This Book is Totally Dedicated to
My One and Only Child
Gregory (J.R.)
For You Have Been Where Most Have Not!

To my husband:
Your words,
"I'll be glad when you write the damn book"

My words:
"Okay, I've written the damn book."

In Loving Memory of My Father
George Cooper

To God Be the Glory:

I am humbled and certainly gracious of the gift that God saw fit to give me. But it is not this gift of writing that makes me give thanks and praise. I am obligated to give God my best praise and my sacrificial praise because of my life. After several times of near death drug induced scares, I knew I was spared for something better. It was to tell others that just in case they were thinking about going down some of those drug-ridden paths, I was put in their lives to be a major delay or a roadblock. Either way, you have to get past God and me. So don't cross my path slinging, smoking, popping or shooting any drugs. Cause I takes my intervention assignment from God seriously. Because God was serious when he saved me!

"I ain't dead
I ain't done
I ain't scared
I ain't run
But still I stand
No matter what people here I am
No matter what remember
I ain't break (neva)
I ain't fold (neva)
They hate me mo'
Yeah I know
Here I go
No matter what Shawty here I go"

(Thanks T.I. … This song was written for me)

To my husband, my soul mate, **Edwin,** who kept pushing me to write because we often talked about my childhood and my time as a crack abuser. Never once did you judge me. You pushed me to open up, write it down and let it go. For your undying love, your total support and never ending encouragement, I thank you from the bottom of my heart.

Throughout every adverse event, throughout every beautiful event, you have been there. I love you Edwin.

My only child, my only son, the love of my life, **Gregory.** To say that we are close is truly an understatement. There are no words to describe the relationship that we have as mother and son. No one can take your place. No one loves me like you do and no one will ever love a son as much as I love you. You were with me through all and not once did you speak a harsh word to me or look down on me as your mother. For this, my beloved son, I love you for all eternity and the next. My greatest joy is hearing you and I laugh together and we do that often. My best friend has nothing on you as we confine in each other. I thank you for being such a beautiful son, both inside and out. Mom loves you J.R. I love you dearly.

My beautiful sister **Marveen**. You are my babygirl. I didn't know what I had been missing until you appeared in my life. Now, I can't breathe without you! You are my right hand. I pour out my heart and soul to no one but you. Your advice, your love, your hugs, your talks, everything that I had been missing from my life for over 40 years has now showed up and showed off. Go on with your bad self SIS! You were the first person I sent the first chapter of this book too. When you called me screaming in the telephone for the rest of the story, I knew then that maybe I just might be able to write this and just maybe I had some skillzs. LOL… Thanks for being such a beautiful, caring and loving Sister. God knew it was time for us to find each other and enjoy our lives together. After so many years of us not really knowing each other, God found a way to make it happen. I am so very thankful for his generosity in bringing us together. I love you Baby Girl. You are my heart. P.S. Please don't take that last drink and do the worm… I just can't take it. RAOTFLMASSOFFF…GIIIRRRLLL….!

I want to thank the following people for their continued support and love. **Keith,** you were there from the beginning. We are old friends from long ago. We had long talks about books and catering and other dreams of ours. Well now that I've written the book, you promised to cater so I'm holding you to that promise. Thanks for you love and support of my project. Love you Boo! **Sherrie**, my Princess and one of my bestest friends…You are my biggest fan. I think you were more excited about this than I was. You are my cheerleader and for that I love you. **Ursula, Derricka** and **Itty Bitty, (Jazmine)**, I want to thank you Ursula for being a great neighbor and good friend. You have been root'n for me for a minute now and for that I thank you. **Jaimon**, what can I say about you. You know I'm shaking my head and laughing as I type this. You are something else; you and them damned suspenders and that **Crass Ass** humor of yours, I love your "**Monkey**" ass Jaimon. **Trevor, "My Jamaican Guy**" thanks for the 8-gig flashdrive. When I told you that I was losing my work because the flashdrive I had was too damned small, the next day, I had an 8-gig flashdrive. Thanks for your love and support. You know I got major mad love for you. **Ann,** my "**Jamaican Firecracker"...** WHOA! You know you my girl. I love you dearly my dear friend. Thanks for your support and love. By the way, your ass is in my next book and don't be cussing me out about your character... Cause, I can't understand a damned thing your butt be saying anyway, especially when get to going in that damned Jamaican.... LMASSOFFF... **Butch**, my **oldest brother**, I love you man, your my heart! You mean the world to me. We share a bond that cannot ever be broken. **Tori,** my **sister-in-law**, thanks for your love and support. You've been there for a many other things that could go in several books...LOL. I love you. **Quentin,** my youngest **brother** I love you. We've come a long way since the doughnuts in the apartment. LOL.. **Antonio**, my friend, you are such a Cool Guy. Your cooler than fan.....LOL. Your smile is contagious. Keep it shining brightly. Thanks for showing me DC. Thanks for your support. **Valencia, Deborah, Dawne, Karen, Valerie, Tonya.** You all are my **oldest and dearest friends**... more than fifteen years and running. We have shared just about everything together... some more than others, yet we have shared, laughed, cried, gossiped and loved one another through all adversities and all wonderful times. Again, I love you ladies.

Gaston my only **nephew**, you make me so very proud of you. Your athleticism will ensure your place in sports history. I love you young man. You will always have your Auntie's heart. **Kaviah,** my **first granddaughter**, I watched in amazement at your birth. I watched you grow from that beautiful baby girl into a teenager. I marvel at this thing called "growing up" that you are doing. I love you dearly my first grandbaby, I am very pleased and proud of you. **Taylor,** my **second granddaughter**, your musical ability will put you in music history. I think you are learning to play every instrument known to man.... LOL... I am proud of you.

My heart loves you to death. **Deirra**, my **third granddaughter**, you are just as full of life as any young rambunctious child should be. You make me and Pap Pap laugh at your antics. You know no fear do you little one? I love you. **Brittany,** my **fourth granddaughter**, you are too funny. Stay out of stuff and stop hitting folks… LOL.. I love you. **Xavier**, my **"adopted" grandson**, you make me laugh. It is a joy to once again have a little boy among all the girls to rumble with. But please outgrow those nine hundred and eleven allergies… I love you my little man. **Sheena,** you are a beautiful mother and a great friend. I love you because you are simply Sheena, no drama, no fuss, no confusion and certainly no disrespect. You let me be Granny anytime I want to be. I thank you for that. But you are also a great friend. I love you Baby Girl, you are my Mommy Diva. **Mona J,** the "Hustler"…Girl you got your little hustle on the side. I remember the first time I took you to "Crossroads"… Girl, we had a ball! And then the second time when you ran that man away from the table by slamming your hand down talk'n bout" "She said NO". Didn't nobody talk to us after that!!! You are stupid…and that's why I love you Boo! What's your saying: "Get you some business!" LMASSOFF

I want to thank some other friends who showed support and love not only for the book but for just being some cool friends. **Sam K**, You always got a smile and something sweet to say to me in the mornings…., **Joelle G**. you are funny as hell. You good peoples. **Brian B** and **Willis G**., the I.T. Gurus who keep my computer happy. You both know how to please a woman… LOL.. **Shamia J**, didn't think I saw you in the magazine with them tatooes, but I saw ya! Hot tattoes Diva…**Derrick J**, a good guy raising a son and daughter on his own. Love you DJ. **Maurice**, Mr. Esquire, my lawyer friend (just in case.) We've been friends for a long time. You've always had my back. Love you Babe! My favorite and only Barbers: **Frank** and **Lavelle**, you two brothers keep my hair cut tight. An author to look out for in the future: **3rd** (Maurice). You got a great thing coming, stay focused. **Tameka**…You are the player of the year. Girl, you be kill'n em'. You always got a story and some juicy ass drama…I don't know what you got that hooks em, but you get's em…LOL… **Frederick,** my laid back and cool ass brotha. Teach me to drive that 530, cause I want one just like yours…You look good driven it boo! Love you Babe! **ZOE,** no body sings like you... Hit that high note for em boy! You need to be signed! Sing to me!!! Sing for me!! To all my other friends and family, I love you and thanks for your support and love.

To everyone who has been a part of my life I thank you for coming into my life and I thank some of you for leaving.

Charisse, Vice President of, The Cartel Publications, I found out just how really cool you are when I couldn't make it for the Christmas Book Signing Party in New Jersey. Your kind words, your empathy and reassurance was what I needed to hear that Friday night because I was so distraught. Thanks for holding a sista down. I am excited to be working with you.

To my extended Cartel Family, I have had the pleasure to be in the company of some of you throughout the Harlem Book Fest, the Grand Opening of the Cartel Café, several book signings and the photo shoot. I am privileged and honored to have made all of your acquaintances.

Toy Styles, Essence best selling Author, CEO, President and Mogul for the Cartel Publications, I don't have the words to begin to justify the feelings that I am having at this moment. I remember your blog on MySpace and I responded with a reply to the blog and when you returned with a second reply to me and told me that what I said sent you into the "Ugly" cry I was touched. Now the favor has been returned by you. When you called me and said you wanted to publish my story, I went into the "Ugly" cry. I am so proud of you for stepping out the box and building your own publishing company and then buying your own book store. The treatment that you lavish on your authors and the promotions that you do for the books is phenomenal. I am very honored and humbled to be a part of a hot new publishing company. We have no where else to go but up. I am a Cartel Diva and a Cartel Pimpette Baby, I'm pimp'n the hell outta my pen! Thank you for giving me this opportunity. You are Mentor and My Friend.

We are the Cartel Baby!

"Stop treating Street Lit like the stepchild to America's bullshit! I represent the hustlers, the pimps, the prostitutes, the abused wives, the crack heads, the unappreciated, the broke, the busted, the liars, the cheats, the single moms, the single dads, the homeless, and every other unimaginable thing you hate or choose to hide from. And until I see a change in a positive direction, my novels will continue to reflect a light on the American's Secrets."
T. Styles, Author, CEO, President and Publisher - The Cartel Publications

What's Up Fam,

Thank you, thank you, thank you!! We at The Cartel Publications humbly and sincerely appreciate your continued support. You are the reason we put out hits. We been in the game now for two years strong but it feels like decades. Your love of our novels has quickly ranked us as one of the best Hip Hop fiction publishers to date. So give yourselves a round of applause! Now, onto today's business.

*************WARNING*************

"Year of the Crack Mom" is one of the truest novels we have ever put out. This book is so official that I had to slap a warning on the front cover in my blurb. Although this is a work of fiction, this story is based on true events. The occurrences weaved within this novel are so detailed, we caution you to be prepared! Trust me, if you are of weak will, be advised!!!

Now that the preliminaries are out the way, we can get to payin' our respects. If you are a follower of The Cartel Publications you know that in each novel we pay homage to an author who has helped to pave the way or may be up and coming. This novel is no exception. The Cartel Publications would like to shout out:

Tushonda Whitaker

Tushonda has penned best selling novels, "Flip Side of the Game"; "Game Over"; "The Ex Factor" and brand new release, "Millionaire Wives Club". She is truly a vet in the game who continues to show us all how to get it done.

Aight' Fam, I'ma sign off now and leave ya'll to it, but remember, I warned you. Lace up ya boots and forward ya mail, you 'bout to go on a journey!

Be easy!!

Charisse "C. Wash" Washington
VP, The Cartel Publications
www.thecartelpublications.com
www.cartelcafeandbooks.com

My life changed the first year I hit the pipe.
But it would take another year for me to realize it.
By then, it was far too late.

Kaneesha Watkins

Reflection

Somewhere in between, I Kaneesha Watkins, became a crack addict, who turned into a five-dollar crack hoe. I lost everything! Yes I did. I lost all my self-respect, my fine ass features, the good sense God gave me and in between that, anything else that was considered morally right.

At first, the indulgence for that sweet drug was few and controllable. But then somewhere between the few became the craving for many and somewhere between the controlled became my total surrender to it. And then the monkey jumped on my back and rode that mutherfucka like a cowboy riding a bucking horse.

Once the first hit was inhaled and that monkey was released, I did all kind of things for the next blast of the pipe. This crack battle was some new shit that I was not prepared for in any sense of the word and the price of smoking crack was a high one to pay.

For me anyway.

My Fuckin Life

I was tired as shit from work and all I wanted to do was go home to my place in Baltimore city, fix a drink and maybe do a couple of lines of coke. That was our thing. I waited for my boyfriend/fiancé', Jarvis, outside in our old ass Honda Accord. He came bouncing out the side door of the bakery and got in the car.

"Come on, let's get the fuck outta here, baby. I'm ready for a blunt, a shower and some of that good pussy." Jarvis said squeezing my phat ass thigh. I reached over and rubbed his dick. It started to swell. Jarvis placed his hand overtop of mine and pushed it harder over his ever-growing thickness.

"Damn, boo, you ready for me huh?" I asked him taking my eyes off the road to seductively gaze at my man.

"I been thinkin' 'bout that ass all damn day!" He replied. I giggled and looked back at the road.

"Before we do anything, I wanna swing by the spot and pick up some nose candy. You wanna ride, or do you want me to drop you off home first?" I asked Jarvis.

"Naw, I ain't ridin' wit you. I just wanna get these funky ass clothes off me, and take a shower. I'll be waiting in the bedroom when you get back. Is your dad bringing home Lil Man or do you have to pick him up?" Jarvis asked.

"No, my dad is gonna bring him home later tonight. I think they're goin' to a baseball game." I replied stopping the car in front of our house and immediately spotting the paper posted up on the door.

"Why somebody always trynna sell some shit?" I said thinking out loud.

"What you talkin' 'bout, Neesha?" Jarvis asked.

I pointed, "Look at the paper up on the front door.

Whatever they're advertisin' I ain't buying." I said.

Jarvis was already out the car and at the front door. He snatched the paper off and began to read it.

"What the fuck!? I know this mutherfucka don't say we gotta move and shit!" Jarvis shouted. I rolled up behind him and snatched the paper from his hands.

"Let me see!" My eyes quickly read the words.

"Jarvis, do you understand what the fuck this is?" I asked him.

"Yeah, that mutherfuckin' landlord trynna put us the fuck outta here in two weeks." He stated.

"Jarvis, what the hell are we gonna do? A foreclosure? We gotta to find another place fast!" I shouted.

"Where the fuck we supposed to find a place in two weeks? Man...I'm goin' over to the landlord's office right now and find that mutherfucka. He ain't gettin' away with pullin' this shit. Fuck that, Kaneesha! Give me the keys and go in the house. I'll be back in a few." Jarvis said holding out his hand for the keys.

"Oh hell no, Jarvis! I'm going with you. That's all I need is to get a phone call cause your black ass is locked the fuck up. I ain't got no money to be comin' down to central booking to pick a nigga up." I told him.

"You ain't gotta worry 'bout me goin' to jail, Neesh. When I see that mutherfucka, he won't have time to see what the fuck hit him, let alone who hit him. I'm takin' his mutherfuckin' head off." Jarvis hissed.

"That's what I'm scared of, Jarvis, you and that temper of yours. Now, let's just go around there and see if we can work out somethin' with him." I coaxed.

"Fuck that, I ain't workin' out shit. I'm straight bangin' that mutherfucka on sight!" Jarvis and I got back in the Accord and drove to the landlord's office.

"Ain't that his car right there, Jarvis?" I asked pointing to an old eighties black Mercedes.

"Yeah that's it. Pull around the side of the building. I don't want him seein' us."

I parked the car like Jarvis suggested and killed the motor. Jarvis looked over at me.

"I want you to stay here!" he said.

"No, I'm goin' with you. Cause if you bang that mutherfucka, Jarvis, I want in on the action too!" I shouted.

"I don't want you gettin' in the middle of this, Kaneesha! I want you to stay here! I don't need to be worryin"bout you gettin' hurt." He said.

"Jarvis, ain't a damn thing happenin' to me. Believe that shit. I got your back. Come on, cause I wanna know why this mutherfucka didn't have the balls to come to us when he knew the damn house was going through foreclosure. That foreclosure shit takes several months to do."

We got out the car and walked to the office door. After several knocks and no answer, Jarvis told me to be quiet and stay at the front door. I watched as Jarvis silently disappeared around the side of the building. I tried to look in the windows but couldn't see anything. The office was pitch black inside. I was just about to go around and look in the side window when I heard loud voices coming from the back of the building. With catlike reflexes I was down the steps and around the back of the building in under two seconds and found Jarvis and the landlord going at it verbally.

"What the fuck you mean you ain't givin' us more time? How the fuck you think we supposed to find a place in the matter of two weeks? Where the fuck we supposed to stay in the meantime if we don't find nothin'? Huh? What we gonna do...come up in your neighborhood and stay with your sorry ass? Is that what we supposed to do?" Jarvis shouted in his face.

"Mr. Henderson, I'm sorry about this, but the matter is out of my hands. Like I told you, there is nothing that I can do nor can I extend you any more time. So you are going to have to make arrangements to move within the allotted time that was specified on the notice." He said to Jarvis.

"Oh hell no!" I walked up to the landlord and put my finger

in his face.

"Mr. Levine, I don't know what kind of fuckin' game you think you playin', but I have a son and a job. Just what the fuck was you doin' with the rent money we was payin' you anyway?" I yelled.

Me and Jarvis waited for the answer. Mr. Levine cleared his throat.

"As I was telling Mr. Henderson, the bank now owns the house and this situation is out of my hands. You have two weeks to move." He sternly stated.

"And if we don't?" Jarvis asked.

"You can either move on your own or the bank will send the sheriff to move your black asses." He retorted.

"What the fuck you just say!!?" Jarvis shouted.

"You niggers heard what I said. If you don't-," He was stopped in mid statement by Jarvis.

Next thing I saw was Mr. Levine's head being snapped back as Jarvis pulled his fist back after hauling off and cold cocking his white ass with a right jab. But Mr. Levine regained his composure and reached inside his jacket pocket and pulled out a small caliber handgun. He pointed it at Jarvis and then at me.

"Come another step and I will splatter your nigger asses all over the sidewalk." He hissed.

"You pullin' a gun on me, mutherfucka!!!?" Jarvis said moving closer to the landlord.

"Stop it! Stop right there or I swear I will shoot you!" Mr. Levine promised.

The gun was shaking in his hands and he was sweating above his brow. I pulled Jarvis by the arm stopping him from going any closer to Mr. Levine.

"That's right you better get his black ass. I don't want to use this but I will pull the trigger and blow your asses away. You *two* niggers have *two* weeks to get the hell outta my house!!" He shouted.

I watched spit fly from the side of his mouth and land on the hood of his black Mercedes. That did it. I let Jarvis' arm go, planted my hands on my hips and stepped in front of Jarvis. I leaned back on my left leg and got my neck ready to roll. I was officially in my "Read Your Ass" stance.

"You wanna shoot me? Then you pull that mutherfuckin' trigger right now!" I egged on, walking closer to Mr. Levine. He slowly began to back up while trying to keep his shaking hand steady.

"If you don't stop right there, I will have no choice but to defend myself." He stammered.

"Defend yourself? Look the fuck around. Ain't no body got no weapons but you, Mr. Levine. Me and Jarvis are empty handed. What the fuck are you defending yourself from?" I questioned.

"Well your boyfriend struck me! And I'm pressing charges!" Mr. Levine said.

"Pressing charges? You must be out your mind. You the mutherfucka standing there with a gun!" Jarvis shouted moving from behind me to my right.

"Fuck that! Kaneesha, call the police!" Jarvis instructed. "He ain't getting away with pulling no gun out on us!"

"Call them! I know most of the cops in this area anyway. And who you think they're going to believe, you or me? I can say that you two were trying to break into my office. And then you two niggers won't have to worry about where you're going to live because you'll be in jail. Do I make myself clear?" He said as he took his eyes off of Jarvis to look on the inside of his coat pocket for his cell phone.

Jarvis stole the moment and rushed Mr. Levine, pushing him against his Mercedes and snatched the gun from his grasp. Jarvis took the butt of the gun and struck the landlord in a rapid succession on the right side of his skull. I shook my head at the beating that I knew Jarvis was about to render on the man. He done fucked up now.

Mr. Levine tried to cover up his head with his arms but that proved not to be an effective shield of protection for him. He screamed for help as he slid down the side of his car and onto the ground. Jarvis continued to strike him with the butt of the gun landing blows on his mouth, sending two teeth and blood flying out. With each blow of the gun, Jarvis talked to him as if he was giving a child a beating.

"DO-I-MAKE-MYSELF-PER-FEC-TLY-CLEAR-MOTH-A-FUCK-A-HUH-HUH!!?" Jarvis scolded then went back to normal speech.

"You think you was just gonna pull a gun out on me and my lady and walk away from here like that?! Kaneesha come get you some!" Jarvis yelled over his shoulder to me.

I didn't waste anytime running over and swiftly kicking the shit out of Mr. Levine with my steel toe work boots.

"That's for callin' me a nigger. I'm nobody's nigger mutherfucka!" I screamed at him as I delivered several more severe kicks into the landlord's ribs.

Mr. Levine stopped fighting back after the last blow of the gun to his head. Jarvis had broken his jaw and I saw his eyes roll to the back of his sockets as he laid there motionless. Jarvis threw the gun, picked the landlords' bloody head up off the ground and wrapped his hands around his neck. He brought Mr. Levine's face within two inches of his own.

"Listen good mutherfucka, cause I know you hear me. I know where you and your family live. If the police come to my door for any reason, your lily-white cracker ass is dead. D.E.A.D...Do you fuckin' understand me?" Jarvis shook Mr. Levine's head until he steadied his gaze onto Jarvis.

"And you're gonna give me a month to find a new place to live. And I ain't paying no rent this month either. You heard with the fuck I said right?" Jarvis waited for the landlord to acknowledge what he heard and that he also understood.

Jarvis reared back to deliver another blow when the landlord's barely audible voice said, "Yes," stopping Jarvis in mid air.

"Good! You did the right thing. And remember your family!" Jarvis stated as he mushed the landlord's head back down to the ground.

My baby stood up and looked down at his handiwork. Seeing it was good, we got away from the scene.

We found out later that his ribs were broken and that it took a while for the ambulance to come. When questioned about what happened he told them he didn't see his attackers.

Turns out the old bastard was smarter than we thought.

Chapter One

Within three weeks, Jarvis found a place for us to move. A friend from our job told Jarvis about a spot in Annapolis Maryland that was having a move in special that month. Jarvis filled out the paperwork and with God's grace, we were approved. We didn't need any additional money other than the first month's rent. Me, Jarvis and my handsome son all moved into a two-bedroom apartment in another hood called the "Heights".

My son Hysear, who we call Lil Man, was eight years old. The name, "Hysear" means to the highest flame. His name was poetic because his little ass decided to enter the world on July 7th, one the hottest months and days in July that year. He has beautiful eyes that resemble mine, long lashes, soft little hands and short curly jet-black hair. All the woman tell him how handsome he is. However, he hates that, "mushy stuff" as he calls it. Being only eight years old, he's not into girls yet. Although Hysear is not biologically Jarvis' son, he treats him just like his own. Jarvis had no kids, which was rare for a black man these days.

Jarvis is from Cherry Hill, a violent project in Baltimore City. He don't take no shit and will straight step to you first before a word leaves his mouth as you have been exposed to. He's a caramel colored brotha with sandy curly hair and six feet three inches tall. Jarvis loves keeping that body tight. His muscles are well defined and his body screams it out loud and clear. Shit, even a blind bitch can see his muscles. His six-pack is ripped into that perfect "V" that sits right in his pelvic area. His physique makes me wanna drop to my knees and please him anytime of the day or night. Whew, let me get back to the story!

Our new spot was okay. It was clean, and it served its purpose. But the walls were too thin and roaches tried to takeover. Somehow, we made it home. We made friends quickly with our surrounding neighbors. There was a particular family that lived on the first floor of our apartment building, known as the "Dirty Bunch". They were called this because of how they allegedly kept their apartment. Two of the Dirty Bunch boys, Carl and William, quickly became friends with Jarvis. They also had a sister named, Rhonda who would often speak to me. One day Jarvis and I were coming home from work and ran into Carl.

"Hey ya'll, I just got a Mike Epps stand up comedy DVD." Carl said excitedly.

"Oh yeah? I didn't even know he had a new one out. We gotta see that." Jarvis responded tryin' to make polite conversation. That's where he fucked up.

"Shit, Y'all can come watch it with us then." Carl invited.

Naw, man but thanks. We just gettin' home from work and wanna unwind a little. We don't wanna hold ya'll up from lookin' at it either." Jarvis said silently hoping it would be enough.

"Shit...We'll wait. Y'all chill out and come down later." Carl insisted and wouldn't take no for an answer.

We really weren't tryin' to go down to their crib and we didn't know what to expect. We had heard stories but it looks like because of Jarvis' big mouth, we were about to find out for sure.

Later that evening Jarvis and I went down to their apartment and knocked on the door. We didn't want to go empty-handed so we brought some beer and wine in exchange for their hospitality. Carl opened the door and invited us in. We walked inside slowly as the apartment was almost pitch black and stunk of stale air. Only the light from the television illuminated the room. Right the fuck then I should have turned my black ass around and went back upstairs but I felt Jarvis push me in the small of my back to keep me moving further into the apartment. I made my way to the living room and tried to look around.

"Come on in." I heard Carl's voice say.

I didn't want to go any further into this smelly-ass place, but before I could say anything in protest, the rest of the Dirty Bunch came from the back of the apartment to the living room.

"Hey, Kaneesha!" Rhonda said.

"Hi, Rhonda. What's up ya'll?" I said to everyone else.

"Girl, have a seat. We gettin' ready to watch crazy ass Mike Epps. Girl, that nigga had me on the floor when I went to see him live down the arena. Wait 'till you hear the shit he be talkin' 'bout." She laughed.

"Yeah, I went to see him too but I couldn't understand a damn thing he was sayin' cause I was up in the nosebleed seats." I laughed back, and held onto the bag I brought for them as I plopped down on the couch. Jarvis remained standing.

Just as my ass touched the material on the sofa, I lost my balance and fell straight into a hole within the cushion. My ass hit that hard ass concrete floor and I thought I broke my tailbone.

"Oh shit, I'm sorry, Kaneesha!" Carl said as he and Jarvis grabbed my arms as they lifted me out of the hole.

"Damn, man! What the hell?" I laughed to play that shit off. The rest of the Dirty Bunch began apologizing, too.

"It's cool." I said. "No harm done. Just pick up the bags from the floor and make sure they ain't broke. We brought ya'll some house favors." I stated.

Carl grabbed the bag and took it back to the kitchen area or at least that's what I thought it was. It was so dark in there, I couldn't really be sure. I leaned over and whispered into Jarvis' ear.

"I don't know 'bout stayin' up in here, Jarvis! There might be something livin' in this raggedy mutherfucka." I commented. Jarvis just nodded his head in agreement.

We sat carefully on the other end of the sofa. Jarvis

chuckled as I scooted closer to him. Everyone had taken up a seat in the living room and was chattering away while Rhonda was busy fixing the DVD player. Now that my eyes had adjusted to the darkness, I took the liberty to look around the place once more. A beat up loveseat was pushed against the wall opposite from where we sat. On the wall behind the loveseat, a picture hung haphazardly. It looked like any minute now, it would say fuck it and fall.

The coffee table's glass top was non-existent and was just a frame. Why not just throw this shit away? You can't put a damn-thing on this mutherfucka anyway. What the fuck! There were no lamps, which explained why the only light I saw came from the TV. I couldn't look at the filth any more and pretend to be interested in what Rhonda was doing with the DVD player. Jarvis and I stole looks at one another once again.

"Here you go, Kaneesha." Carl said handing me a glass of wine from nowhere.

"No, that's okay. I don't want any wine." I said in my attempt to avoid a disease I could catch by drinkin' out of their glasses.

"Awe come on and have a drink with us." Carl insisted.

I reached for the glass tryin' not to be rude.

"Jarvis, what you want to drink, man?" Carl asked.

"A beer is cool." Jarvis answered back.

Carl handed Jarvis a can of bear. I took a small sip of my wine and waited for the DVD to load. I had no intentions on finishing the rest. Since there was no glass top to the coffee table, I put the glass on the floor beside my feet. Twenty minutes later, Carl wanted to make a toast to his new friends, Jarvis and me.

"Girl, give me your glass so I can put some more wine in it for you." He said.

Before I could reach down and get it, Carl grabbed it for me.

"Girl, you ain't finish the first glass of wine, go on and drink some of it down so I can pour you some more." I held the glass out in front of me and said, "No I'm good."

"Oh come on, you know damn well you want some more! Drink some down!" He insisted.

Trying to get him out my face, I put the glass to my lips and swallowed. What the fuck? I felt something in my mouth and immediately spit the wine out in my hand. What the hell is this? I looked again and saw that a large dark spot covered the center of my palm. A fucking roach! A roach had climbed up in my glass. Not a fucking baby roach, but a big mother roach with the fucking egg sack still attached to her underbelly! I ran my tongue over the roof of my mouth and felt nothing but slime. I started gagging.

"Kaneesha, the bathroom dat way!" Carl said as he pointed down the hall.

I ran to the bathroom and was horrified when I turned on the light. The stench from the tub wafted through the air. The bathtub was full of stagnant water and clothes. The tub was so dirty that I thought the basin was the color gray instead of white. The toilet didn't even have water in it. The bowl was brown and rusty and the top of the tank was missing. That wasn't it! The mirror on the medicine cabinet was broken-and the cabinet was hanging crooked on the wall. Floor tiles were missing in some areas and the sink was so dirty, that I gagged some more when looking at it. This was just fucking nasty! I turned around and ran back to the living room. Fuck these nasty mutherfuckas!

I returned to the living area and Jarvis was standing up waiting for me.

"Jarvis, we need to roll right now!" I told him.

"Baby, you okay?" Before I could answer him, Carl asked me the same question.

"Naw, man, I just drank a fuckin' roach. I'm ready to go!" I yelled.

"Y'all don't want to stay and watch the rest of the stand up?" Rhonda asked.

I snapped my head around to face her and Jarvis saw the

look on my face. He knew I was getting ready to get ignorant.

"Fuck no! I'm takin' my ass home!" I said as politely as I could. "And thank you for the triflin' invite." I continued to yell.

"Well, if you wanna come back down later, come on then." Carl said.

"Ya'll too nasty for me. Don't ever worry 'bout us steppin' foot down here. Dirty bitches." Fuck a polite!

Before I could say another word, Jarvis grabbed me by the arm and pushed me out their front door.

"Keep movin', Kaneesha." Jarvis said as he continued to push me up the steps.

"You said one thing too many and I just wasn't in mood to have to beat a nigga down tonight." Jarvis admitted.

We approached the last set of stairs before we got to the top of the landing and Jarvis laughed so hard he was crying.

"Woman, you should have seen your face when you spit that roach out in your hand." He laughed.

I was trying to figure out what the fuck was funny.

"That shit ain't funny, Jarvis. Dem dirty muthafuckas need to be shot livin' in filth like that! And we need to have our asses beat for goin' the fuck down there! No wonder them nigga's get talked about so bad, Damn!" I yelled.

"Man, fuck them dirty bastards. As long as you're okay, that's all that counts. Come on, I wanna blow a few smoke rings before Lil Man gets here. Besides, I've been waitin' for a phone call." Jarvis said.

I kept walking up the steps when I asked, "Who you waitin' to call?"

"Ummm," Jarvis cleared his throat. The trepidation in his voice should have told me that he was hiding something.

"Jarvis?".

"Yeah, Kaneesha?"

"Who is supposed to be callin' you?" I re-stated.

"Stone." He answered with contempt.

"Stone? Why is Stone callin' you?" Jarvis cleared his

throat again and put the key in the door.

"We gonna talk a little business that's all, Kaneesha." He explained.

"Hold the fuck up! What in the world would you want with that drug dealer, Jarvis?"

Jarvis opened the door to the apartment and allowed me to walk in first. Before he could step foot inside, I turned around and awaited his answer.

"Man, I ain't tryin' to have everyone up in my business." Jarvis said because he would be explaining while still in the hallway.

"You not answerin' my question!"

"Lower your voice, Kaneesha." He said ushering me inside, closing the door behind us. I stopped in the middle of our living room and turned to Jarvis again.

"Jarvis, what type of business you got with Stone?" I needed to know.

"Damn, Kaneesha. It ain't nothin' big. I'm just gonna talk to him about makin' some extra money. Maybe he could use another foot solider. Shit, I don't know." He shrugs. "That's why I'm waitin' to hear from him." He told me.

"Jarvis, when did you decide that you wanted to dabble in bein' a drug dealer?"

"Come off it, Kaneesha. You wildin' out again. You act like I'm pushin' major weight. I ain't even done nothin' yet."

"Nigga, lets get one thing clear. First off, you didn't talk to me about jack shit, Second, you sling any type of weight and get caught, your ass is gone. Third, you got a fuckin' temper and the first time some shit go wrong, you gonna fly off the handle. Forth, your ass is gonna need protection.

"So that means you gotta get a piece and I ain't feeling that shit either! Lastly," I said pointing my finger at him, "you got me and Hysear who love you and I ain't trying to buy no fuck'n black dress 'cause your ass is laid up in some casket."

Jarvis rolled his eyes to the top of his head and exhaled.

In an exasperated tone he replied, "See, this is exactly why

I didn't want to say shit to you. I knew you was gonna act like this."

"Act like what? You think I'm supposed to be happy that overnight my fiancé has decided to sling drugs part-time?"

Jarvis walked away from me and into the kitchen. I was on that ass though, not missin' a step. He opened up the cabinet and retrieved a glass and poured himself some water.

"And furthermore, what the fuck you need to be out there slingin' for anyway? It ain't like we at death's door or anything. There's food in here and the lights and gas are on and the rent is late but that shit will get paid before the end of the month."

He slammed the glass down so hard on the counter that it broke in his hand cutting his knuckles across the top.

"Shit, Kaneesha! You and your mouth! Can you please just shut the fuck up for a minute! Damn woman!"

He let go of the broken glass and snatched his hand off the counter and rinsed it under some cold water. The blood ran clear for a moment and then the red returned full force. The cut looked pretty deep. I grabbed some paper towels and wrapped his hand up.

"Kaneesha, listen. I wanna make some extra cash. I wanna get a couple of things. I don't like you drivin' that raggedy ass car out there. So I wanna make some extra paper to go to the auction and get a nice ride for you. Plus, I want some new gear for all of us and some paper to fall back on. I'm tired of workin' that whack ass job all day to bring home nothin'."

"Jarvis, that whack ass job is what pays the rent and keeps the lights on. I don't care about the car. I can always catch a bus."

"That's just it. I don't want my baby catchin' no goddamn bus. I'm tired of livin' fuckin' paycheck to pay check. How much money you got in the bank?"

"I don't know," I shrugged, "maybe twenty dollars, Jarvis."

"How much you got in your wallet?" He continued drilling me.

"None, I used the last for gas."

"And as the man of the house, who is supposed to take care of my family, you think I'm happy with this?" I remained silent because he was beyond angry.

"Listen to me, baby," he continued, "I know what I'm doin'. I'm gonna deal for a couple of weeks and put some paper up and then I'm out. Okay?"

"I ain't got no choice now do I, Jarvis? You done already made up your mind." Jarvis sniffed hard.

He turned around to cut the water off and grabbed and wrapped more paper towels around his bloody knuckles.

"No, but what I really would like is for you to have my back in this, Kaneesha." He softly said. He pulled me into his arms and looked down into my eyes.

"Whatever." I said melting into his embrace.

"I ain't about to let nothin' happen to me, you or Lil Man." He squeezed me tighter. "You believe me right? You believe I got our family don't you?"

"Yes." I said.

He smiled, bent down and softly kissed my lips as his one good hand found its way to my ass. We tongue wrestled briefly before he pushed me back up against the fridge. He smoothly slid the good hand down the front of my jeans and found my pearl. He gently stroked me with his middle finger making my hips wind to grind my clit against it.

"Yeah, that's it, baby. That's it. Get yours!" He cheered.

Before I could say another word, Jarvis grabbed my face and plunged his tongue in my mouth and worked it like he was deep sea searching for lost treasure. He continued to push his fingers in my wetness and rubbed his thumb over my throbbing button. I was on my tiptoes, against the fridge, getting finger fucked so good that I would have agreed to anything.

"You got a nigga's back right, boo?" he asked me.

And with precision and rhythm, Jarvis worked his thumb over the top of my clit and his fingers in and out of my pussy making me cum so hard that I instantly yelled, "Yes, yes, yes!"

He pulled his hand out of my still quivering pussy and said,

"That's what the fucks up. I knew you would come through for a nigga."

"Jarvis, you're a damn manipulator. You used sexual warfare to get what you wanted. That shit wasn't right." I said as I pushed past him.

Jarvis chuckled and replied, "You came like you was pregnant and your water broke. Look at the big wet spot in your jeans, girl." Jarvis laughed.

I looked down and sure enough my jeans were wet.

"I need to clean up and change." I said as I headed to the bedroom.

On the way down the hall I heard his cell phone ring. Jarvis answered it and then I heard the front door of the apartment open and close. Several minutes later, I returned to the front room and Jarvis was gone. I opened the door of my apartment and peeked out in the hallway. I saw Jarvis talking on his phone in a low voice. I was surprised he chose to talk out there when all of ten minutes ago, he refused to discuss his business in the hall.

I was dying to hear the conversation but I knew if I stepped out, Jarvis would go the fuck off. Better to close the door and wait to hear what he's going to tell me later. I might as well try to work with Jarvis because once he makes his mind up about something, he doesn't stop until it's accomplished.

Since Lil Man is coming home, I started dinner. Approximately fifteen minutes later the front door opened and I heard his voice.

"Moooom, I'm home." I dried my hands off on the dishtowel and waited for him to round the corner. My son came bouncing through the kitchen with his jacket halfway on and his infamous book bag dragging behind him.

"I'm hungry. What's for dinner?" He said looking around wide-eyed.

"Darn, I don't get a kiss or hello or nothing huh? Just what's for dinner?" I said playfully hitting him.

"Awe, mom, shoot!"

"Shoot what?" I stare. "And why do you always look like you've been wrestling in your clothes? Why can't you stay neat, baby?"

My son looked at himself and then shrugged his shoulders.

"We wasn't doing nothing but throwing Damon's hat around outside. We was playin' *Keep Away* with it."

I looked at my son and replied, "You know sometimes playin' *Keep Away* makes people mad."

My son swelled his chest up in defense.

"Shoot, I ain't scared of none of them boys."

I stopped stirring the spaghetti sauce and faced my son.

"Hysear, I just want you to be aware that everyone doesn't like to have jokes played on them. I better not find out you gettin' in trouble at school." I said sternly.

"You won't."

"Oh yeah, mom, Pap Pap said he's taking me with him this weekend. He's going to Pittsburgh. Can I go with him?"

"Yeah. But for now, go wash up."

My son rambunctiously ran out the kitchen down the hall as Jarvis had come in from outside. I eyed him briefly trying to peg what he may have talked about on the phone. He didn't bother volunteering any information. So we finished dinner and I had Lil Man do his homework in his room after he ate. There would be no peace in my home tonight until Jarvis told me everything about his new money venture and my new problem.

Dishes and homework done and Hysear bathed and slept so I slid over on the couch next to Jarvis.

"Okay, I don't know why you're waiting. So tell me what's up? And I want the truth, Jarvis. No bullshit!"

"Stone stopping by Friday night to see me. I asked him to come over here so we can talk in private."

He snatched a Newport from his pack and lit it. He pulled heavily and let out the smoke. I watched the smoke ascend to the ceiling and wondered if this shit that Jarvis was about to get in was gonna have us up in smoke as I listened to him talk.

"Well?"

"Well nothin'. Until he gets here and lays down some groundwork, there's nothin' else to tell you. You're gonna have to wait until Friday. You'll be alright."

I don't trust Stone or Jarvis right now.

But he was right, there was nothing I could do but wait.

Chapter Two

Jarvis and I went to work as usual putting up with the same old bullshit on our jobs. I worked at a restaurant that was new in the area. It served gourmet burgers with homemade rolls and baked goods. Jarvis worked in the bakery down the street that made the baked goods for the restaurant. The pay was just barely seventy cents more above minimum wage. I wasn't complaining too much 'cause it beat the welfare check I was receiving once a month and the food stamps that didn't buy shit but a two-week supply of food.

On welfare, after two weeks of eating *good*, the food supply would dwindle. Then came the noodles. I thought Hysear and me were going to have high blood pressure from all the sodium. I put every imaginable thing in them to make them different. I used boiled eggs, cheese, hotdogs and anything else that would make it into a meal.

Hysear never grew tired of them though. He ate them and never said a word. He was just happy to be eating. So I was happy to be working and collecting a paycheck every two weeks. Shit, one paycheck alone equaled what I was receiving on welfare for an entire month. My ass was thankful but Jarvis wasn't.

After work, Jarvis and I stopped by one of his spots so he could get some smoke. We chatted about the workday and what we were gonna do for the summer coming up. We talked about taking Lil Man to Six Flags and maybe to Ocean City but the problem was getting there. The raggedy ass car that we owned wasn't going to make a trip to DC to Six Flags or the Eastern Shore.

"We gonna have to rent a car if we going to Six Flags." I told Jarvis.

As soon as I let that statement slide outta my mouth I

knew it would lead right into a conversation that would only perpetuate Jarvis's belief that he needed to sling.

"See that's what I'm talkin' 'bout, Neesh. We can't even take a ride up to DC without wonderin' if this bitch ass car is gonna break down."

"Jarvis, all I'm sayin' is that we're gonna have to rent a car. Stop tryin' to turn this into a reason to sling. If you gonna do it, just do it."

"That's not what I'm sayin'. We need a credit card to rent a car and we don't have one."

"I found a place called Rent-A-Wreck. They take cash."

Jarvis looked at me quizzically. "Kaneesha, you fuckin' around right?" He laughed.

"No, I'm serious. I saw some of their cars. They're three times better than what the fuck we sittin' in right now!" Jarvis stopped laughing and wiped the tears from his eyes and I found his laughing offensive.

"For real, Kaneesha. I ain't about to pay for no rental that comes from a company called 'Rent a Wreck'." He snickered.

"Fuck it! You tell Lil Man that he ain't goin' no where this summer." I said angrily.

"Oh stop bein' so Goddamn dramatic! It ain't that serious, woman. Hysear ain't gonna lay down and die if his little ass don't get to Six Flags this year. Shit, most of the muthefucka's in the neighborhood don't even know what Six Flags is. He'll be aight."

There was something behind his tone and I felt he didn't care. All he cared about was slinging drugs.

"Every night, lately, he asks me if we're gonna keep our promise this time and not stand him up like we did last summer. Stop makin' promises to *my* son if you're not goin' to keep them!" I yelled.

"Wait, hold the fuck up. First off, who you talkin' to like that, Neesh? I ain't one of your girlfriends. I will knock your fuckin' head off. I'm still the man and I'm holdin' shit down. Now, I got this. I'ma get the money to rent a real fuckin' car and take *your* son to Six Flags. Everyday you give me a reason to do what I gotta do." He threw in.

I rolled my eyes at Jarvis and sat back in the car with a pout on my face. *Fuck him* I said to myself. *He better do what the hell he said.* I looked out the window as we drove in silence.

Jarvis's cell phone rang out scaring me out of my contempt for him but I listened intently. Lately Jarvis was having sneaky conversations that he didn't want me to hear. He was also talking in a code, which could only mean that he was talking to Stone.

"So when a nigga gonna get laced?" Jarvis paused to let the caller talk. "Word? Cool. You know the spot. See you then." He said as he ended the call.

Jarvis flipped his phone shut and put it back in the carrying case attached to his hip. I was still seething about the conversation we just had so I felt uncomfortable asking him what was up. But his secrecy was causing a riff in our relationship.

"Stone's comin' over tonight." He broke the silence with bullshit. I didn't respond and continued to look out the car window.

"Kaneesha, you hear me? I said Stone is comin' over in a little while."

"What the fuck eva, Jarvis." I sighed. "He the only one you still keep your promises to."

"Why you always gotta act like a spoiled bitch?"

I snapped my head around and mean mugged him.

"I got your bitch, Jarvis." I told him heated.

"Fuck you!" He hollered.

I knew then he was tryin' to start a fight on purpose. I guess to feel better about neglecting his family and our relationship, but I still couldn't make myself stop.

"No fuck you!" I yelled back and before I knew it I had slapped Jarvis in the back of his head. He snatched the wheel to the side of road, slammed on the brakes and stopped the car.

He got out and walked around to the passenger sidecar

door and snatched it open. Before I could react, Jarvis grabbed me by the arms and pulled me out of the car. He slammed the door shut, threw me up against it and got in my face.

"Bitch, I ought to beat your ass right here and right now! Why the fuck you hittin' me while I'm drivin'? Bitch, is you crazy!!? He yelled into my face.

"You wanna see crazy!" I screamed.

"Don't disrespect me out in public like this! I will beat you down out here!" He promised through clenched teeth.

I didn't give a damn anymore about the consequences. I snatched my hands out of Jarvis's grip and smacked him across the face. Silence filled our space and he looked fed up.

"Get in this car! And if you put your hands on me again and Kaneesha, so help me God, I can not be held responsible for my actions!" He spit, as he applied more pressure to my arms and my back.

He pulled me toward him, opened my door back up and pushed me down in the seat immediately slamming my door shut again. He got in and turned the key in the ignition. The car sputtered and then shut off. He tried the ignition again with the same results.

"Come on Goddamn it! Come on, Betsy!" He pleaded to the car as he tried again to turn the engine over with the same results as the last time. Jarvis slammed his fist into the middle of the steering wheel and then he snatched the keys out of the car and threw them out the window and into the street. He looked over at me and said, "Don't say a mutherfuckin' thing!"

He got out of the car and walked away. I watched him make a call on his phone. He stood outside against the hood of the car and smoked a cigarette. If we really wanted to, we could just catch a bus or walk. If we walked it would take about an hour. But I knew Jarvis wasn't doing either of those things.

After fifteen or so minutes, a black Range Rover pulled up in back of our car. Jarvis went over to the driver side window and began to talk to the driver. I sat in our raggedy car gawking at the truck of my dreams. It was the Flagship autobiography Range Rover. You couldn't see shit inside. Even the license plate had a tinted cover over it so that when you looked at it, the numbers were blurred. The Range was floatin' on 26 inch Asanti black iced rims. Who was pushing that mutherfucka?

Jarvis finished talking to the mystery driver and came back to our car. He opened the door and directed me to get my shit and to come on. We had a ride. Jarvis didn't waste no time getting back to the truck, leaving me to get our shit along consisting of several CD cases and our workbags. I felt like a Princess whose prince had come to rescue her and then I remembered that my crazy ass boyfriend was riding shotgun and I would be in the back. At least the bastard had the decency to get out and open up the back door so I could get in.

I could smell new car scent the minute the door was opened. I couldn't believe the interior of the ride as I slid into the buttery leather seats and inhaled the scent. I wasn't surprised it was Stone.

Stone was beautifully black because of his dark chocolate complexion. He had a thin precisely squared cut goatee. His eyes were big and penetrating and looking into them made you want to tell him the truth. His head was razor cut bald and his were manicured. And I had heard from MeMe, a neighborhood gossip, that his workouts with his personal trainer were consistent and efficient.

"Wow. This is tight." I said to no one in particular.

"Thanks." Stone replied with a slight Jamaican accent. "I just got her today. A nigga likes the best things. I take it you do to?"

"Yep, this is one that I've had my eye on for a long time myself." I responded not knowing if I liked him or not. After all, he was the current reason for my dismay. "It's on my wish list."

"I bet you would look great pushing one of these."

Just then Jarvis spoke up and I almost forgot he was even

in the truck.

"Yeah, it won't be on my baby's wish list anymore." Now I'm his baby. A minute ago he was manhandling me into the broken down piece of shit back there and now I'm his baby? "We gonna get one, just as soon as I'm put on." Jarvis said looking at Stone. "She's gonna look good in this."

"Yeah mon, she looks good alright."

Jarvis didn't hear his comment. He was too busy talking about business. I glanced up from looking around and caught Stone looking at me in his rearview mirror. He kept sneaking glances at me and smiling. Stone was giving Jarvis just enough focus to answer his questions, while keeping his real attention on me.

We got to our apartment building and before we jumped out, Stone looked at me with an inquisitive stare. I could tell he wanted to know was I interested. I gave him a look back that said hell yeah! I guess I like Stone after all.

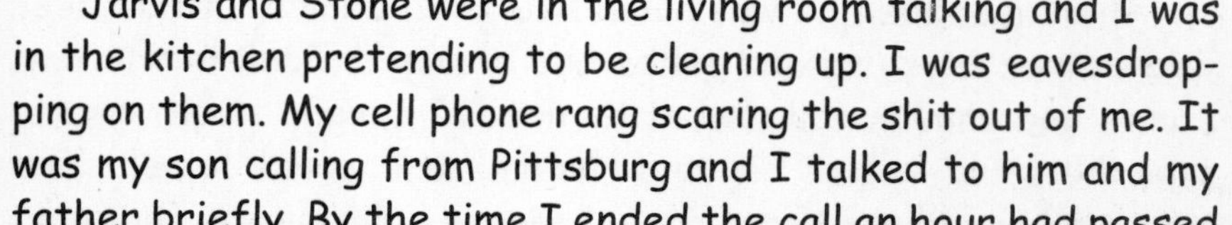

Jarvis and Stone were in the living room talking and I was in the kitchen pretending to be cleaning up. I was eavesdropping on them. My cell phone rang scaring the shit out of me. It was my son calling from Pittsburg and I talked to him and my father briefly. By the time I ended the call an hour had passed and I was angry I didn't get a chance to hear what Jarvis and Stone were talking about.

I put my phone in my sweatpants pocket and continued to clean the kitchen until I heard, "She holdin'?" Jarvis asked.

I wondered who he was talking about.

"Yeah. Come here, Reds." I heard Stone say.

"Okay." A female's voice responded.

I couldn't get out the kitchen fast enough. I waltzed into the living room and was taken aback by another woman in my home. When did this bitch roll up in here? I recognized her as a well-known Crack-head in the neighborhood.

Even still, Reds was a pretty young lady. Her skin was flawless other than a few red freckles that adorned her face. Her long red hair was gathered in a ponytail and gracefully fell down her back. Most people would say that Reds has "good" hair. Thick, long eyelashes and light red eyebrows made up the rest of her pretty facial features. She was on the thin side but she had a big gut. A closer look led me to believe that she was pretty far along in a pregnancy. She just carried it a little differently because she was thin.

"Who dis?" I questioned with my hands on my hips.

"Chill, Kaneesha!" Jarvis said. I rolled my eyes at him.

Stone looked over at me and gave a slight wink and then he said, "This is Reds. She's one of my associates. I called her to come over. She and I got some business to 'tend to. I hope you don't mind now, do you?" he asserted.

"What kind of business you talkin' 'bout, Stone?" I asked.

"Nothin' serious. She just droppin' off something' for me and Jarvis." He replied.

"Neesha, we 'bout to do a little bizzness. Disappear." Jarvis told me.

All of a sudden he was some BIG drug dealer. It had been years since he slung and times had changed. Back in the day, Jarvis had enough pull that if he needed a nigga to get a message, he could make a call and the message would be sent. But that was over eight years ago. Niggas is killin' niggas for sport now.

"Whatever, Jarvis. I ain't goin' nowhere." I said reluctantly.

I looked back over my shoulder just in time to see Reds lift her shirt up, reach around to the back of her clothing and pull out a huge plastic baggie from her stomach, and hand it to Stone.

She pulled her shirt down and I heard Jarvis ask, "So when you due Reds?"

"In two months." she replied."

What kinda of shit is that?

"Okay everyone, listen up. First and foremost, I need to know what the plan is since Jarvis ain't tryin' to tell me." I demanded.

"Kaneesha, let me holla at cha for a minute in private." Jarvis said.

He walked with attitude towards the kitchen area. I knew he was getting ready to lay into my ass but I didn't care. I didn't know that Stone was going to be bringing drugs up in my crib and shit. I followed him into the kitchen and as soon as I rounded the corner, he snatched me by my arm and pulled me into his face.

"Kaneesha," he snapped, "You tryin' to fuck this up?" He harshly whispered.

"I'm tryin' to find out what's goin' on! You don't talk to me anymore. I didn't expect Stone to bring his ass up in *here* to conduct no business like ya'll fixin' to do. And I *never* condoned the town's crack queen to come up in here makin' deliveries and shit!"

"Listen to me, Kaneesha. I'm tryin' to get my packages tonight. I told Stone he could come here with his business. It was my way of thankin' him for pickin' us up when we was broke down." Jarvis explained. "Or have you forgotten?"

"But why he got *her* bringin' shit up in here?"

"What you jealous?" I don't respond. "Look, we need him. We don't even have a car. Don't you wanna be able to go to the mall and get them designer bags you always got your eye on? Don't you wanna be able to get your hair done weekly? Don't you want Lil Man to have nice shit?"

I sighed long and hard. I rubbed my eyes and then my temples. When I reopened my eyes, Reds was standing in my kitchen.

"Listen, I didn't come up in here to be startin' nothin'. I was just doin' what I was told to do." Reds explained.

"Umph, if you say so." I responded. She came further into the kitchen and leaned against the counter.

"Well, in case you didn't catch my name, it's Reds." She

offered.

"I didn't ask you to throw it." I said sarcastically. She ignored my tone.

"Can I sit down?" she asked.

Jarvis walked out.

I shrugged my shoulders and pointed to a chair at the table. As she pulled out the chair she asked me, "You got something to drink?"

I wanted to tell her hell no but I handed her a cup of City Punch and Kool-Aid. City Punch was the term we used to describe faucet water.

"Thanks," she said gulping it down. "I just wanted to thank you for letting us handle our business over here. And as a woman, I needed to come to the woman of the household personally."

"Just don't stay long." I told her rudely taking my cup from her.

"What's up wit' you? Why you act like such a bitch? You get high?" Reds shot.

"I do lines, but not all the time. I'm not no where near addicted like you." I shot back.

"We're all addicted to something. Men...Drugs, something." She said rubbing her belly. "The only difference between me and you is that I know who I am. We're going to get acquainted real soon. You'll see."

"Doubt it."

Reds pushed the chair away from the table and got up. I followed behind her and we both sat on the couch. Stone and Jarvis seemed to be in a world of their own. Fifteen minutes later, Reds got up and started walking towards the back of the apartment. I jumped off the couch and shouted at her.

"Yo, where you goin'?" I questioned her in the hallway next to the bathroom.

"Neesha, sit down!" Jarvis yelled.

"Shut the fuck up, Jarvis!" I yelled back.

"This fuckin' girl, is gettin' on my last!" Jarvis said to no one in particular.

"I'm goin' to piss if that's fuckin' aight wit' you, unless you want me to pee on your couch." Reds said.

"I'm just checkin'." I said a little embarrassed.

"You ain't gotta be checkin' on nothin' concernin' me. I might smoke crack, but best believe I works for mine and ain't got to steal shit out this bitch."

"Then leave your purse. That way I don't have to worry about you puttin' nothin' in it."

"Girl, please! I got more money in my bag than you've seen in a whole month. I ain't leavin' my purse with you."

"Leave the purse or pee outside." I gave her an ultimatum.

"Here." she said pushing the large brown purse against my stomach.

When I saw the bathroom door was closed, I quickly ran to my room and rummaged through her bag. She had a stack of money that I counted out to be twenty five hundred dollars. That was big money for a crack head. While going through her shit, a small bag fell out. I held the bag of White Girl up in front of my face and shook it. Immediately my mouth began to water and my heart quickened it's beat. I could actually smell it. *Damn, I would love to get a twenty-five cent piece of this to snort.* Upon further inspection, I noticed the coke was beige in color. *Good God, this was good shit in my hands and I had to have some.* I put everything back in order in her purse and headed back to the living room.

Several minutes later Reds came out and met me in the living room. She gave me a knowing stare and sat next to me. We held a conversation. A long one. Let's just say I had a change of attitude, but not heart. I no longer cared what Jarvis and Stone were talking about, I met someone who could supply *my* need. And for right now, that's all that mattered.

Chapter Three

I woke up the next morning and Jarvis wasn't next to me. I didn't have a chance to think about where he'd gone because someone was knocking at my front door. I got out of bed and walked sluggishly towards the knock. It was Reds.

"What you doin' here so early?" I asked opening the door.

"So early? It's 2 o'clock in the afternoon."

I glanced at the clock on the wall and said, "Oh shit! I missed work."

"I got somethin' that will help get your mind off of work," she said waving a bag of White Girl. "You callin' out?"

I disappeared, made the fake sick phone call and rejoined her in the kitchen.

"What did I do to deserve this?"

"Nothin' yet. But we'll revisit it later." Reds said.

"I'm not into no gay shit." I made known.

She laughed and said, "Pour me some of that City Punch and let's get this party started. You got some gear right?"

"You ain't said shit. I'll be right back." I said as I walked out the kitchen.

I took off to my bedroom and returned in less than thirty seconds with a mirror, razor blade and gold plated straw. I placed the mirror on the table and anxiously waited for what Reds was about to do. I watched with anticipated breath as she opened up her prized bag of Beijing coke.

"Get a spoon!" she said.

I snatched open the drawer and grabbed the first thing that looked like a spoon. Reds took it from my hand and put it in her baggie and scooped out a healthy pile of powered beige cocaine and tapped it onto the mirror. The powder was still semi moist. There were several clumps of powder that just rolled off the spoon onto the mirror. My heart immediately started to race. Reds carefully refolded her bag and put it back in her purse. She looked at me and smiled. I smiled back. She was teasing me and it was driving me crazy.

"So, this make up for me rollin' up in your spot like I did last night?" she asked.

"I won't know until-" I cut my own words short when Reds pushed the mirror to me. I took the razor blade and hovered over the beautiful powder that laid before me.

I didn't know which clump to chop up first. I choose the largest clump ball to the left of the mirror. My razor blade made contact and like a chop-o-matic, my hand began chopping up the coke. The sweet smell that wafted through the air made my head swell. Reds sat back in the chair and watched me. I was like a prep cook with short, precision, and controlled cuts down across the coke. I was so busy cuttin' that I hadn't noticed that Reds had pulled out a purple Crown Royal bag and laid it down on the table.

As I picked up the straw and positioned it in my nostril, I nodded my head towards the bag and asked Reds "What's with the bag?"

"Nothin' you should worry about."

I snorted a thick line of coke up my right nostril first. Then I snorted the second line of coke in my left nostril. I stood up straight and snorted loudly again pulling any excess coke back into my nasal passage. Immediately, the effect I was waiting for appeared. My nose was wide open and I could smell a pile of shit a mile away. I felt the familiar numbness in the back of my throat. My appetite instantly vanished and I had to shit. Every time I snorted coke, I had to shit. I did my business and came back.

"Damn, Reds, that's some good shit!" Reds looked at me quizzically.

"You aight?"

"I'm good." I said pushing the mirror to her, which still held lines.

"That's for you, Kaneesha. I'm good. I'm not a snorter. I smoke mine." I sat back in the chair and studied her momentarily.

"Reds, I ain't trynna get all up in yours, but that can't be good for the baby." I said.

"You right. It's not good for the baby. And right now, I want you to get you some other business besides mine." She said staring at me. I stared back. "It ain't like you sittin' in front of me for an intervention. You done called out of work and everything for the love of the high."

"I was just making an observation. That's all. That ain't my baby and what you do *is* your business."

"Let's keep it that way." Reds stated.

"I'm curious though, what's in the bag?"

"You're determined to know what's in here." I nodded. "Well it's *my* gear." She said putting her hand over it as if to protect it.

As long as that bitch didn't pull out a pipe and get to smoking in my house, I didn't really care what was in the bag.

"Let me ask you something, Reds."

"Shoot."

"What you doin' with twenty five hundred in cash?" In an alarmed state, Reds scooted her chair back from the table.

"Bitch, you went in my purse *and* counted my money?" She asked.

I stood up.

"You know I did. That's why you left your purse with me. You wanted me to see you was gettin' it. So tell me, how can I make some extra paper? I ain't tryin' to sling or sell pussy but would gladly do anything else. Maybe like what you're doin'?"

"Jarvis is already on the payroll and Stone ain't gonna be puttin' you on along wit' your man, especially when you got a kid. Plus I don't think you're built for this." I immediately took offense.

"Hold up. What you mean by I ain't built for this? You sayin' I can't carry a package from point A to point B?" I questioned.

"Who said that's what I do?"

"I did."

"Well, it's more to it than just carryin' a package. You gotta know what the fuck your doin' and you can't be no pussy 'bout it either."

She didn't know shit about me but I let it slide.

"Why...don't you think Stone would put me on?" I said.

"First off you were makin' a big ass deal about Jarvis selling and the only reason Stone put Jarvis down is cause Jarvis is smart and knows his shit. Other than that, Stone wouldn't have looked at Jarvis twice."

I sat back in the chair and let what she said marinate.

I grabbed the straw and shot a couple more lines up my nose.

"Reds, how you get hooked up then?" Reds sighed and leaned back in her chair. She patted her little belly and shook her head.

"It's a long story, Kaneesha. I kinda owe Stone for somethin'. So this is my way of repayment."

"But you're gettin' paid wit' coke and money right?"

"Yep, sure am. That's cause I'm good at what I do. But Stone ain't my only form of employment so to speak."

I wanted clarification but I wanted to go about it another way. I had seen Reds around the heights and would see her go over to Me-Me's. Me-Me was another known crack queen who I liked for entertainment purposes. She would only let you in her house if you had something to share with her.

"What all do you do for Stone, Reds?"

"You not goin' to give up are you?"

I laughed.

"I'm a foot mule. I travel to different places takin' packages which means, I only transport on land. I don't fly. Those that do are called "flying mules." I drive to destinations, drop off or pick up."

"Who goes wit' you?"

"Another car rides behind me wit' back up power in case

some shit goes wrong." She explained.

"You ever had any trouble?" I inquired.

"Now that, Kaneesha, I will not and cannot tell you. That would put my life as well as yours in danger. I already gave up too much knowledge as it is. So I'ma move on."

"Reds, talk to Stone for me." I pleaded. "I can do this." I reassured.

"Kaneesha, have you really thought about what you're askin' me to do?"

"I still want it."

She shook her head in defeat and I knew she was breaking down. I think she was spending so much time with me because she was pregnant and lonely. Maybe she saw something in me she could connect with and I wanted to play on that.

"What if you ask him to let me ride wit' you on one of your trips?" I asked with hopeful eyes.

"I don't need no company wit' me. And bringin' another bitch along would only serve as a distraction." I pouted hoping it would work as it had with Jarvis. "You know how to use a nine?"

"I've shot a gun a time or two." Reds burst out laughing." What?"

"Take some lessons." Reds said.

"I will!" I lit up. I don't even know what my obsession was for wanting to be put on, especially since I fought so hard with Jarvis.

"And you betta be willin' to take the fall yourself if you get caught." she continued rubbing her belly.

"I ain't gettin' caught. I'll be ridin' wit' you. Right?"

"That don't mean shit." She let me know.

"If I get caught, I'm on my own." I reassured her.

"Okay, I'll talk to Stone once. But don't hold your breath, Kaneesha. Stone ain't easily persuaded to let new comers enter his world. You just pray that your pretty little ass makes an impression on him enough that he'll even think about it."

"I think I already have." I said smiling.

She excused my comment and a washed over glow took over

her.

"You mind if I take care of myself?" She said pulling a crack pipe out of the purple bag.

I pointed down the hall. "Help yourself."

She wobbled toward the bathroom and out of sight.

And that was just the beginning of me breaking my own rules.

Chapter Four

"Lil Man, come! You're gonna miss your bus!" I shouted down the hall.

Several minutes later, Hysear came running down the hall. I could hear his shoes thumping against the floor and knew that he had not tied his Jordan's like I have asked a thousand times. He hit the table with his oversized book bag and knocked over the milk.

"Tie your shoes, boy!" I demanded as I wiped the milk from the table.

I was in no mood to take his butt to school today because I had shit to do. So I was making sure he got the hell outta of the house on time to catch that bus. And when he was done tying his shoes, he took a few sips of the glass of milk that I gave him, grabbed a few cookies and ran out the door.

Jarvis was in the bathroom getting ready for work. Tonight I had the closing shift and although I hated it, it did have its advantages.

We were some stealing mutherfucka's at closing time. The garbage was always the last thing to pull at the end of the night and we dumped cases of beer, wine, chicken and steaks inside of them, pulled them bitches out the store and to the back of the building. Jarvis or one of my co-workers that I could trust was always waiting in the back with a car. We would load that shit up and haul ass.

Jarvis came into the kitchen and snatched a piece of bacon off the stove. "I'm gone, boo. When you get home later tonight we'll talk a little about my new job." He said grinning.

"Yeah, we'll do that." I said totally uninterested now.

I wanted him and my son to get gone so I could wait on Reds. After what seemed like hours, both of my men finally left. I finished the dishwashing and sat down in the living room to watch T.V. I couldn't focus on what I was watching and got up only to begin pacing back and fourth. The knocking at the door halted my steps. I quickly went over to the peephole and saw Reds behind the door. I opened it and invited her in. She went straight to the kitchen and sat down. I was on her ass.

"So?" I asked.

"Kaneesha, are you sure? This may not be right for you." She said a little loudly looking around. It seemed staged.

I sucked my teeth and said, "Is that what he said?"

"No, it's what I'm sayin'."

"You just scared," I said not sure where my observation was coming from.

She smiled, sat up straight and asked. "Did Jarvis go to work?"

"Yeah, he's gone why?"

She held up her hand indicating for me to be quiet.

She grabbed her cell phone to make a call. The caller picked up and I heard Reds say, "It's cool." Reds closed her phone ending the call. "Kaneesha, Stone is on his way over okay? So wait for him."

"Well, at least give me somethin' to chew on. Did he flat out say no?" I dug deeper.

Reds chuckled. "Damn, girl, you act like you borrowing money from the mafia. Why you_so amped?" She laughed.

"I'm not."

"Then you need to wait on Stone." A few minutes later he came.

"Go wait for me in the car." He said to Reds once inside.

She didn't hesitate. When the door closed, I caught my breath. Standing in front of me was Stone. He crossed his arms over his chest and looked me up and down.

"Let's talk in the livin' room." He followed me there. "Sit down."

He sat down across from me on the loveseat. I had seen Stone a few times but today it seemed like the first. The

Creed Neroli Saugave cologne that he wore jumped off his body and attacked my senses. His cashmere *Dolce' and Gabbana* hand painted T-shirt was neatly tucked into his *APO* jeans that hugged that tight, firm ass. The platinum cross that swung from his neck only added to his quiet arrogance. I caught myself looking at this man with a salivating lust. I put my head down and scratched the back of it, a gesture I use when I know I need to be thinking of something else. And if I looked at him any longer I might commit a crime of passion by killing Jarvis for not looking like Stone.

"I hear you wanna work? Is this true?" His Jamaican accent fell from his thick luscious lips.

"Yes."

"Ever done any ting like this be for?"

"It's a first time for everything." I said hopeful.

"Why? Are you bored wit' your life or broke?"

"Both." He smiled and I figured I must've answered correctly.

"I usually don't hire people for adventure, but I see someting in you. For me, it will be a first. But if I bring you in, you will answer to no one but me. You will do *exactly* as I tell you to do and not even your man can challenge that." I nodded in agreement. "I'm strictly 'bout the paper. I could give a flying blood clot 'bout any ting else. I have Replacement Killa's on payroll and I'd hate for you to meet one of them. So let me ask you one last time, are you sure?" I stood up and walked over to the loveseat. I kneeled down in front of Stone and looked into his eyes.

With a boastful and sure attitude, I said, "Hell yeah."

"That's what the fuck I'm talk'n 'bout." He whispered.

And out of nowhere, Stone grabbed the back of my hair and pulled my face up within an inch of his.

"I like you, Kaneesha. But don't ever fuck me over or I will kill you with my bare hands."

Before I could reply, he snaked his tongue in my mouth and I met him swirl for swirl. Suddenly Stone stopped kissing me and let my head go. I fell back on my ass to the floor trying to catch my breath. He withdrew a small baggie of coke from his pants pocket.

"Wanna a hit?"

"Yes, I do." I mumbled.

"Get some shit to do this on." He ordered.

I jumped up and went to the bedroom to get the mirror. I set it down on the table in front of Stone. He shook some coke out, cut up four lines and snorted up the first two. He passed me the mirror and I snorted mine. He put the baggie back in his pocket and I looked at the door. I hoped Jarvis wasn't doubling back for anything because nothing about this situation could be explained.

"Who you looking for?"

"Nobody," I lied.

"Then worry 'bout me. Come." He said. "And bring the mirror."

Stone was headed to the back of my apartment. There were only two things back that way, the bathroom and my bedroom. I soon found out which one he wanted.

"Come." He said again waving his hand for me to enter my bedroom.

As soon as I walked in the door, Stone pushed it shut with his foot and locked it. I put the White Girl on the table next to the bed and we jumped on the bed and removed our clothes. I wanted him and the White Girl made me feel like I was on ecstasy.

Before I had time to react, Stone leaned in and kissed me again pulling me onto him. He kissed me so passionately that I began to grind myself on his dick. He slid his hands between my legs and found my clitoris. He took his middle finger and gently starting making a circular motion on the tip of my clitoris. My pussy was getting wetter by the minute. We kissed and grinded on each other for several minutes.

I couldn't believe what I was doing and that I didn't care. He flipped me onto my back and got on his knees and began to lick my clitoris. He stopped and directed me to hand him the mirror. I reached over and carefully grabbed it. His tongue was giving my pussy a beating that had my legs buckling.

He scooped some coke off the mirror with a matchbook and then opened up the lips to my pussy and blew the coke off the matchbook onto my clitoris. Seconds later, my clitoris was numb. I had never felt this type of sensation before. He stuck his tongue dead center on my clitoris as I held his head in my hands and guided his tongue as he licked and sucked and licked and sucked until I was completely at his mercy. Stone was relentless with his tongue assault on my pussy. The added stimulation of the coke on my clitoris sent me into overdrive.

He stopped his attack on my clit and lifted up. He pushed my legs apart with his knee, lowered himself down onto me and pushed his hard thick dick into my pussy. When we joined together, we both let out a satisfied moan. Stone slowly fucked me. He kissed my neck and cradled my body in his strong arms, looking into my eyes.

He moved into a new position where he placed my legs over his shoulders and banged rapidly using the dagger move. He was in my pussy so deep and hard that I could feel him in my stomach. I grabbed his back and pulled him back down onto me to slow his rhythm and bring his body closer to mine. Stone obliged and we went back and forth in sync. Stone was fucking the shit outta of me and I could feel the start of my orgasm. I dug in his back with my nails and threw my pussy back on his dick. With two more thrusts of Stone's hips into my wetness, my orgasm was released. I lay convulsing on the bed with Stone on top of me.

When he left to go to the bathroom, I got dressed and went back to the kitchen. I didn't want this ruining business but hindsight is twenty-twenty. Minutes later, Stone came into the kitchen smoking a Blunt. He snatched me by my arms and pulled me into him for a kiss. My pussy was wet all over again and I wondered what he wanted with me.

"I like how you handled yourself." he said blowing out

smoke. "You never once mentioned Jarvis knowing he could come home at any minute. You took a risk and I like risk takers. So...I'm goin' to try you out for one job. You can ride with Reds. I have someting comin' up on next Thursday afternoon and..."

I cut Stone off.

"Thursday? What time? My son is in school and Jarvis will probably be at work."

Stone cut me short and said, "Kaneesha, this job requires that you be ready at any time and any day of the week. When I need a mule, I need a mule right then and there. This is exactly why I didn't want to put you on. You're goin' to have to make a decision tonight. You think about this before I feed you."

"I'll find a way to make it work. Just give me the job on Thursday."

"I'll think 'bout it." He said leaving out the door.

I had a chance and fucked it up. How could I be so stupid? I come to realize my desire to work for him was not about money. I needed excitement. I needed another life outside of being a girlfriend and a mother. As I was cursing myself out, my cell phone rang. I reached for it without looking at the caller ID with major attitude.

"What?!" I yelled.

"Is that anyway to be talkin' to your new boss?" Stone asked.

"I'm sorry. I didn't realize it was you." I calmed down.

"Reds gonna give you the brief. She'll be over in a minute."

Within a few minutes Reds came back over.

"Sit down." I did. "I ain't for no fuck ups. All you doin' is ridin' and watchin' my back. You need to be at the Deep Valley Inn at exactly 9:00am sharp. This is a local run so we shouldn't be out any longer than five hours. We're runnin' to the eastern shore, Washington County. Normally, we would do this thing at 5:00am but since Stone wants to let you shadow me, he's givin' you time to get your son's little ass off to school."

"Why I gotta go to Deep Valley Inn, Reds? Why can't you just pick me up here?"

"Kaneesha, it's already hot in this camp with Dubbs, Stones' competition slinging shit across the hallway from you."

Dubbs was another dealer who just happened to live in the corner apartment from us. He was small time and wanted to act and be like Stone. He even tried to get Stone to put him on. But when Stone told him to fuck off, he became his rival instead. There's something about Dubbs that rubs me the wrong way. It could be the awkward looks he gives me when I run into him, which I purposely tried to make few and far between.

"Alright, cool. So you gotta key to the room?" I asked.

Reds reached into her Balenciaga bag, pulled out several bills and handed them to me. I quickly stuffed them into my bra.

"Rent the room and wait. Don't bring nothin' extra, just you and don't open the door for shit! I'll be there exactly at 9:00am. I'ma knock once and then get back in the car."

"What are you pushin?" I asked.

"You'll see me sittin' in the driver's side. Just be on time, Kaneesha." I nodded.

"So I took by how long I was outside that he broke you in on the rules of engagement?"

She gave me a knowing look.

"He explained everything to me clearly." I smiled.

"Cool, but don't think you're special. He's a ruthless Jamaican with one thing on his mind and it ain't love."

There was something behind Red's words. And for some reason, I wondered what their relationship was really about.

One thing's for sure, time tells all.

Chapter Five

"Lil Man said he wants a pair of high top shoes from the Billionaire Boy's Club." I joked to Jarvis.

"How much are they?" He asked.

"About two and a quarter." I quoted.

"So get 'em." He told me.

"Jarvis, I'm not buyin' my eight year old son no Pharrell sneakers for two hundred dollars."

"Then why you bring it up? You already know what I'ma say."

"It's not the point."

"Look, he makes good grades in school and I ain't got no problem wit' him havin' 'em."

He hands me a wad of cash.

"Jarvis, is this money from your paycheck?"

"Yeah, why?" He asked.

"Well as far as I know, Stone ain't called you to do shit and I ain't seen no additional money rolling in."

"Well I guess you don't know much now do you?" Jarvis spat.

He grabbed the keys off the counter and bounced.

Something's up and I have no idea what.

I made dinner for us but Jarvis hadn't come back from wherever it was that he went so he missed eating with Lil Man and me. I called his cell phone several times but no answer. I tried not to sweat it and enjoyed dinner with my son. After my son's bath, I gave Lil Man some milk and two cookies for desert. An hour later he was in the bed watching TV and I went in to tuck him in and to turn the TV off.

"Son, it's time for you to go to sleep. You'll be getting up in a couple hours.

"Don't worry, mom, tomorrow is pizza day in the cafeteria so I'll be up."

"You like the food at school?" I asked surprised.

"Only the pizza." He admitted.

I laughed and turned off the light but before I left I asked Hysear the question I always ask him before he goes to sleep.

"Hysear?"

"Yes?"

"Did you talk to God and pray tonight?"

"Yes, I did, mommy."

"And what did God say?"

"He said that he is protecting you."

"Did he say he was protecting you too?"

"No, he told me he was protecting you cause you would need it." I froze.

His comment sent chills up my spine.

"Okay," I paused. "Good." I said still shocked.

"Mom?"

"Yes?"

"Please be careful." He stated as he stared into my eyes.

"I will, Hysear," I reassured him as if he knew what I was in to. "Why did you say that?"

"'Cause you look different. Like you not happy being my mommy. Are you happy being my mommy?"

"Oh God yes! I love being your mommy." I said hugging him.

He smiled and said, "And I'm happy being your Lil Man. Goodnight."

I released my embrace and walked out of his bedroom and back to mine. We just had a strange conversation and it bothered me. Eventually I shrug it off and got ready for bed.

Many hours later Jarvis trying to sneak into the bed awaked me. When I glanced at the clock I saw it was 2:30am.

Jarvis turned his back to me and pulled the covers up over his head and he smelled funny. It wasn't a sexual smell. It smelled more like a perfumed cigarette. I was too tired to deal with him now. I'll make dealing with him in the morning the first thing I do.

Chapter Six

I served Hysear his breakfast and I saw him off to school. As soon as the door closed behind my son, I confronted Jarvis.

"Jarvis, you didn't come home last night 'till way after two o'clock. That ain't like you." I started in with my back to him as I washed the breakfast dishes.

"I was out, Neesha." he replied while opening the fridge and sticking his head in it. And I'm sick of you bein' in my shit."

"Yeah, nigga, I know you was out. But out where?"

"I was out wit' some friends, Neesh." He sighed. "That's it and that's all. We smoked and drank a little and it got late. I got home when I could."

"Well, what was you smokin' cause it was all over you last night. That couldn't have been no Ganja smellin' like that."

Jarvis leaned against the counter and said, "I didn't say that it was."

"Well, what was it?"

"Coke." he replied looking into my eyes. He wanted to fight me but why?

"Coke? What the hell you mean Coke, Jarvis?"

"Coke, Kaneesha, C.O.K.E. I smoked some Coke." I immediately snatched my hands out of the water and faced him.

"Like in freebasing, baseballin', hittin' the pipe or all the above?" I asked needing clarification.

"I smoked a little piece of crack, Neesh. Nothin' major! Just wanted to try somethin' different." He admitted drinking some milk before putting the cup in the sink. He grabbed a napkin and wiped his hands. "So stop trippin."

Did this nigga just say, nothing major and he wanted to try something different by smoking crack? Is this mutherfucka for real?

"Somethin' different? Tryin' something different is buying another type of beer, alcohol, or a new brand of cigarettes. It ain't smoking crack, nigga! What the fuck is wrong wit' you?"

Jarvis immediately went into defense mode.

"Stop bein' a drama queen. You sniff, so we in the same boat!" He threw at me.

"No the fuck we not either!"

"You fuckin' delusional! We both do drugs, so it is the same thing, Kaneesha." He said. "That's why I don't talk to you no more 'cause you think you better than me when you not."

"Better than you?"

"You heard what the fuck I said. I'm sick of your shit. So I'ma ask you, do you want to be the man in this relationship?" He asked nodding his head.

"I'll do a damn better job than you!"

"Then be it," he said throwing a napkin he had in his hand in my face. "'Cause I'm outta here."

As he had done a lot lately, he left out and slammed the door.

I thought about bringing it up again later but decided to drop the subject. Besides, I too had my own secrets. In a few days, I would be doing my first job for Stone behind Jarvis's back.

I would have to have faith in Reds with this job and that wasn't like me. Besides, I didn't even know here. But she did seem to know what the fuck she was doing. All of a sudden I became lightheaded and the pit of my stomach churned. I sure hope I know what I'm doing.

Chapter Seven

"Welcome to Deep Valley Inn. How long will you be staying?" the clerk asked.

"Just today." I replied fidgeting with my purse. I was more nervous than I thought.

"Okay, let me see what we have available," she said as she typed away on the keyboard and looked on the computer for a vacant room.

I took the time to look around the lobby. The wrong shit was running through my mind like lying to Jarvis. Because as much as he got on my nerves, he was still my best friend and I felt an overwhelming sense of betrayal.

This morning when he asked me what I was going to do on my day off, I told him that I was going to take Reds to a doctor's appointment. He looked at me like I was crazy until I convinced him that me and Reds had been talking and getting to know one another. Which was the truth. Reds and I had been texting and talking non-stop for the past week. What we were talking about is a different story.

"Okay, I have room number 312 open. I hope you will find everything to your liking. The ice machine is down the hall to the right," she pointed, "and the pool is on the first floor past the work out area. How would you like to pay for this today?" She cheerfully asked.

"Cash."

"Okay that's one-hundred fifty two dollars. That includes the taxes. However, if you use the phone for any calls outside of the local area there will be an additional charge. There is also Wi-Fi service that is provided free of charge. Room service is excellent and the food is great. Would you be needing anything else, Ms. Anderson?"

Damn this bitch is long winded. "No, I'm fine."

"Great. Here is your information along with your card keys and oh yeah, let me give you your ID back. I see you're from Michigan. I went to school there. Did you?"

"No, I moved there a couple years ago." I lied.

"Are you on vacation here in Maryland?"

Okay, a bitch was asking too many questions now. I took the papers, the card key and the fake I.D. from her hands and said, "Thanks."

I walked abruptly out of the lobby. If something kicked off, and she was subpoenaed, she'd most definitely be able to identify me. I got back in the car and went around to the left of the building where my room was located. My watch read, 8:30am. I quickly got out of the car and found my room. When I walked in I was pleasantly surprised at the room's expansiveness. From the outside, it didn't look that big. I did a once over checking out the room from the front of the door to the bedroom and noticed it was beautifully decorated. It was a shame that it would go to waste since I was only here to wait for a knock at the door before leaving. I pulled the covers back on the bed, rearranged the pillows and pushed the covers around. I then sat on the sofa and waited for the one knock. I made sure all the paperwork was safely in my purse along with the hotel key card.

The knock at the door made me jump. I grabbed my purse and got to the door. I stood there briefly regulating my breathing before I opened it and walked out. I walked down the hall expecting to find Reds walking in front of me. Instead I saw a man dressed in Army fatigues swiftly walking several hundred yards ahead. As I got to the elevator, expecting to find him waiting, I didn't. The door to the elevator was slowly shutting. I punched the button and waited for the slow ass elevator to make its stop on floor three. Once outside, I scanned the lot. First to my left and then to my right. I didn't see any signs of Reds. Just as I was about to pull out my phone a silver Maxima pulled up. Reds was sitting behind the wheel. I quickly got in and before I could close the door, she pulled off.

"Damn, bitch, can a nigga get in good." I laughed.

"Close the door so your ass don't fall out cause I ain't stopping to take a bitch to the hospital." Reds cut the corner speeding out of the parking lot. She cut the corner so sharp I swore we were on two wheels.

"Shit, slow down, girl. We on time ain't we?" I asked.

"Relax, I got this. And yes, we on time. I'm just getting out into traffic that's all. It's still rush hour. I got us some coffee. That one's yours." She said pointing at the second cup in the cup holder. "I got it with cream and four sugars."

"Thanks, I need this." I gratefully accepted.

"You nervous?"

"Not about the run." I assured her.

"About misleading Jarvis?"

"Yeah. If he finds out he's goin' kirk the fuck out."

"As long as you do what the fuck you're supposed to do, you ain't got shit to worry 'bout. For real, all you should be worried about is Stone. Jarvis will be fine."

"Just drive, Reds." I told her not wanting to talk about it anymore.

She looked over at me and I looked out the window and let my mind wander. We drove in silence for about ten minutes when Reds let out a small yelp.

"What's wrong? You okay?" I asked genuinely concerned.

"My stomach, I felt a sharp pain." Reds gripped the steering wheel tighter.

"Pull over!" I shouted.

"No, Kaneesha, we gotta schedule to keep! I can't be late."

Buckled over the steering wheel, she appeared in extreme pain. The car swerved barely missing another vehicle.

"Stop this mutherfucka right now, Reds! You ain't killin' my black ass. Pull over now!" I yelled.

I guess she wasn't physically able to argue with me so we got out and traded places. The moment I did, I noticed a black Navigator pull about fifteen yards away from us and Reds phone rang.

"Yeah," she answered. "No, everything is cool. I'm in a little pain but I'm good. We're staying on schedule. Let's just keep goin' to grandma's!"

Reds closed her phone. I looked over at her and said, "Reds, do we need to stop and get you something?"

"Like what, Kaneesha!" she panted back.

"Oh I don't know, maybe an aspirin or a damn doctor! You can't travel like this! How you gonna make the run like this, Reds? Whoever you droppin' off to might mistake you're pain look as nervousness and become uneasy. That ain't the signal we want to give is it?"

Reds began to pant through her nose. With gapped breaths she replied, "Okay, okay, you're gonna have to make the drop yourself."

I gripped the steering wheel and said, "I got it."

I knew this was my only chance to prove myself and I had to man up. I was uneasy because this was not how it was supposed to happen but fuck it. Reds had explained earlier that Stone had already told the customer, that I would be accompanying her today on the run. So there should be no problem. I looked in the rearview mirror and didn't see the truck behind us.

"Reds, how come the Navigator isn't following us?"

"Because there's a tracking device on the car so they don't need to be all up our asses. They know what they doin'. We just need to focus on gettin' to our destination." She paused and breathed heavily again. "Pull off at the next exit."

I did and we drove another hour with Reds in pain. An hour and thirty minutes later, Reds told me to pull over so we could make the switch. She got in the back seat and lifted up her shirt. She pulled the tape from around her belly and pulled off several packages that were duct taped all around her waist. They were so flat, you would have never guessed Reds was strapped up.

What really got me was the liquid escaping her legs, rolling onto the leather seats and then the floor.

"Your water broke! You gotta get to the hospital."

"Fuck that!" She said panting. "This ain't been the first baby I had and it probably won't be the last."

"You didn't say you had any kids."

"I don't," she said looking at me. "I said I had babies, I ain't keep none of 'em. Now stop asking questions. You're gonna have to put this shit under your shirt before going in. Go to the trunk and get the clear packing tape. And there should be some scissors on the side." I scampered to the back and retrieved the items.

"Lift up your shirt." She commanded raising from the backseat.

I did as I was told.

"Hold this." she said pressing a package against my stomach. She tore off a long piece of tape and put it across the package.

"Hold these two on your sides." I pressed the remaining packages on my body, one on the left and one on the right. Reds pulled another piece of duct tape off the roll and began to wrap it around the packages and around my waist. When she was satisfied with her work she nodded her head in approval.

"Get out and put your shirt down." I did and she got out with me holding her belly.

"Good, looks like nothin's on you." She said.

"Damn, Reds, I can't breathe and I can hardly move."

"Don't worry. You won't be in there long. The man you're going to see is Carlos. He knows me and probably won't expect you, so I have texted the ride-along so they can send word to Stone that we have switched. I'm waiting for the confirmation now. So hold on." I stood outside the car sweating because of the plastic tape stuck to my skin. Reds' phone rang out and she answered.

"Okay, Kaneesha. You're on. You know what you're supposed to do right?"

"Yeah." I nodded.

"Okay, let's rock and roll."

I got back in the driver's side and Reds got back in the passenger seat. She gave me directions that led to a mansion. There was a gate that strangers could not enter unless welcomed in by the owner of the home. I drove up to the gate and the guard waved us in. I nervously continued up the winding driveway towards the front of the house when Reds scared the shit out of me.

"No girl, we can't be parking this shit out front! Follow the driveway around the back!" She yelled in pain.

"Reds, I hope you gonna be okay."

"I'm fine! Stop askin' 'cause it's not makin' it no better!"

I continued driving to the back.

"Stop right here and get out." She said. "Wait for someone to come and get you. From there you know what to do." I looked at Reds. She was still in quite a bit of pain. She grabbed my hand and said, "Kaneesha, you got some gangsta in you that's been dying to come out. Handle your business like I know you will. Check your shit too before you get outta of this car."

I reached in the small of back and checked that the holster was snuggly in place. I pulled out my "Public Defender". It was a new .22 caliber short handgun, the newest model on the market. It was almost perfect with the exception of the small scratch on the side of it. I checked my weapon inside the car.

Last week, as soon as Jarvis and Hysear left for school and work, Reds and Stone took me to the shooting range all week long, I had the late shift at work, which allowed my mornings to be free so I was good. I found out Reds knew her shit when it came to firearms. Both of them schooled me on being a mule. I was taught everything I would need to know to do the job. After two mock runs that included me pulling my Defender and posting it near a pigeon's head for target practice, before he could react, I had graduated.

I secured my toaster back into its carrier and not a moment too soon Reds said, "Get out. There's one of Carlos' boys."

I gave her a nod and exited the car. I waited for the man

to come to me. He walked up on me and asked, "You Mary 2?"

"Yeah, I'm Mary 2." This was my working name. He looked in the car at Reds. "Is that Mary 1?"

"Yes."

"She okay?" he asked seeing the pain in her eyes.

"No, she's goin' into labor. So if you don't mind, I want to get this over and take her to a hospital." I informed trying to get down to business.

He looked back at Reds, sucked his teeth and said, "Follow me."

We walked down a path that lead out to a wooded area. Several minutes later, I was in a guesthouse that was located away from the main house.

"Stay here, wait and don't touch shit!" He sternly said.

"Mutherfucka, you ain't talkin' to a child." I spat back.

"Wait." He repeated before walking out the door.

I stood frozen in the spot, running my hand carefully over my back to check my shit, again.

"So you're the new girl?" Someone asked behind me.

I quickly turned around to face a short fat Columbian looking man who was overly tanned. He had on several thick gold chains and an open shirt. He wore shorts and sandals and thick curly black hairy covered his entire body. The man was ugly.

"Are you Carlos?" I asked.

"No, Carlos can't be here. He sends his regrets," the man said walking around me, looking me up and down.

"Then who the hell are you?"

"My name is Luchi."

"Well, Luchi, I'm supposed to meet Carlos. Do you have a time of his return?" Luchi continued to walk around me and I could tell he was testing me. He was getting on my nerves already. I didn't come in here for all of that.

"Look, Luchi, is Carlos comin' or not? Cause if he's not I'm out."

"Why are you in a hurry? Sit down. Why don't you let me pour you a drink?" He offered.

"I came to see Carlos." I said straight to the point.

"Well Carlos ain't here, so why don't we get to know one another. Mary number two right?" He said sarcastically.

He came closer standing directly in front of me, so I slowly put my hand behind my back. He hadn't noticed. He touched my face and my skin crawled.

"Relax," He coaxed. "We have forty minutes until Carlos returns."

"If Carlos isn't coming back for forty minutes, I'll wait in the car." I turned my back on Luchi.

But the moment I did, what Reds told me a week ago came flooding into my memory.

"Never turn your back on anyone. Walk out the room facing everyone you see."

Hindsight is 20/20. Because before I could turn back around, Luchi pushed me toward the large oak sofa table. I maintained my balance, turned around and immediately pushed him back. He pushed me forcefully again and I fell on my back, hitting the table.

"Oh you want me to come and get it? Huh?" Luchi said as he lowered his body onto me.

I couldn't get to the gun as my back was pinned against the table.

"Get your short ugly ass up off of me! What the fuck is wrong wit' you?!" I screeched trying to get out of his grips.

The man was strong no denying that. We wrestled for a brief moment until I kneed him in the groin.

He released me, buckled over and I ran for the door, but it was locked.

"Bitch, you think you're gettin' outta here? Fuck you! You black bitch! You think Luchi's ugly do you?" He screamed at me as I felt his fist crash against my face.

I saw stars as I staggered to the side of the couch. The doubled vision I had going on didn't help me as I tried to make out where Luchi was. I found out when he jumped on my back bringing both of us down to the floor. I rolled over on my stomach to get leverage to push myself up off the floor. But Luchi was on my back trying to get my shirt off. I pushed myself up with my hands like I was doing pushups and Luchi fell off to the side. He grabbed me around the waist just as I positioned my Defender to his temple and pulled back the hammer. All movement stopped. Luchi's eyes were wide and fearful. He instantly put his hands up in a truce like manner. My own fear had given way to protecting my life..

"Don't fuckin' move or I will slide one right between your goofy eyes you butt ugly motherfucker." I hissed as I got to my feet. "Get the fuck up right now, you piece of shit! Get up!" I ordered as I checked my waist to ensure the packages were still intact.

Luchi slowly got up.

"Sit your ass down in that chair!"

He sat down. I stood behind him and repositioned the gun to back of his skull. I wrapped my arm around his neck and started squeezing his throat.

I whispered in his ear, "You think you can just try to take some shit from me like that. "I should just pop your dumb ass right...."

My sentence was cut short by an army of men who swarmed into the room like swat. With more than several big ass weapons posted up at me, my arm had a mind of it's own and fell immediately from around Luchi's neck. I put my gun down at my side.

"Whoa, fella's! It ain't what you think. I came to see Carlos and he was trynna rape me." I said slowly backing away from Luchi.

No one moved or said a word back. Then I heard another door open and in walked a man with a cane. He wore an impeccably fitted pin stripped suit, a straw fedora was perched on his head and black and white wing tipped shoes dressed his feet. He walked with a slight limp and went over to the half circle bar on the side of the room. He didn't say a word as he carefully chose a bottle from his bar. We all watched as he prepared a drink.

"I am, Carlos." He started. "Who are you?"

"I thought I was someone who came to do business. But your partner tried to violate me." I immediately said hoping he believed me.

He pointed to Luchi.-"Is this true?"

"Boss, I don't know what she's talking about. I came in to get the package when I found her going through the drawers in here. She was looking for something, boss. She might be undercover. I didn't trust her the moment she came. She's not like the other girl that we deal with." He lied.

"Enough." Carlos said. Luchi shut up immediately. Carlos took a sip of his drink and then looked at me. "Are you legit?"

"I was told to speak to a man named Carlos. I was then told to wait here, which is what I was doin' until he beat me down for my pussy. That's when your boys stormed in and found me about to pop his head off his shoulders." I seethed.

He got in Luchi's face and said, "I gave you a chance to come clean and you didn't."

"What do you mean?" Luchi asked.

"I saw the whole thing on tape. You could've ruined my business relationship. No worries though. I'll deal with you privately." Carlos told him.

And with a nod of his head, two of the gunmen lifted Luchi's ass out of the chair and hauled him out the door. The man went back to the bar and prepared another drink.

He turned around, looked at his crew and said, "Put your toys away. She's harmless. Aren't you?" He asked.

I didn't respond but they lowered their weapons.

"I apologize for what happened to you. He's my wife's brother. You try to give a guy work and look what happens." He said hunching his shoulders. "I can certainly make it worth your while to keep this between us. I wouldn't want to upset Stone with the details and ruin our business relationship. I will see to it that Luchi is punished. Five grand ought to make you forget about this little incident. Say in cash?" He asked giving a penetrating stare.

"I just want to deliver my package and go home." I let him know.

"Very well, the choice is yours. Now, let us get to the business at hand. I think you have something that I want." Someone handed him a pair of scissors. "Give it to me."

Carlos watched me intensively as I lifted my shirt and cut the tape from around me. He helped take the packages off of me. When all three were safely on the desk, he stuck the scissors into each of the packages to break it open. When he stuck his finger in the holes and tasted the contents of each one, a smile crept across his face. He went over to a large bookcase and pressed on it. The bookcase opened out to expose a room with large safe in it. He walked in the small room that housed the safe and came back out with a small black bag.

"For Stone." I accepted the bag. "My man Lupe' there," he said pointing to one of his gunman, "will show you out. Well done, give Stone my regards."

With that Carlos turned on his wing tipped shoes and walked away. I'm not going to lie, I never envisioned my first job turning out this way. I guess the saying's true, you should be careful what you ask for...you just may get it.

Chapter Eight

"What are you doin' out?" I said opening the door for Reds.

"What?"

"What?" I repeated. "You just had a baby!"

"That's right and now I'm ready to get on with my life." She said walking around me and into the living room.

"Where's the baby?" I said locking the door.

"With my cousin. She thinking about taking him like she did the rest of my kids."

"The rest of your kids?" She nodded and smiled. "So it's a boy?"

"Yep."

"Well I guess it's good cause if they found out about your habit, they might have called social services."

"Trust, Kaneesha! That mutherfuckin' doctor already ran tests and I'm sure my blood came back dirty. He just didn't want to have to fill out all the paperwork if he reported me to Social Services. And what the fuck happened to your face?"

"Oh that's right! You had already gone by the time I got back to the car to the hospital. I had my hands full with one of Carlos' men. A fight and all."

"Oh...the fight." She nodded. "Is that how you got the knot the size of a golf ball on your head?"

I handed Reds a glass of water and sat down beside her on the couch.

"It's a long story that turned violent but I held my own." I informed her.

"You gonna make Stone look at you in a different light behind that shit. And just so you know, Stone knows about everything. He didn't give me details, but he did say he liked how you handled yourself. But you shoulda told him instead of Carlos." Reds advised.

"I didn't want the drama." I told her.

"Just tellin' you."

"I know. Do you know that nigga tried to offer me hush money? I ain't take it though."

"Good, cause Stone would have went the fuck off if you had taken the bribe from Carlos to keep that type of shit away from him. Carlos and Stone will handle what happened to you. So don't vex over that. I'm 'bout to bounce though. I just came by to check you. I'll holla later."

"Before you leave, are you holding?"

She smiled and said, "I'ma have to start chargin' you soon enough."

"What...you want me to pay you now?" I said with an attitude. "Cause if I'm not mistaken, I still haven't gotten my cut from the drop yet."

"Naw...don't pay me now, but you owe me later," she said reaching in her purse and handing me some blow.

"Fuck her." I thought out loud. "I'ma have enough money to buy my own shit."

After Reds left, I went to my bedroom, closed the door, dropped to my knees and did some lines. I reflected back on yesterday's events as I inhaled each one and satisfaction and my high got me aroused. I guess the near death experience was payback for my lying to Jarvis about my new life.

"Thanks for keeping me safe, Lord." I said wiping my nose, and licking the residue. "I"ma get it together."

I guess I need to stop lyin' to God 'though, cause I'm sure if anybody knows my heart, he does. And I don't have any intentions on changing, not right now anyway.

"Hey, boo." I woke up and looked at the clock it read 9:28pm.

"You were knocked out and I didn't want to wake you so I let you sleep. Lil Man and me had Checkers and I brought you a Champ burger with cheese. It's in the microwave." Jarvis leaned down and kissed my forehead. "Damn, you take some sleepin' pills or something? 'Cause I shook six times and you didn't move."

I sat up and pushed back the covers. I didn't remember dosing off and I didn't remember putting up my gun. When I looked on the dresser, I saw it was partially covered by my purse.

"I was just tired." I replied looking at him and then my gun. I was surprised he was speaking to me because lately he's been avoiding me. "So I guess you not mad at me no more."

"Naw. How's your head?" He asked rubbing the knot. "I can't believe you fell that hard."

"It's fine, Jarvis."

"So how is Reds? I heard she had the baby." He continued his with his twenty questions.

I froze in place.

"How you know about Reds?" Jarvis got up off the bed and looked at himself in the mirror.

"I know everything about you, girl. Look, I gotta go. I got work to put in." He smiled. "Hysear had his bath and is in his room playing Wii. I'll be home around twelve." He kissed me.

"Why aren't you ever home anymore? Do you even live here?"

"I'll be home later." He said ignoring me then leaving out our home.

Since I needed to put up my gun, I let him leave without a fuss, but we needed to talk about us. Here I was living a dangerous life and he wasn't even home enough to know. I was hoping he'd be a little jealous at my newfound freedom but it wasn't working.

Once I put the gun up, I checked on Hysear. Good...he was fast asleep. I went to the bedroom, opened up my Coach bag and found my phone. I had several missed texts. One was from my dad saying that he wanted Lil Man to hang out with him this weekend. The second and third texts were from Reds saying my bank was waiting for me and that she took her cut from the Coke she gave me. Bitch. I was to meet her tomorrow before I went to work to collect. After reading them, I erased them all from my phone.

I was up now, so wasn't no sense in going back to sleep. I opted to surf the net for a while. When I finally turned off the computer, it was 2:00 o'clock in the morning and Jarvis was still not home. But my phone rang.

"Hello?"

No one said a word and the caller's number were blocked.

"Hello? Who is this?"

The caller hung up and I finished surfing the net. My mind soon found Jarvis again. Jarvis told me that he would only be slinging a couple nights a week and wouldn't stay out past twelve. And for the first week Jarvis stuck to this plan. But lately he's been coming in later and later. I wasn't feeling this shit and something in my gut said something wasn't right. But for now, what could I do? And, who was I to point fingers?

Chapter Nine

Over the next several weeks, Reds and me became inseparable and so did me and Stone. All the while I had managed to keep my lie a secret from Jarvis. I even managed to hold onto my job.

I was getting ready for work when my phone rang.

"Come." The call ended and I knew what it meant. Stone had taught me codes over the weeks we'd worked together to throw people off.

I snatched up my work shit and my purse, headed out my apartment and sprinted down the steps. The black double R was waiting. I jumped in and Stone floated that beauty out of the Heights.

"Hey, Princess. Give me some." I leaned over and kissed him on the lips.

"That's what I'm talkin' 'bout. Ah, why you going to work? I have someting for you to do."

"My king, you know I can't just quit my job. Jarvis will get suspicious. I'll stop when I get enough saved. But even then, the money won't last forever, Stone."

"Listen, don't talk to me 'bout Jarvis. In me eyes, him nawt real man. If he was, he wouldn't have his woman working."

"I know, but we're still together."

"For now, Princess. For now."

Stone and I drove to our spot to make love. After we were dressed, I was sitting on the side of the bed waiting for Stone to finish the conversation he was having with someone on the phone.

Stone was furious about something and every other word that fell from his mouth was a curse word either in Patois (foreign language) or English. In any language, whoever it was, was getting cursed the fuck out. I looked at my watch and saw I only had thirty minutes to get to work or I would be late. I caught Stone's attention and pointed to my watch. He turned his back on me and continued to rant and rave on his Blackberry. I grabbed my shit and headed for the door. In one swift movement, Stone grabbed my arm and pulled me back in inside.

"Bumbleclot! Where are you going? Don't open no doors here!"

"Stone, I've gotta get to work."

"Hold on!" he told the person on the phone. He faced me, "Why ya not say so? Give me a minute, den I take you! Stop trying to be the man in this here ting," he said pointing at him and then me, "cause with us, there's only one...me! Now...wait in the truck!"

I opened up the door and went outside and got in the truck. I was going to have to put some distance between Stone and me. We had been seeing each other for several weeks now and he could act a little crazy when it came to me and business. As much as he didn't want to admit it, I knew Stone was catching feelings. And I had already caught mine for him. After ten minutes, the driver's side door opened and he got in. He put the key in the ignition and then turned to me to touch my face.

"I didn't mean to vex out on you. Got some shit I gotta handle that a mutherfucka was supposed to do and didn't. You cool?" He asked as he ran his soft hands along my cheek.

"Yes." He threw a stack of cash in my lap and I picked it up examining its thickness. I hadn't had this much money in all my life.

I looked at Stone's handsome face and said, "Thank You". He pulled me into him for a passionate kiss. When we let go, we both stared at one another.

"Your mine." He said.

"I know." I replied not knowing if it were totally true.

"Don't make me prove it to the world."

I didn't know what that meant, but it sounded like a threat. We drove in silence and when I made it through the door to work, I punched in two minutes after my scheduled time.

I went to my locker and put my stuff in it and then leaned against it to count the number of bills that Stone gave to me. I counted fifteen hundred dollars. Suddenly when I looked around my job, I was starting to hate it. Look at how much paper I was making. I'd stay with the gig for now but for real, I couldn't make any promises.

Stone put me on a few more runs with Reds but most of the time she made the drops and pickups by herself. When she made over thirty-five hundred, she laced me up with five hundred of it. I was stashing money from left to right.

When Jarvis asked me where all the money was coming from, I told him that Reds had me look out for her while she made runs from time to time. He bought it and as he had lately, he seemed to not care.

I put the money in my new Dolce and Gabbana wallet and secured the door to my locker. It was time for me to do my regular work when all I really wanted to do was say, "Fuck this job!"

Chapter Ten

Reds and I were walking in the mall when her phone rang indicating she had a message. She paused to read it and showed it to me. We had a major job that meant both of us would be laced. We were to be downtown at the Radisson hotel in Baltimore city tomorrow night and the time for drop off was 12:30am.

We were in Nordstrom's trying on shoes and I had several pair of Steve Maddens sitting around my feet.

"Don't hurt no body in 'em!" A strange voice said. I followed Reds eyes as the owner of the voice came from behind me, and stood in front of me.

"Umph, umph, umph, Jarvis must not know what he got. 'Cause someone as fine as you should not be out the house without an escort. If I was your man, you'd be my Cinderella and I'd place the shoes on your feet." Dubbs, my next-door neighbor said licking his lips.

"What?" I laughed looking at Reds. "Stupid and corny."

"You know you fine as shit don't you?" Dubbs continued ignoring my insult.

A slight smile crossed my face as I said, "Thank you."

"Every time I see you my dick gets hard," he whispered grabbing himself.

What the fuck?! What kinda of shit is that to say to someone you hardly knew? Let me remain calm before I go on this ignorant bastard.

I leaned back and replied, "You should take care of that. I hear you get blue balls when you don't get none." I coolly stated.

"Exactly, that's my point. I ain't gettin' none of that." He stated.

"Nigga, you will never be gettin' any of this either." I

snapped.

"Why you tryin' to play hard to get? I've seen your ass come out the house and look at me. I know you want this!" He said and pulled my hand over toward his hard dick.

I jumped up.

"What the fuck are you doin', Dubbs?!" I shouted.

I forgot where I was and people had begun to stare at us. Reds didn't say a word. She was sitting down in the chair across from me, with her legs crossed, swinging her top leg and loudly popping gum. Dubbs looked around and appeared to be embarrassed by my comment.

"You ain't got to put a nigga out there like that. Damn!" He said.

"Well you shouldn't be so fuckin' stupid! How dare you treat me like that! I see why you ain't got nobody! I gotta man at home if I wanna feel dick!"

I sat back down to finish trying on the shoes. Dubbs stood over me looking down.

"Yeah, but I bet your man don't know you layin' underneath that black ass Jamaican now does he?"

Instantly my heart leaped out my chest. How the fuck this nigga know that? I played it off.

"Nigga, what the fuck are you implyin'?" I asked irritated.

"I've seen you wit' Stone a couple times. And I know Stone. You ain't just ridin' in his truck to be ridin'. You givin' that Jamaican nigga all that good pussy. It's written all over your face." He accused.

"That's a lie! I ain't sleepin' wit' Stone. I work for Stone." In that moment of time, I knew I let the cat out the bag in the heat of an argument with Dubb's simple ass.

"Ahhh, you workin' for Stone huh?" he said smiling mischievously. "Well excuse me."

Reds finally interjected. "You know what, Dubbs, you're an ass. Why don't you take your wanna be ballin' ass up outta here. Don't nobody want what you peddling, nigga!"

Dubbs turned around to face Reds.

"So what you peddlin'? That stank ass pregnant pussy or them dried up dick suckin' lips?" Reds stood up and walked over to Dubbs and mashed him in the forehead with her finger.

"Well if that bitch you call a mother keeps sellin' her pussy, I won't have to sell mine!" She said with her hands on her hips. "You don't know me like that, so I suggest you leave before you show up missin'." Reds warned.

Dubbs jumped into Reds face.

"Bitch, I will whoop your pregnant ass!" He yelled back.

Dubbs and Reds stood toe-to-toe staring each other down. I grabbed Reds by the arm.

"Come on, Reds. Let's go. Fuck Dubbs!" I said as we walked away leaving all the shoes I was trying on by Dubbs' feet.

"Yeah, fuck ya'll too. You two nasty bitches! Don't nobody want ya'll no way, especially you, Kaneesha. You ain't all that!" Dubbs yelled to our backs as we made our way out of the store. We didn't stop until we got to the car.

"Girl, Dubbs is crazy! He wants to be like Stone so bad. He lucky I didn't have my iron on me or I would have pulled it. Who the fuck he think he is? I gotta good mind to call Stone and set Dubbs ass blazin'." Reds seethed.

"If you call Stone and tell him this, what would happen?" I asked hoping for a dangerous answer.

Reds looked at me like I had two heads.

"Come on, Kaneesha! Think."

"I know...that's why I want you to call him." I chuckled.

"Well let it go. I'm just fucking with you. You never call in the troops unless you really ready for war!" Reds stated.

We pulled out the lot and proceeded to my house. It was time for me to go to work and for Jarvis to get off. Lil Man was with my Dad as usual and I was glad. Reds let me out in front of my building; I retrieved my shopping bags and went inside.

The moment I closed the door, my phone rang with the words, 'Me and my crew got the whole city locked'. It was my cell phone singing "*Elephant Man's Message*".

I threw my stuff down on the bed and reached in my bag to get the phone. I looked at the caller ID and didn't recognize the number, but sometimes my Dad would call me from different locations. So I answered it.

"Hello."

"I'm watchin' you, bitch!" And then the line went dead.

I looked at the screen and immediately pressed the button on my phone to automatically dial the number back. It rang and then gave two long beeps and disconnected. I tried several more times and each time I got the same results. I deleted it out my phone's call history.

Who the fuck was that? And how did they get my number? It made me nervous because that was the second time I received a strange message. I took a quick shower, put on my work gear, grabbed my purse and keys and headed out the door.

I bopped down the steps to my car. The hairs on the back of my neck stood up and I turned around. Dubbs was leaning against the wall, smoking a cigarette, and watching me.

"Don't know why you're going to work? Don't you have a job with Stone? Ain't that what you told me?" He heckled.

I didn't answer Dubbs I just continued out the building as if he wasn't there. I got in my car and pulled off quickly. Only when I got to the bottom of the hill did I pull over to collect myself. Dubbs was becoming a thorn in my side and if he wasn't careful, whatever family he had might be pulling the thorns off the roses that would lay on his casket. It may come down to his life or mine...and it ain't goin' be mine.

Chapter Eleven

Finally, the house was empty as I waited for Reds to come through. A soft knock let me know that it was her and I snatched open the door and pulled her inside.

"Girl, what's goin' on? Your text sounded like you was in trouble? Did you tell Jarvis that you would be out tomorrow night?" She asked looking at me with nervous suspicion.

"No, Reds, I ain't told him nothin' yet." I said pacing back and forth.

She threw her hands up.

"Kaneesha, you better think of something to tell him tonight. Stone is countin' on you to make this drop with me. Everything is in motion. Think of something! Shit, tell him you and I are going to DC to my cousin's and we won't be back 'till late. I got your back. Just make sure your ass is downtown at the Radisson by 11:00pm."

"I'll handle Jarvis, but, Reds, I texted you cause lately Dubbs has been like watchin' me and shit. And I've been getting strange texts and calls. I'm scared. You don't think it's related to what we do, do you?"

"Watchin' you? What you mean watchin' you, Kaneesha? Like how?"

"Well yesterday when I was goin' to work, I had this weird feelin' then I noticed Dubbs standing up on the landing watching me. He said, he didn't know why I was going to work since I was working for Stone." I informed her.

"Shit, Kaneesha, fuck Dubbs! Worry about Stone and get ready for our job. Okay?"

"I guess so."

"You better. I have to go, I'll talk to you later."

I closed the door behind her. And after our conversation, I could have sworn that I heard Dubb's door open as mine was closing. But I didn't look out of the peephole because I knew I needed to stop worryin' about his ass, and focus on me. Instead I opted to lie down and rest. And the moment I closed my eyes, Dubbs entered my mind again.

I rolled over and checked the clock. Again, Jarvis was not home. It was four fucking o'clock in the goddamn morning. Where the fuck was my man? I got up and went to the living room to wait for Jarvis. I wanted to be the first thing he saw when he comes through the front door.-When he finally opened the door, he jumped back when he saw me sitting there in the dark.

He threw his keys down on the coffee table and walked past me and into the kitchen. I continued to sit in the chair in the dark...waiting.

From the kitchen he hollered, "Why you sittin' in the dark?" I shifted in the chair.

"Waiting for your ass, Jarvis. Where you been?"

"Out."

"You've been doing that a lot lately."

"What difference does it make, Kaneesha? I got my life and you got yours. So live it."

"What's going on between us? Are we a family or not?"

"You're askin' the wrong person." He said, entering the living room.

"I thought I was asking my man. You've changed, Jarvis. You come home when you want and lately you have been having this spaced out look on your face. So I'm askin' you...my man...what you been doin' in the streets."

"Kaneesha, if you must know, I been smokin'."

"Crack?"

"What do you think?"

"Why, Jarvis? I thought you would've given that up by now."

"You said you didn't want me smokin' in the house, so I took it to the streets. So right now you can't say a damn thing to me. I'm doing what the fuck you asked me to do."

"Why crack, Jarvis? You know what that shit does to people! I don't understand."

"Cause I fuckin' love the high. Better than I love going up in that soft ass pussy of yours. Nothin' beats the feeling I get, not even you."

"Fine, Jarvis!" I yelled fighting back tears. "You do what the fuck you want!"

"I already have," he smiled slyly walking away. I followed him.

"I'm goin' wit' Reds to her cousin's house tomorrow night and probably won't be back until Saturday morning." I said trying to draw some emotion from him.

"With Reds huh? When you talk to her, tell her I have to holla at her about somethin'"

"Holler at her about what?" I asked enraged.

"Fuck it, I'll tell her myself." He said entering the bedroom. "And just so you know, I ain't baby sittin', Kaneesha. Find anotha sucka to watch your kid." He shot back.

"My kid huh?"

"Yep, I finally get it. He's your son and not mine."

"Get out of my bedroom!" I yelled throwing him a pillow. "You sleep on the couch!"

He took the pillow with a smile on his face and slammed the door. Me? Well I cried myself to sleep.

The next morning I expected Jarvis to apologize for hurting me. But when I walked to the living room, he was still on the couch sleep so I gently shook him.

"Jarvis, get up and get ready for work." I said and walked away.

I went back to bed and waited for him to come to the bedroom to get his clothes on. Hoping he'd want to talk about us and that our making up, would give me comfort for the rest of the day. When thirty minutes passed and he didn't enter, I went back out. He was still on the couch sleep.

I yelled, "Jarvis, get up! You gotta go to work." He opened his eyes and looked at me.

"What time is it?" He mumbled.

"5:45."

"Shit, I'm tired. I ain't goin' in today. Call off for me, Kaneesha."

"No! Had you come home at a decent hour last night, you could have gotten the rest you needed and been up and out the door."

Jarvis laughed. "You love playing the role of the nagging bitch don't you? I can tell why though...you're good at it. Don't matter anyway 'cause I ain't goin' to work. I'm tired and I'm lampin' around the house all day today. Besides, I got bank. I ain't just out smokin' you know."

"If you don't go to work, you can't sleep here."

He looked at me and said, "Have it your way. I'll go where I'm wanted."

He quickly got up and went to the bedroom to grab his things. I was angry and hurt that he had somewhere else to go. Was he dating already and if so what was she like? The emotions of losing him filled me and I did something I couldn't believe.

I reached in my drawer, pulled out my gun and aimed at him.

"You're...not leaving."

"Where did you get that?" he said with his hands up. A frightened look took over his face.

"Don't worry about it. You're not leaving until you talk to me."

Jarvis walked up to me, placed the barrel of the gun to his chest and said, "You can't kill somebody who's already dead. Bye, Kaneesha."

Chapter Twelve

"Ya'll ready?" Stone asked.

"Yes!" we both replied.

"Okay. We're here. I'ma drop ya'll off and then fall back. The ride alongs will be on their jobs as usual. Just go in, make the drop, collect and come back. In and out as usual."

Reds and I acknowledged Stones orders and got out the rental car and walked into the hotel. Although Stone just reminded us that this drop was business as usual, there was nothing usual to me about Stone himself dropping us off. I had a funny feeling about this job and silently prayed that all would go smooth.

Prior to getting off the hotel elevator, we checked our shit. Red's had a Dessert Eagle as her choice of weapon. I stuck with my Defender. We got to the room and knocked. The door opened and we were ushered in by what appeared to be a solider manning the door. The room was dimly lit. We walked in further into the living room part of the suite.

"Hey, Red's." Manny said.

I couldn't believe that it was Manny. He is another well-known dealer in the Annapolis Baltimore area, but he was not who we were there to see. He sat on the couch smiling at us. I gave Reds a puzzled look. She shook her head and I kept my mouth shut.

"Where's Cappy?" Reds asked.

"In the adjoining room." Manny replied.

"Go get his ass." she demanded.

"Just hold your thong, babe." Manny said as he stood up and walked into what looked like the bedroom.

I heard the toilet flush and immediately whipped around to see who was coming out of the bathroom. I slowly an unnoticeably placed my hand in my back, on my weapon and waited.

When the door opened up, that mutherfuckin' Dubbs came walking out. What the fuck!!? He stopped mid stride when he saw me. I do not like how this shit is panning out!

"Well, well, well. Ain't this some shit? I guess you *are* working for Stone huh?" Dubbs came up closer to me. I put my hand out to stop him.

"Don't get up in my space, Dubbs." I warned him.

"You ain't got to worry 'bout that. I ain't trynna to do nothin'. At least not here anyway." He said.

"And what does that mean?" I asked.

He slowly walked past me making sure to press his body against mine as he did.

"Don't touch me no more, nigga!"

When Reds saw him she immediately went the fuck off.

"Oh hell no! What the fuck is you even doing here?" Reds spat.

"I'm here on business, baby. Shit, your man Stone ain't the only mutherfucka who gettin' cake. I'm tryin' to eat too. I got soldiers to feed and we all hungry. You gotta fuckin' problem wit' that?" Dubbs asked.

I tapped Reds on the shoulder and whispered, "Just chill. Let's get this over with."

"Yeah, you right, Neesh. Fuck him!" She said.

Reds relaxed when an older looking gentleman who I figured was Cappy came out of the room behind Manny. Cappy was supposed to be one of New York's biggest distributers. All he did was buy large quantities of coke, "E" pills, and push them throughout his city. I figured that Dubbs went through Cappy to get his weight. Lord knows Stone ain't fuck with him.

He smiled widely when he saw Reds.

"Hey, baby girl. Come on over here." He grabbed Reds in a bear hug.

"Hey, Cappy! How you been?" Reds said as she was pulled into his grip.

He pointed to me, "Is this the other half of your team I been hearing about? Come here girl. I ain't gonna bite you, that is unless you want me too." He laughed heartedly.

Manny laughed with him but Dubbs had a scowl on his face. It was like I was his girl. I went over to be introduced to him and he released his grip on Reds and bear hugged me instead.

"Alright, let's get down to business." He gave me a seductive look and said, "You girls go in there and strip. I'll be right back with drinks." He said.

Reds motioned her head for me to follow her into the adjacent room. We quickly reached in our purses and took out the scissors and cut the packages off our bodies. We put them in the bag that was laying on the floor under the table and straightened our clothes back up. Cappy came in with three plastic cups. He sat them down on the table. After he examined the packages, he nodded his head to a solider that was posted up at the door. He came over and took the bag from Cappy and left the hotel room.

"Sit down for a moment and have a drink with ole Cappy." He turned to Reds and handed her a cup and then handed me one. He picked up his cup and put it in the air. Although we moved closer to Cappy, we did not sit down.

"Raise your cups." We did. "Here's to never having to say you're sorry or broke!" he toasted. Reds and me touched the cups with him and then put them down on the table.

"Why ain't ya'll drinking? You know it's bad luck to make a toast and not drink to it."

"Cappy, we're on the job. I don't drink on the job." Reds explained.

Cappy turned to me and said, "What about you?" He asked. "From what I hear, you like to mix business and pleasure."

"None for me. I respect my employer," I said with all seriousness.

Cappy bellowed out a hearty laugh.

"Mr. Cappy, we ain't trying to rush you but we need an ETA on when we will receive the bag to carry back." Cappy stopped drinking and looked at me.

"What did you say?" he asked

"I said, we need to know where is the money so we can snag it and bounce?" I told him more directly.

"Are you trying to rush a nigga?"

"We trying to get paid," I continued.

Reds cocked her head, looked at Cappy and pursed her lips. And she assumed her, 'get ready for some shit to go down', stance. She had my back.

"That Jamaican nigga Stone has trained you both well. He makes you bitches believe you're more than just runners. Tell me, has he broken you world down yet? Removed everyone you love from your life?" He continued.

Reds hurriedly said, "Cappy, just give us what we came for."

I wanted to know what he meant.

"Either sit your pretty little asses down and wait for the bag, or go back to your "employer" and tell him to suck my dick. Your call," he said mockingly.

"Cappy, chill. We just want to do our jobs and go home. So look, make it easier for us and let us know how long it will be." Reds asked. "You know I got mad love for you." Reds crooned.

Cappy looked at me and pointed.

"Next time, check that bitch! She must think she's 007 or some shit." Cappy spat.

Reds cut her eyes at me in a threatening manner. I bite my tongue but wondered why she ain't say anything before. I would have just chilled the fuck out.

Cappy pulled out his phone and hit a button. He turned his back on us and began talking.

Reds whispered to me, "Be cool, Neesh. Cause if not, Stone will be up here with the ride alongs and it ain't gonna be good." Cappy turned back around and faced us.

"It's going to be another ten or so minutes. You know we don't keep that type of cake with us. So chill out and lighten up." He said.

He grabbed his cup and walked back into the living room area. We followed behind him. When I came out the door I noticed Dubbs fiddling with what appeared to be a cell phone.

He looked at me and half smirked.

I felt the vibration on my belt and looked down to see the phone Stone gave me. I read it clearly then erased it. I gave Reds a knowing nod and she nodded back. We both drew in our breath and waited. A knock at the door made the solider that was posted by it jump. Cappy pointed to the door and the solider looked out the peephole.

"It's Stone." He acknowledged.

"Open the door." Cappy said and before any reactions could be made, the ride alongs bum rushed the door with guns drawn. They were six deep.

"Stand down!" Cappy shouted. "Stand down!"

The ride alongs pointed guns at the solider, Cappy, Manny and Dubbs. No one made a move as they were all targets. Stone came in the door last. He looked around and then nodded to his ride alongs. They positioned their weapons by their sides.

"Damn, nigga. Why you gotta always make a fuckin' grand entrance. You better be glad that you my dawg." Cappy said.

"Why is this shit takin' so long? What the bloodclot problem?!" Stone inquired. He continued, "You givin' me girls a hard time, Cappy?"

"Like I told your girls, you know we don't keep shit here. It's on the way, Stone. Just hold your fuckin' horses. Shit!" Cappy responded. Stone nodded his head at Reds and me.

"Well I'm involved now. Bring me money. Now."

"Easy big fella, I'll make the call." Cappy replied. Stone looked at the ride alongs and nodded. "Bring it," Cappy continued on the phone. When he was done he said. "It should be arriving in a minute." He told Stone.

We all stood motionless, hoping for the best.

Within two minutes of Cappy's call, the door opened and the ridealongs posted their glocks back up at everyone that wasn't a part of Stone's team. Stone ordered one of the ride alongs to look out the peephole. He nodded his head and Stone told him to open the door. As she walked in carrying a leather pouch, Stone motioned to his goons to lower their heat again.

The woman handed the bag to Stone. He snatched it from her and threw it to one of the ride alongs. Once he had the money in is possession he started asking questions.

"Why are you two here?" he asked to Manny and Dubbs.

"We conductin' business with Cappy. Our bein' here doesn't concern you none, Stone." Dubbs retorted. "You got your hands full enough with your own business." He said looking at me.

Stone mean mugged Dubbs.

"Your bein' here *is* of my concern!" Stone said to him then turned to Cappy. "Cappy, the next time only *we* deal! *If* we deal again, I want never to see either of those faces again. Especially his," he said pointing at Dubbs. "Understood?" He motioned for all of us to walk to the door without waiting on Cappy's response. "Later."

"I think it will be sooner than that," Dubbs said.

"We'll see." Stone responded. "We'll see."

Chapter Thirteen

After the meeting with Cappy, I took some of the cash I earned and got a hotel room. So far I had been here for two days. Hysear was still with my father and I was happy because I just wanted to be alone. And, I was certain that Jarvis wasn't at our apartment waiting on me.

"You still at the hotel?" Reds asked me on the phone.

"Yeah. Why? You need me to do something?"

"Naw, just checkin'."

"I been thinkin' 'bout Jarvis. I miss him a lot."

"Try not to think about him. It's done, and ya'll will be back together. Besides, your mind should be on Stone. I know he been laying down the pipe on you lately."

"Not the same. I love Jarvis."

"Maybe you shoulda thought about that before you pulled the gun on him."

My heart stopped and I tried to regain my composure. You don't understand, I never told her about our fight because I was too embarrassed.

"How did you know about that? I didn't tell anybody about that."

"Look...Jarvis has been over my house for the past couple of days."

"Your house?"

"Yes. He says you don't let him live. That you be naggin' him all the time. Look, Kaneesha, there's nothing for you to worry about. My keeping Jarvis under my watchful eyes for a couple of days is just business related. Don't forget, I work for Stone, and you do too. If one part of the business fails, we all fail."

"Why wouldn't you tell me?"

"Because we had a job to do and I needed your mind on it."

"But you are my friend."

"I still am, I'm just his too."

"Are you fuckin' my man?" I huffed.

"I already told you I'm not interested in him. So relax, all we share is a love of the pipe. Now get some sleep. Okay?"

When she ended the call I sat up in bed stuck. Too say I was angry didn't do my emotions justice. I tried to remember every detail of Red's body. Was her butt thicker than mine? Was she prettier than me? Suddenly my questions boiled down to one fact. They shared love for the most important thing in his life right now. The love of crack. And because of it, I risked a major chance at losing him.

Not being able to spend another night in the hotel room alone, I decided to go home. The moment I put the key in my apartment door, Jarvis snatched it open.

"Where the fuck you been?" He yelled.

I didn't get a chance to answer him as he grabbed me by my jacket and pulled me through the door. He pushed me down onto the couch and I quickly jumped back up onto my feet.

"Kaneesha, I said where the fuck have you been!?" He breathed heavily into my face.

"You were at Reds so why are you asking me where I've been? You can't be serious, Jarvis. Why didn't you just ask her where I was, since it's obvious she's playing both sides." I yelled back.

"Reds allows me to be me, but there's nothin' going on between us. I work for Stone just like you do, remember?"

"You know?" I asked feeling my heart race within the walls of my chest.

"I told you along time ago Kaneesha, I know everything about you."

"If that's the case, why are you all up in my face? Do you...like you want me to do me!" I yelled at him.

Jarvis looked at me like I was crazy. He grabbed my jacket by the collar and pulled me to his face.

"You must think I'm fuckin' stupid. You been gone for two days fuckin' some other nigga. I bet it was Stone. I know 'bout ya'll. So you fuckin' him *and* workin' for him, huh? You whorin' for money now?!"

Either Reds told him, or someone else did, either way I was fucked.

"Fuck you, Jarvis. I ain't whorin' for shit!" I spit back.

I reached up and pushed Jarvis away from me. He grabbed me by my arms and threw me down on the couch again. He began to choke me and push my head into the cushions. My hands were free, and I used both of them to rake both sides of his face with my nails. He continued choking me and suddenly, the fight in me had gone away.

I tried to plead to him with my eyes but he was in a murderous rage and emotionally disconnected from me. I knew then, that he was wired up on crack.

Only stopping to hurt me more, he kicked me several times and punched me all over my body. When he tired of that, he took off his belt and started beating me like I was his child. With every strike Jarvis delivered to me, he shouted Stone's name and kept repeating that I was a whore and that I betrayed him. I had nothing left in me to fight with.

With my body weakened, I gave up and after some time, felt no more pain. It was the last thing I remembered, and the thing I'd never be able to forget.

Chapter Fourteen

I woke up to my father being in my apartment. He spent the next few days nursing me back to health. And when I was a little better, he left me alone, taking Hysear with him so that I could get some much needed rest. I walked past mirrors unable to get over how badly beaten my face was. Amazingly, all I wanted to do was get high. So I called the one person I should hate and she quickly came over.

"Oh hell no, girl! We need to tell Stone. Look at your shit! Your grill is all fucked up!" She yelled.

"No, Reds, leave it alone. Jarvis has every right to be mad as hell at me," I told her. "Did you tell him? About me and Stone?"

"Don't ask me somethin' you know the answer too. I'm his friend, but I'm more yours. You do trust me right?"

"Yeah. I guess."

"Here, do a couple of lines," she said quieting me with a habit I wanted no longer to keep. I did a few lines and sat back in my seat in ecstasy. I was better already.

"Where the fuck is his punk ass at anyway?!" She spat.

If she wasn't mad she was doing a damn good acting job.

"I don't know. He left here early this morning and I haven't heard from him since. He just grabs his clothes and leaves."

"Well he better not come the fuck up in here while I'm here. That's all I gotta say. Damn, Neesh, this shit done gave me a headache. I needs to calm my nerves. I need a hit. I'll be back in 'bout a hour."

"No, where you goin', Reds? Don't leave." I whined. In my heart I wanted to keep her in my sight. If she was with me, it meant she couldn't be with him.

"Girl, I needs a blast and you don't smoke so I'm goin' to Me-Me's and get a hit. My mother's home and I can't do nothin' at my house right now." She replied.

"Well, stay here and do your shit. I don't care. You ain't gotta go down Me-Me's." Reds gave me a puzzled look.

"You sure?"

"Yeah, it don't even bother me no more."

"Okay...you got your ass beat and it done fucked with your head."

"No, it's cool, Reds. Go on and do you. Shit, I might wanna a hit of that shit myself to calm my nerves down. I ain't got no more snort and I'm still on edge." Reds gawked at me.

"You ain't doin' this to keep Jarvis are you?"

"No, but I do want to know what the hype is about."

"That ain't nothin' but a word. Let me find out!" she giggled.

Reds opened her purse and took out her famous purple bag. She took out all the gear she used. After she was done mixing up stuff and putting flame to a spoon, she had produced a little white ball. She cut the ball up into smaller pieces.

"Okay, Kaneesha. I'ma show you how to do this. Watch me," she turned to me and said.

I watched as Reds scooped up some cigarette ashes and put them in the screen of her pipe. She placed one of the pieces of the stone on top of the ashes and hoisted the pipe up to her face.

"I'm going to gently touch the coke with my lighter and pull easy and then hold the smoke in and let it out, like this. Watch." She taught.

Reds put the pipe in her mouth, flicked the lighter and touched the flame to the pebble. I saw the stone vanish into the ashes. Reds pulled on the pipe and white smoke wafted through the small bowl then into the glass neck and into Reds' mouth. She held the smoke for a few seconds and then blew it out. She closed her eyes and let out a sigh. She sat back in the chair spaced out, then closed her eyes. I just watched as she seemed oblivious to me sitting there.

"Reds?" I softly said. She opened her eyes.

"Damn that's good shit. Your turn, Kaneesha. Now listen to

what I say."

"Reds, I don't know 'bout this shit. I ain't never smoked no coke and I'm scared."

"Your idea not mine. But remember, that's why your man is hanging over your friend's house and not yours."

Tears welled up in my eyes.

"Cryin' is for suckas. Just take a hit and save your relationship. Jarvis too fine for you to let him get away. Take a journey into his world." Her acknowledgement of his looks scared me and I wondered if they were fucking after all. "If you don't like it, then do you a couple lines." She said pointing to the bag of coke.

I nodded okay and waited for Reds to prepare the pipe for me. She repeated the same steps from before and gave me the pipe.

"Okay, pull slow and hold it." She coached.

I put the pipe to my mouth and waited for Reds to apply the flame. When she lit the lighter, she nodded and I pulled on the pipe.

"That's it. Slow. Now hold it." she coaxed.

I held the smoke for a quick second and let it out. Reds was waiting for my reaction. I waited too.

"I don't feel nothin' yet, Reds." I said as I shrugged my shoulders.

"Let me fix you another hit then. That was just a small piece. Let me give you a bigger one and hold it in a little longer this time." Reds said.

"No, I don't want no more of that." I said secretly feeling the creeping sensation that would be my demise. "Just give me the powder and I'm fine." I told her.

"You sure, Kaneesha? You really don't know what you're missing girl." She said fixing the pipe up for another hit.

"No, I'm good." I protested.

Reds smoked and I snorted well into the night. Jarvis didn't call or come home and I was not about to call him either.

I was just satisfied that he wasn't with Reds.

I called work and put on an Oscar award performance like I was sick with the Swine Flu. There was no way I could go to work looking like I did. The Swine Flu or H1N1 was the newest strain of a virus that had everyone scared, so my boss didn't argue when I told him I had it. Several deaths were reported in the Maryland area that were attributed to it. He even told me not to come back for a couple days until I got rid of whatever it was he thought I had. I would go to the doctor's office and get a slip on Wednesday.

Days turned into months and still no Jarvis. I can't believe we had been apart for six months. The only signs I could see of him still being around, were his shirts disappearing little by little. Still, I never ran into him physically. I was thankful for my father because he kept Hysear regularly.

Most of the bruises had gone down but my spirit was broken. Nothing remained by a small gash over my left eye that I don't even know how it got there. Missing him like crazy, I called the job to speak to him but strangely, they said Jarvis didn't work there anymore. He must have told them to say that if I called.

I decided to clean up my house. I put clothes up and straighten up my shoes in the closet. I made sure my Defender was securely in its hiding place. There was underwear in the laundry basket that needed attention since last week. I began to fold them up and put them away in the dresser drawers. I put mine away first and then went over to Jarvis's side of the dresser. I opened it and moved some underwear over to make room for the T-shirts that I had in my hand when my eyes caught sight of something in the corner of the drawer. I pushed his boxers out the way, reached in and pulled out the pipe. Upon further investigation, I saw a small baggie. I snatched it up and held it in front of me.

There were several large rocks inside of it. This nigga had

crack and a crack pipe in my house. Jarvis was serious about smoking this shit. The ringing of my cell phone startled me and I dropped both the crack pipe and the baggie. The crack pipe broke into several pieces. Shit! I shouted. I ignored my ringing phone for the moment as I bent down to pick up the broken pipe. When I was done cleaning up the glass, I put the baggie back in the drawer. I would take care of that later. I got my phone out of my purse and looked at the missed call. It was Jarvis's number. He left a message. I pushed the button on my phone and listened to it.

"*Kaneesha, I'ma be back today. We need to talk.*"

I erased the message and closed my phone. My head began to pound. My heart was beating in my chest and my stomach was doing flip-flops. I was on edge about what Jarvis might say or do. I loved Jarvis. He was still my man and no matter what, I still had his back. But if we're going to stay together, then I knew that both him and me would have to stop working for Stone, and Jarvis was going to have to stop smoking. We needed clear heads to get through this...together.

"Mom, I'm home." Lil Man hollered as he came running through the door. I was in the kitchen preparing Sunday dinner. Maybe Jarvis and I could talk better if he had some home cooking.

"Is Pap Pap with you?" I hollered back praying his answer would be no.

"No, he's gone. He said he gotta buy some flowers for his lady friend. What happened to your face, mom?" My son exclaimed.

"Nothing, Hysear. It's okay."

"No it's not, mom. Your eye is all black and the side of your face looks big. What happened?" He quizzed.

"Son, nothing happened. I fell, okay?" My son stood there momentarily and looked at me.

"Did you and Jarvis fight again?"

I turned around and stirred the pot on the stove hoping that Hysear would find something else to talk about. But he didn't.

"No, son like I said, I fell."

"Mom, you're telling me a story!" he yelled. "I told you God said you needed protection but you didn't listen."

"I know, and I'm still here which means I'm fine. Now go and get your stuff out for school tomorrow. Is all your homework done?"

"Yep. I did it Friday before I left with Pap Pap. Can I wear my new Timberlands with my Ed Hardy jeans and shirt tomorrow, mom? Please? I've been waiting to put them on!" He asked.

I smiled at how quickly a child's attention could be taken away from the grim, to return to happiness.

"Yes, Hysear. Go and pull them out and lay them across the chair so I can see what they look like together. I'll be in to see you in a few minutes. Let me finish cooking dinner."

"Okay. I got a new game from Pap Pap so I'm going to play with my Wii." He said and ran out of the kitchen, down the hallway hollering all the way into his room.

I had to laugh at my little boy. He was the light of my life. I continued to fix my dinner of collard greens, potato salad, candied yams and baked chicken. I even tried my hand at baking a cake from scratch rather than the box. I just finished icing the cake and stood back to admire it when I heard the keys in the front door. I took a breath and waited. Jarvis came into view and threw the keys on the coffee table and then he walked into the kitchen.

"Hey."

"Hey, boo." I replied with a smile, trying to make things okay.

He reached in the cabinet and withdrew a glass. He proceeded to the fridge and took out the kool-aid. I watched him pour it and was glad he was home, with me. He sat the glass on the counter, and just stared at me. I pulled the sweet potatoes out of the oven and put them on the stovetop.

"I was putting away your clothes when I found your stash." I watched Jarvis's eyes grow big and then narrow.

"So did you leave my shit where it was?"

"Actually, I took it out to look at it and dropped your pipe. It broke." I confessed.

"Why you touch my shit anyway, Kaneesha. It was safe where it was. So where's my baggie. I know you got it so hand it over." He replied.

"Jarvis, how long you goin' keep smokin' that shit?" I questioned. "Look what you did to me. Look at my face. You can't have me and it."

"I didn't come home for you to question me. I need to be questioning your ass some more about what the fuck you been up to. You got my head fucked up, man. You need to be telling me just what the fuck is up with you and Stone!" He hollered.

"Shhh! Lower your voice. Hysear's home. And he ain't happy about how my face looks either, Jarvis." I told him.

"Kaneesha, I didn't mean to hurt you like I did. But you left me no choice. You're *my* mutherfuckin' woman and to find out that you out here sleeping around with Stone and then working for him, fucks me up!"

"I'm not fuckin' him!"

"I need you to tell me what the fuck is up and I need to know right fuckin' now!" He implored.

"How did you find out I was workin' for Stone? Was it Reds?"

"No, she wouldn't tell me anything, but someone else who saw you around did."

"Who was it?" He ignored me at first. "If we gonna work on us I have to know who told you."

"Dubbs." The room felt like it was spinning. "He sent me this picture."

When I looked at the picture in his cell phone, I saw me and Reds in a hotel room. It was from the night we were with Cappy.

"Oh. Well...uh...Dubbs is a liar." I said under my breath. "I'm not fuckin' Stone."

"So why you ain't just tell me you were workin' for him?" He badgered.

"I don't know, but I'm sorry. I wanted my own money."

"But I was taking that chance, not you."

"I was bored. I don't know. Maybe part of me resented you for being involved."

"But I didn't want you involved in this. You the reason I started smoking crack. It was too hard knowing you were working for him when I was forced into secrecy. Saying something to you meant losing my job with him."

"Speaking of losing your job, so you don't have your legal one anymore?"

"No. It's ridiculous when I make more money in one day with Stone than I do in five weeks at work. Now answer my question...why the lies?"

"I'm sorry, baby. I really am. What can I do?"

"I don't know. When was the last time you seen, Stone?" Jarvis asked.

"Friday." I replied. Jarvis didn't say anyting. For a moment he looked defeated then scared. "Jarvis, what's wrong?"

"Nothin', Kaneesha. Listen, if you tellin' me the truth now about you and him, then I guess I can dig why you did it. I don't agree with it though and want you to stop working for him. Stone has me and that's enough. I better not ever see you around him again. Do I make myself clear?"

"What about you and Reds? You giving her up to?"

"You don't have to ask."

"I will talk to Stone. I'll cut it all off."

"Yeah, you do that. The sooner the better." He said.

After we finished our conversation, and he held me in his arms, I thought about Stone. Giving up the work would be easy but giving up his bed would be another story. Because no matter how ruthless Stone was to the outside world, once he got in the bedroom and we made love, Stone was the most sensuous man who ever touched me. My mind continued to drift off to thoughts of Stone until Jarvis pulled me in for an intimate hug. I snapped out of it and focused back on Jarvis. What was I gonna do?

Chapter Fifteen

Reds hit me up on my cell phone and I deciphered the code. Stone wanted us to do a job tonight. I told her I would be at the hotel as required. As soon as I finished my text back to Reds I went to talk to Jarvis. Wasn't no sense in me lyin' to him, so I opted for the truth. He saw me hesitate in the doorway of our bedroom. His eyes zeroed in on my phone. He turned his head away from me and slammed his hands down on the dresser. Several perfume bottles fell over from the tremble. I casually walked over to the dresser and began to set them back up. He walked away and sat on the edge of the bed.

"I have a job to, Jarvis and I need to go." I said with my back turned to him still picking up the perfume bottles from the floor. I looked in the mirror at him. "Jarvis, I know you hear me. I need to leave tonight and I'll only be gone a few hours."

"You're gonna do what the fuck you wanna do anyway, huh? I'm just wasting my time and my breath. All I ask is that this be your last job with Stone." He said.

"Yes, Jarvis. I plan to talk to him tonight." I said moving away from the dresser and going into the closet to get my gun.

I pulled the piece from its resting place and checked it. Yep, one in the chamber and five in the barrel. I slipped it back in the holster and pulled my jeans down. I grabbed my purse, checked for the fake ID and disposable phone. When all items were cleared and secure, I turned around to face Jarvis.

"I'll be back. You gonna be here when I get home?"

"I don't know."

"I need you to."

"We'll see. Go save the day."

"Reds, you pregnant? Again?" I asked noticing the belly I saw months ago had reappeared. She had to be about seven months pregnant. Damn! She was always so covered up because of what we did that I didn't pay her much mind.

"Yeah, why?" She said with an attitude.

"Cause you just had *and* gave up a baby."

"Mind your business."

"You know what, you're right about that," I said waving her off. "Anyway, Jarvis and I talked and I think it's best if I quit." I said as I turned on the signal to make a left. I felt her stares. I was driving the rental car this time.

"You gonna give up this easy money, girl? *Shiiit*, that's exactly why I don't fuck with niggas."

"No...you just fuck 'em."

"I'm serious," she said waving me off, "you worry about the wrong shit. You could keep Jarvis simply by doing what he likes to do. Get high. I sure hope he ain't tell you no lie like he gonna stop."

"Why, you gonna let him run over to your house if I don't?"

"It's not about that, I'm my own, person."

"I can't tell because for a while, you were all open home."

"Me and Jarvis were business partners who became friends cause of what we do. Stop feeling threatened because it ain't that deep. That ain't got shit to do with you giving up this money."

"Reds, I don't feel comfortable with you and Jarvis's friendship and I'd like it to stop." She ignored me. "Reds, are you listening to me?"

"Don't tell me, tell him."

"I'm telling both of you. I want my family back and I shoulda never jumped into this shit to begin with. This choice is best for all of us." I said looking at her.

"Don't convince me, convince Stone cause he sure not gonna

like this shit."

Reds and I did the drop and the pick up without any problems. We were getting back in the rental to leave when her phone vibrated.

"Stone just texted me. He wants to see us. We need to go back to the motel and wait for him. So come on." Reds informed me.

She seemed short with me and I figured it was because I told her to stay away from Jarvis, but fuck her. We arrived back at the place of origin and went inside. Reds immediately pulled out her pipe and went to work. She offered me some coke but I declined. I didn't want to be high when Stone came and I'm surprised she opted to smoke right now. I saw her stomach move and knew the baby was having an objection to her drug of choice.

"Can you do that in the bathroom?" I asked.

"Whatever," she said walking inside, closing the door behind her.

Approximately thirty minutes later Stone was coming through the door. He stopped and sniffed the air. "What the Bumbleclot!. Where she at?" He growled.

I was scared as I pointed to the bathroom. Stone rushed in and she ran out.

"Bloodclot woman! What de the fuck I tell you 'bout smokin' that shit on the job!?" He screamed at her.

He snatched her by her hair and pulled her down onto the floor.

"I don't want anyone workin' for me smokin' that shit on the job! And you wit' child too! American women are loose in their actions!" He spat. "What's the matta wit you?!"

Reds lay on the floor and took the lashing that Stone was giving her both mentally and physically. She was in pain and I was scared for the baby.

I spoke up. "Stone! Please stop you're hurting the baby." I begged.

Stone shot a look so deadly at me that I felt a chill run through my body. "Stone! Please let her go. Please!" I continued to beg.

He released Reds' hair and walked off. Reds remained whimpering softly on the floor.

"Get up and go!" he commanded.

Reds quickly retrieved her things and rushed out of the motel room.

Stone sat down at the desk with his legs crossed and began to pick his nails. I sat on the edge of the bed.

"Come." Stone beckoned to me as Reds walked out the door. I didn't move. "You disobey me? Come I said!"

I slowly got up off the bed and walked over to the desk and stood in front of him. He reached out and took my hands in his.

"I didn't wanna have ta hurt Reds but she know that's a fuckin' no-no in my book."

"But she said you pay her in coke sometimes. So I thought it was cool with you."

"Well it's nawt. Coke one thing Crack anotha. I don't ever want ta see you wit no pipe in ya mouth! Do you hear what I tell you, Kaneesha? The minute I find out you turned to crack, I forever turn my back on you." He said snapping his fingers.

I nodded to acknowledge what he was saying but I had bigger issues to discuss with him. "Stone, Jarvis found out that I'm workin' for you."

"So what's the problem?"

"He wants me to stop."

"How did he find out!?" He questioned.

"Dubbs sent Jarvis a picture of all of us at the hotel room the night we were there with Cappy." I said hanging my head. "And, he suspects we're sleeping together too. Dubbs gave him his theory on that also. We fought about this some months back. It was really bad and he just came back home."

"I'll take care of Dubbs. So, this fight tween you and Jarvis is why ya have a gash over ya eye that won't go away?" Stone asked as he reached up and caressed my face gently. I melted into his touch.

"Yes, he was upset when he found out and went off." I admitted.

"I kill him!" Stone said as his nostrils flared.

"No, Stone! I was wrong, Jarvis had the right to be mad at me. He's my man and look how he found out. You gotta stay out of it! I want to work on us, please. If you get in the mix he'll know the the truth. I can't have that! Let *me* handle my home, please!" I begged.

"Why be wit a man wit no self control?"

"What do you mean?"

"He's on crack isn't he? He was weak enough ta allow the drug to consume him. He's no good for you."

"How...how did you know?"

"I turned him on to it."

I backed away and looked at him. "What....why? I...I don't understand. You just said you didn't like people smokin' on the job."

"Yes...on the job, but at Reds place it's okay."

Tears ran down my face.

"Don't cry. I wanted you ta see he's no good for you, and then maybe we could be."

"Stone...this is awful!"

"No awful...just real, now come. I've been tinking about the way ya suck my dick all day. On your knees now and handle a real man."

Chapter Sixteen

For the next two weeks, Jarvis and I squashed any beef between us and carried on like the couple we were before Stone came into our lives, somewhat. Secretly, I still snuck off twice a week to be with Stone. I know I should be mad at him, but by sleeping with him I had the best of both worlds. Money without having to work and good dick.

But the last time we were together, we had an unusual conversation. We were lying in the bed and I was lying on his chest rubbing his six-pack. He was smoking a blunt and had just exhaled the smoke before he spoke.

"Where is the gun me gave you when you worked for me?"

"At home...why?"

"Look, it's very important that ya give it back. I gave you a weapon that has bodies on it."

"What? What do you mean?"

"Don't say noting else. Just bring me back the weapon."

"Okay."

"Love, has Jarvis been bringing home work?" I sat up and my breathing quickened in my chest. I snuggled up closer to Stone.

"Hell no? What makes you ask that?" I asked inquisitively.

Stone nudged me and I moved off of him. He sat up and looked at me. I averted my eyes to the TV. Stone took another hit from the blunt.

"Kaneesha, I'm going to ask you again. Is Jarvis bringing home work?" He repeated. "I've been having large amounts of stash missing and we can't figure out who it is."

"Stone, didn't I just tell you no? Why do you keep askin' me that?"

"Look at me, Kaneesha." Stone demanded. "Are you protecting him?" Stone asked.

My defense mode kicked in. Regardless of what Stone and I did, Jarvis was still my man so I had to protect him.

"Stone, I don't know where the hell you got that from, but Jarvis would never steal from you. What about Reds?" I offered.

"Reds would never do such a ting. She's crazy but not stupid."

"What makes you think its Jarvis?"

"I heard some tings I don't like lately. Some tings that make me wonder. But if you say he's not bringing home my product, and you should know because you live with he, then for now, I will drop the subject. But I implore you not to mention this conversation to Jarvis I still have one more thing to find out!" He said as he got up to get dressed.

He went to the bathroom and I put my clothes on wondering what the hell was going on. Jarvis had been bringing home bags of crack lately. He had so much of it, that I was finding it everywhere. He smoked it all day everyday and I quickly realized it was something I'd have to accept. But I never…ever…once thought he was stealing from Stone. I knew I couldn't say anything to Jarvis about it because I was not supposed to be still seeing Stone to begin with. But maybe I could drop a hint to Jarvis so he could watch his.

I could hear Stone on phone in the bathroom taking in Patios. I opened my phone to see if I had any missed calls or texts. There was one missed text. I opened it and read it. It said "*I'm watching you…still.*"

I instantly looked around the room and then crept to the window and pulled back the shade just enough to look around the parking lot. The same cars that were there when we pulled up were still there and I didn't see anyone around.

"What are you doing?" Stone hollered. I jumped away from the window and my phone fell out of my hand.

"Damn, Stone, you scared the shit outta me!" He crossed his arms across his chest and stared at me.

"What you looking out the window for? You expecting someone?" he implied.

"No, Stone. Someone sent me this message," I said showing him.

"Bloodclot! Whose number is this?" He screamed dialing the number. When he did, the phone clicked and rang once before ending. "Why they not answer?"

"I don't know. That's the second time I got a message like this. The first time it was a voice mail and when..."

I cut myself off as I remember Jarvis later saying that when he first got the picture mail from Dubbs, he tried to call back the number and got the same ringing and clicking tone.

"I don't care, troe this wicked pussyclot phone away and here." He said reaching in his pocket and peeling off three hundred dollar bills. "Take this and buy a new one. Give me that phone!"

Stone snatched it back from my hand and put it in his bag.

"But I got numbers on there, Stone, that I need to get off." I pleaded.

"Then get a pen and paper and write dem down. I'm gettin' rid of dis shit today." He stated.

After I wrote down the numbers, Stone and I left the hotel. While driving, he kept looking in his rearview mirror. The messages put him on edge too. Stone dropped me off a block away from the Heights. Before I climbed out of his truck, he affirmed that the conversation we had at the hotel was between us. I concurred and proceeded to my house.

When I opened the apartment door and walked in, I saw Baggs, Patrick and Man-Man, a few guys I knew and had seen around the neighborhood, sitting in my living room. Jarvis hung out with them a time or two, but they never came to the apartment before. So I was surprised to find their asses sitting around the coffee table.

"What the hell is going in on here?" I asked.

Everyone looked up at me, but no one said a thing.

"What cha'll deaf? I asked what the hell is going on?" I repeated.

Baggs spoke up. "Hey, Kaneesha. We just in here chillin.' That's all."

"What you mean you in here chillin'? I ain't never seen you niggas up in here before so what cha doin' here now! And what the hell is that shit ya'll got on my coffee table?" I looked sternly at Baggs.

"We just came over to see Jarvis and he said it was okay if we chilled here for a minute."

Just then Jarvis came bopping out from the back of the apartment. I stopped him before he got into the living room.

"Jarvis, I need to talk to you for moment?" I said, giving him the come here finger.

Jarvis rolled his eyes and turned around to head to the bedroom. Before I followed him I took another look at the items on the table. I saw a mirror, an empty baggie, and some cigarette ashes along with a miniature Nottyhead bottle lying on its side. Nottyhead was a cheap bottle of alcohol and if you drank too much you'd have a headache, hence the name, Nottyhead. The bottle had been molded into a pipe. I shook my head and walked to the room. I slammed the door shut and pointed my finger at Jarvis's face.

"What the hell is wrong wit' you? Why you sweatin' like that? Look at your eyes? You look like you've seen a damn ghost! What the fuck is going on out there, Jarvis?" I yelled.

He was sweating profusely and his eyes were bigger than normal, and his hands were shaking. His jaws were clenched together very tightly, and he kept grinding his teeth. This was not the same man I had left before I went out. Some new shit had come up in here and had transformed my boyfriend. Jarvis sat down on the bed across from me.

"Kaneesha, I wanted to get high in my own damn house. So I invited some of my boys up. We just smokin' a couple blunts and I a few rocks." He said.

"And where did you get the rocks from?"

"What...what you mean?" He asked in a guilty tone. "Did Stone say something?"

My heart dropped.

"I haven't seen him and if I did, what would he say to me about this? You stealin' from him or somethin'?"

"What? No...look, I'ma go back out there and have a good time. You stay the fuck back here." Jarvis exhaled loudly and left the bedroom. I began pacing around talking to myself.

What the fuck is he thinking? Oh hell no! I was not having that shit up in here! I'ma 'bout to kill this action right the fuck now. That nigga is crazy if he thinks he gonna be smoking crack and bringin' them bamma ass niggas in here too! Man, I'll come home and find my whole fucking apartment gone. I heard Jarvis call my name from the living room. What the fuck does he want! I ain't for no bullshit. They better be gone when I get out there. I walked down the hall and into our living room and everyone was gone except Baggs.

"Hey, Kaneesha," Baggs said.

"Why are you still here?"

Baggs didn't pay me any attention. He just pulled out the plastic baggie from his pocket that held about a quarter of a kilo of what looked like cocaine. He always had weight, but Baggs would sometimes step on his product so bad that it would drive his customers to other dealers. He proceeded to shake some girl onto the mirror.

"Yeah, I know you don't freebase, so that's why I'm givin' you a little something for your trouble. Now me and Jarvis wanna continue to get lifted, so if you don't mind, I'd like to lay here for a minute." he said steady shaking coke onto the mirror. Baggs put a generous amount on it. There must have been about a fifty-cent piece.

"Is that all mine?" I asked, my mouth already watering at the prospect of a freeze on my teeth.

"Yep, that's all yours." Baggs told me.

"Fuck it, I could use a pick me up. Put that shit right in

this!" I told him as I handed him a dollar bill that was in my pocket. Baggs scooped the coke off the mirror and into the dollar. I turned towards Jarvis.

"Once Baggs is done, I don't want him runnin' back in forth through my door. It's too fuckin' hot out there with this type of shit floating around." I turned my attention back to Baggs. "And don't you be goin' out there tellin' folks our business, Baggs. I mean it. If I hear anything about what you did in my house, you will never darken my doorway again. You got that?" I told him.

"Kaneesha, I'm not gonna tell no one, I ain't 'bout to blow this set up." He said.

"What the hell do you mean by blow this set up? This is just a one time thing."

"Didn't your boy tell you about my proposition?" Baggs asked. I froze in my tracks and looked over at Jarvis.

"What the fuck is he talkin' about?" I questioned.

Jarvis looked over at Baggs, and I saw him put his hand up in air signaling for Baggs to be quiet.

"Come with me, Kaneesha." We walked to the kitchen.

Jarvis couldn't even look at me and turned towards the sink.

"Kaneesha, Baggs asked me if it would be alright if he could use our apartment to produce some of his product." He started. "And I said yes."

"Why in the fuck would you tell that nigga he could come in our home to do that type of shit? Did your ass forget that I have an eight-year-old son who also lives here? You didn't even ask me first. I managed to live six months when you were gone and I would like to live six more. I thought you worked for Stone."

"Yeah well Stone ain't been treating me too good. I'm thinkin' about leaving and working with Baggs."

"Jarvis, I fixed you something on the mirror." Baggs interrupted. "You go on in there like a good little dog and let me talk to your woman." Without hesitation Jarvis left and Baggs walked up to me. I knew then Jarvis was not the same man.

"Look, I don't know what you feeding Jarvis, but I'm not on it. I want you to take your shit and get out of my house. As a matter of fact, take this back and go." I handed Baggs the dollar bill with the coke in it that he had given to me earlier. Now I know I must be crazy for real to give back this nice weight.

"No, you keep that. I want you to have it no matter what," Baggs said, pushing the dollar bill back into my hand. "Kaneesha, I'm willin' to lay some change in your hand if you could help me out of a pinch."

"Go on." I said with my hands on my hips.

"I'ma be straight wit'chu, the place where I used to go, the girl there got stupid. At first, all she wanted was money for the use of her kitchen. I'd go there every other night and do my thing and I'd leave her a hundred dollars every single time I used her shit. But about three months into this arrangement, she started asking me to leave her a little coke cause she said she like to snort every once and a while. So I would leave her some along with the money. I didn't know that she had started sucking on the pipe, too. It got to the point that she didn't want the money no more. All she wanted was Coke and for me to fuck her every now and again.

"But then she got outta control. Blowin' up my pager all hours of the day and night, demandin' that I come over there and give her some powder or rock. When I told her no, she threatened to call Five-0 on me. So I had to put a stop to that arrangement quick. You know that woman as Reds, and I understand she's working for Stone. I just hope she's not stealing from him like she was from me. But he's my competition so fuck him."

I was blown away by his words and his involvement with Reds.

"I only need to use the kitchen to cook up my product and bag it. It shouldn't take any more than three to four hours to do the whole thing. I ain't bringin' nobody with me, and I would come late at night after your son is asleep. I'ma leave you a hundred dollars and some powder for your nose." He propositioned. "And I'll go. Deal?"

I looked at Baggs and let what he said marinate in my mind. It sounded easy, but it's never as simple as that.

"Why did you come to me and Jarvis for this shit?" I wanted to know.

"Cause I know that you don't smoke no rock, you only snort coke occasionally. So there's no threat," he said grinning all hard.

"Yeah well what about Jarvis."

He gave me a sinister look and said, "He's not crazy."

"Baggs, I don't think this is a good idea. I mean, I got my son here man and I ain't trying to get nothing started in here that will be hard to stop. Your gonna have to find somewhere else to cook and bag your product, man. I'm sorry." I said finally.

"It's cool, Kaneesha. I understand and I respect that." He said sounding defeated.

Just then we hear Jarvis coughing in the living room. He had taken too big of a hit off the blunt he was smoking.

"Jarvis, are you alright?" I asked.

"Yeah, I'm fine, that shit is the bomb!" He said still coughing out smoke.

"I'm goin' in the room to lay down. Please finish up your little session so Baggs can be on his way." I told them. Neither one of them acknowledged my statement just continued in their own world.

A hour later Jarvis came into the bedroom and said he was leaving out for awhile. I still needed to let him know about Stone.

"Jarvis, just so you know I turned down Baggs' offer." I told him.

"You did what? Why would you turn down that good easy

money? I need that money!"

"Boy, I don't need that type of drama in here! I quit workin' for Stone so that I can be outta this game and you think I'ma open my home up to it for some punk ass $100 a night? Please, Jarvis!" I yelled.

"Well where did you get this from?" He asked showing me the money Stone had given me earlier.

"Unlike you, I saved my money," I said hoping he'd buy it.

"Yeah right," he said throwing it in my face.

I scooped the bills and said, "What you need with Baggs? And why you not workin' for Stone?"

"Let's just say we had irreconcilable differences."

"Jarvis, what the fuck does that mean?"

"Kaneesha, we just ain't vibin' no more and the situation with you two fucked me up."

"But nothin' happened."

"That's what you say."

"Well look, Stone been askin' around 'bout you. He askin' people if you been workin' on the side. Have you?"

"Just stay outta my business, Kaneesha! I'll be back." He said as he grabbed his keys.

There he goes leaving again.

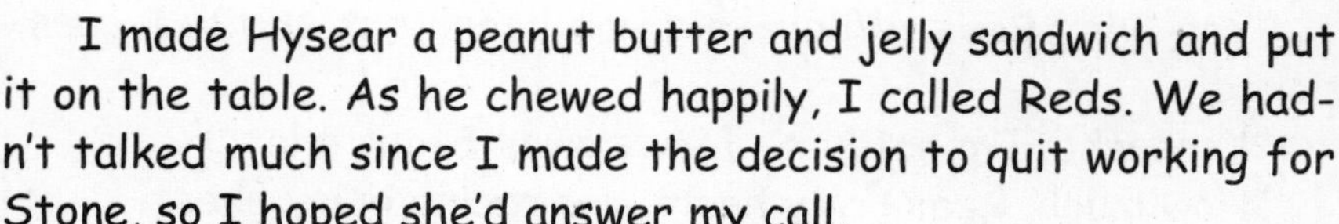

I made Hysear a peanut butter and jelly sandwich and put it on the table. As he chewed happily, I called Reds. We hadn't talked much since I made the decision to quit working for Stone, so I hoped she'd answer my call.

"Hey, Reds. How you been?"

"He's not here," she said being smart, but secretly relieving my frustration.

"Oh...I'm not calling about Jarvis. I was calling to see if you could come over.

She paused for a moment and said, "I'm on my way."

Fifteen minutes later, Reds and me were in my bedroom

chillin'.

"So since you ain't workin' for Stone no more, how you holdin'up with money?" she asked.

"The stash of money that I had has dwindled down some but I got a little change left. They cut my hours on the job so I really need to hold on to what I got. And Jarvis hasn't been contributing anything extra. I don't understand it. He was workin' for Stone and if Stone was payin' him like he was payin' me then I don't get why Jarvis ain't bringin' more to the table." I saw Reds facial expression change when I mentioned Jarvis working for Stone. "It seems mighty funny that Jarvis ain't producin'." I rambled on. I waited for a response from Reds. She didn't give any. So I went directly in. "Reds, do you know what's going on between Stone and Jarvis?"

Reds tightened her lips and shook her head no.

"Come on, Reds. You know somethin'." I persisted. Reds sat up in the chair before she spoke.

"Kaneesha, you know Stone don't divulge anything to anyone about his dealings. But you my girl, so I'ma tell you somethin' that you gotta keep under your hat." She warned me.

"What?" I asked, half excited to get to the bottom of this mystery and half afraid of what she might tell me.

"Swear your ass is not goin' say anything!"

"Stop bullshittin' and tell a bitch what she need to know."

"Jarvis owes Stone money." She replied.

"You lyin', Reds. Where did you hear that shit?" I questioned.

"Kaneesha, I'm not lyin'. Jarvis owes Stone a lot."

"How much, Reds?" My heart was racing in my chest.

"I don't know. The story is that Jarvis, Big Willie and Sammy all got a package to sell. Big Willie and Sammy say they put the package in their usual hiding place and when they went back to re-up, the package was gone. The package was ready rock and the bag was worth sixteen hundred dollars."

"You can't be serious."

"I am, and Big Willie and Sammy think Jarvis stole it."

"I don't believe it! Jarvis wouldn't steal from Stone. It ain't like he ain't been havin' no extra ends, so what would he do wit' two O's?" I asked. Reds looked up to the ceiling and took a deep breath.

"Kaneesha, Jarvis is smokin' crack like no tomorrow. Did you know that shit?" she asked. My silence must have told her all she needed to know.

"He be down Me-Me's smokin' wit' me and everyone else in there 'cause I ain't let him in my place since me and you talked. He had large quantities of it a couple weeks ago. That's prolly where all his side money was goin', until it ran out. Now I ain't sayin' he did anything cause my yellow ass wasn't there, but as a fair warnin', you need to be ready for anything that might come down the pipe. Literally. You know as well as I do that if Jarvis really did take that package the repercussions will be devastating." Reds warned.

If this was true, then it was just a matter of time before it would catch up with Jarvis and for that matter me too.

I was nervous for the rest of the evening ever since Reds told me about the missing package and Jarvis smoking down Me-Me's. That would explain why Jarvis didn't have no damn money like he should have had. I was in my room snorting a couple of lines when Jarvis came in and kissed me on the cheek. Just looking at him and knowing what I knew made me nervous.

Jarvis sat down in the chair across from me. He looked spaced out.

"You okay?" I asked him.

"Yeah, I'm fine. Let me get a hit of that."

I passed him the mirror and watched him snort up two thick lines. He snorted hard and sat back in the chair.

"Let's smoke some. I'll show you how to do it!" He said all excited like a damn kid.

He didn't know that I'd already had my lessons from Reds

and was not really impressed.

"You know damn well, I'm not 'bout to put no pipe in my mouth and smoke no cocaine. Why would you ask me to do that?" I asked.

"Kaneesha, the high you will experience will put that snorting shit to shame. I'm telling you, girl. Ain't nothing like this rush."

"I don't want to smoke, Jarvis." I said.

"Well, I do so give me some of your stash cause I ain't got none." He held out his hand.

"No, Jarvis."

"Well give me some money."

"Where the fuck is yours?"

"Are you gonna take care of your man or not?"

"I thought you wanted to take care of me. What happened to that?" He was silent and I saw for a brief moment, he even felt bad. "Look Jarvis, I'm not wasting my little bit of shit by putting it in a pipe and I'm not giving you no money." I snipped.

I had an uneasy feeling about sitting on the bed with this mirror of coke on my lap and Jarvis just watching me. He looked like he wanted to hurt me for it. I was scared.

"Jarvis, if I give you some, will you please leave me alone after that?"

"Yeah, baby, just break me off some, and I'll go in the bathroom and do me. No problem." He grinned.

He pulled out a dollar bill from his pants pocket. I took the dollar bill out his hand and put it on the mirror and scraped some of my coke into it. I handed it back to him and watched him walk out the room. Several minutes later, I heard the bathroom door shut and then the familiar smell of coke being smoked wafted through my bedroom.

I tuned into the remainder of the David Letterman show. But for some reason, I still had the nervous feeling. Twenty minutes later, Jarvis emerged from the bathroom with that fucking crazy spaced out look on his face. His eyes were wide as saucers, and sweat was beading up around his forehead. He sat back down in the chair with a fucking plastic pipe in his hand. I didn't say a word. I continued to watch David Letterman and prayed that Jarvis would go back into the bathroom to finish what the hell he was doing. No such luck.

"Kaneesha, you got any more coke?" He asked.

"You look like you don't need any more coke. Ain't you high enough?" I replied.

"Just give me some please." He begged.

"I already gave you some. You said you would leave me alone, remember?"

"Yeah, girl, but shit, it wasn't but about a dime piece anyway after I cooked it up. That don't do nothing but tease you. So now I need to get a good blast. So give me some."

"I ain't got no stash, Jarvis. All the coke I got is on my mirror and that ain't much."

"Let me see." He walked over to the bed looking under it for my mirror.

"Jarvis, why you taking my shit? Go buy your own. Call Baggs or go see Dubbs. Stay out of my shit!" I yelled.

"You told Baggs to stay away remember? If you woulda let him work here, I wouldn't be all up in your face." Jarvis continued on his rampage.

I knew this shit was gonna turn wrong. Things were getting out of hand. I was not trying to give him the mirror and what was left of my coke.

"Kaneesha, I don't want to hurt you. So don't make me...okay? Just give it to me."

"You would hurt me? Is this that important to you?"

"More important than your life."

Without my consent, he took all of it and walked out the bedroom. I wanted to run down the hall and slap the shit out of him but I was scared and hurt. Instead, I just laid back on the bed. Just as I was about to turn out the light, Jarvis came back in the bedroom with the mirror. He sat down on the bed

"Kaneesha, I know you mad at me, but I want you to try this one time for me." Jarvis said.

"Jarvis, please stop askin' me to do this. You took it so take it."

"Baby, the high you get from this will blow your mind. Try it one time. If you don't like it, you ain't gotta do it no more. But you're wasting your high snorting it."

At first I felt I said and meant no, but the more he worked my nerves, the more I needed relief. It got to a point when I woulda done heroin, if it were in front of me.

"If I try this will you leave me alone?" I asked hoping to get him off my back once and for all about this.

"Yeah, but I guarantee that once you try this you are going to like it. Just do what I tell you to do." He said.

"Whatever," I said.

I snatched back the covers and sat on the bed to await instructions from Jarvis.

"Kaneesha, I'ma go get some the stuff we gonna need to cook with okay?" He said. I nodded my head and rolled my eyes.

Jarvis ran out the bedroom. When he returned, he had one of my serving trays in his hands. He put the tray on the bed and I saw that it held a spoon, a candle, a box of baking soda, a glass of water, a lighter, a piece of a wire coat hanger about three and half inches long and a crazy looking plastic pipe that he had fashioned out of a miniature nottyhead alcohol bottle. I watched him as he intensely began to go to work. He seemed like he was a pro at this shit. This man wasn't my Jarvis. I don't know this person. I don't like this person but yet I felt defeated and stayed in his presence.

He lit the candle and sat it in the candleholder that I didn't even know we had. Jarvis must have bought it purposely for this. He took the coke and put some in the spoon. Next he took a pinch of baking soda and put it on top of the cane in the spoon. He took his fingers and dipped it in the glass of water and let the water drip from his finger onto the spoon. He did this several times, making sure not to add too much. He took the spoon and put it over the flame of the candle. The wire coat hanger was used to mix everything in the spoon.

"Kaneesha, look."

"What am I looking for?" I asked, moving closer to him.

"See the way the coke gets oily."

"Yeah." I replied still looking.

"That's what I want, I don't want it to be too watery, and you only cook it enough to melt the coke until you see it form to an oil state like this. See?"

Sure enough there was an oil circle in the middle of the spoon.

"That ain't no rock, so how do you get it to come to that rock form?" I asked.

Personally, this shit was intriguing to me. I had seen Reds do it but only from afar. I didn't know how she mixed the shit. I moved in even closer to Jarvis.

He took the spoon away from the flame and dipped his fingers back into the glass of water. He let the water drip from his fingers into the spoon again and began stirring the oil. I saw the oil begin to solidify around the end of the hanger. Jarvis kept going around in a circle making sure that he got all the oil to cling to the hanger. As the coke started to cool down, it became hard. Jarvis pulled the wire out of the spoon and showed me the end result. A huge white rock was attached to the end of the hanger. Jarvis was sweating like he was performing a life and death operation. Damn, that shit was amazing to see the transformation of powder to a rock formation. After that I was curious as hell to try it.

"Sit right here and watch me." Jarvis said. I scooted down towards the end of the bed.

"Light a Newport and let it burn. We need the ashes." He told me.

I reached over on the nightstand and picked up my half a pack of Newports. I lit the Newport and laid it down in the ashtray. Jarvis was busy cutting the solid rock off the end of the hanger. I watched as he carefully cut around the hanger scrapping it, ensuring that every speck of it was scraped off and onto the mirror. He cut the rock, which was about the size of an aspirin into several pieces. He picked up the pipe and inspected it before he used it. He blew into it while he hovered his hand around it at the same time.

"Why you doin' that?" I asked.

"Makin' sure ain't no holes for air leakage." he replied while inspecting his pipe.

When he was satisfied that he could feel no air, he put the pipe back down on the mirror. Jarvis got up off the bed and began rummaging around on the dresser.

"What are you looking for now?" I said.

"Any type of pin or needle so I can open the holes on the top of the pipe." He replied

"Look in the jewelry box. Should be some straight pins in there." I told him.

"I got one." He took a matchbook and tore the cover off. Then he picked up the pin and stuck it in the holes that were already in the aluminum foil.

"Watch, Kaneesha. You have to open up the holes once in a while to make sure the smoke gets through. But don't make them too big. If you do, you'll burn up your rock, and you won't be able to pull the smoke like you want. Just watch me, okay?" He schooled.

For some reason, my disgust turned into attraction. Although we were dealing with something deadly, the way he handled himself with it was surgical. He was a doctor who had passion for his work. He was patient and anxious all at once. Patient enough to cook it right, yet he was so anxious, that every part of his body vibrated, except his hands.

Jarvis took the straight pin and began opening up some of the holes that were already in the foil. When he was done, he took the torn match book cover and used it to scoop up some of the cigarette ashes in the ashtray and put them on the top of the aluminum foil.

"Hold this so it doesn't fall over." I held the pipe on the mirror while Jarvis cut a piece of the rock. He put the little piece of coke on top of the ashes and then brought the pipe up to his mouth. He grabbed the lighter, and just as he was about to put the straw end of the pipe in his mouth he told me to get ready, he wanted me to have the first hit.

"Put the pipe in your mouth. When I say pull, I want you to gently pull in and get some of the smoke in your mouth. Hold the smoke in for a couple of seconds before letting it go. And let the smoke out your mouth slowly. Okay?" He said.

I was nervous as fuck. But there was no turning back now. I might as well get this over with. Jarvis handed me the pipe and placed it in my mouth. My eyes were crossed as I watched him flick the lighter and very gently and barely touch the stone.

"Pull easy, Kaneesha." He coached me. "Pull it nice and slow."

I pulled in the smoke easy like he said.

"That's it. Hold it, baby." He coached, his tone extremely sexual.

I held the smoke in my mouth like my teacher taught me, wanting to make him proud. Hoping he'd see my love was so strong, I'd push my own boundaries.

"Let it out slow." I exhaled the smoke out slowly and Jarvis watched my reaction. Several seconds later, my heart began to race.

"Kaneesha, look at me." He said, and I glazed over his face.

"Kaneesha, are you okay?" He asked sounding nervous.

I couldn't answer him at that moment. I was beginning to feel euphoric. I felt like I was being transported to another dimension in time. I was on a cloud where nobody could reach me. I was floating. My ears rang and my heart was beating fast. I felt a rush of heat resonate throughout my body. I was listless and could not move. I didn't want to move. I was in fucking heaven and I was angry that God held this from me for so long. This was the answer to my sadness, to my happiness and to my life.

"Kaneesha, girl, talk to me. You okay?" He asked in a worried tone.

"I'm fine," I managed to say.

With confirmation of my well being, he took the pipe and put it into his mouth and lit what was left of the rock. Several minutes later, Jarvis joined me in freebase heaven. He didn't talk much after that himself. We exchanged non-verbal dialogue and he knew I was ready for another taste.

He fixed the pipe up for me again and nodded his head in approval as he watched me put the flame to the coke and take lift off. I held it again for several seconds and then slowly let it out. Here comes that feeling again. An incredible airy, heart-racing, and body-sweating feeling. This time, I too had begun to clench my jaws tightly as I have seen Jarvis do on so many occasions. When I stood up, I was lightheaded. I closed my eyes, and next thing I knew I was on the floor semi-conscious. I felt Jarvis pulling me up into a sitting position.

"Kaneesha, I'ma go get a cold washcloth. Don't go anywhere!" He ordered.

I scooted up next the bed so my back could rest on it and Jarvis came back into the bedroom with a cold washrag. He put it around my neck and then wiped my forehead with it.

"Baby, you okay? You may have hit the pipe too hard and took in too much that last time. You gotta be careful with this shit, baby. It can make you have a seizure or even a heart attack. I ain't trying to scare you, but I want you to know this okay?"

"Damn, Jarvis," I said ignoring his pleas. "I've never…ever…felt anything like that before."

Jarvis had put the mirror on the dresser and was sitting beside me on the bed. I was feeling good now since the light-headedness had passed. Jarvis reached over and pulled me close to him. I don't know what was going on but when he touched me it was like my body was suddenly sexually charged.

Jarvis pulled me on top of him and began to kiss me softly. We locked ourselves in a passionate tongue battle. I felt Jarvis's dick swell in his jeans and I grinded myself against him. We kissed deeply. Jarvis reached around my back and pulled my T-shirt up and over my head, throwing it to the floor.

He unhooked my bra, snatched it off my arms and flung it above his head. I heard it fall down softly behind the headboard. He stopped kissing me and began to run his tongue down the side of my neck, down my throat and down the middle of my breast. He began to kiss each one of my breasts softly. He took my right breast in his hand and suckled the nipple like a baby. I felt his tongue run across it making it stand up at attention. He bit my nipple and I moaned.

"Bite me harder." I begged.

Jarvis obliged. He bit each nipple harder sending small slivers of pain and pleasure through me. I continued to grind on his ever-growing erection, but I wanted to taste him. So I stopped and unbuckled his pants. I slid my hands down into his boxers and found what I wanted. Jarvis and I hadn't really been with each other sexually in a while because I was content with my secret escapades with Stone. But now, Jarvis was my master and I was his slave.

Jarvis slid out of this boxers and let them hang at his ankles.

"Where are your candles?" he asked.

I walked over to the drawer where I kept my special occasion underwear, teddies, and nightgowns and found three new candles. I set them around the bed and lit them. I turned off the light and walked over to Jarvis.

"Wait, go back and walk slowly towards me." he said.

I went back over towards the candlelight and seductively walked towards Jarvis. Jarvis was stroking his dick up and down while he watched me walk to him. He was long, hard and thick. Just what the fuck I wanted. I was still in a euphoric state of high so I was really feeling freaky. The more seductively I walked, the more Jarvis kept beating his dick. I got to him and stopped. I knelt down in front of him and let my mouth take over where his hands were. I wrapped my hands around his dick and looked up at my man. He was going to get the best head I could give him. I brought my mouth down onto him and ran my tongue over the top of his head. For some reason, I thought about the pipe that had been in my mouth moments earlier and my pussy throbbed. Then, I heard him moan. I ran my tongue down one side of his shaft and up the other side. I teased him relentlessly.

I purposely licked every inch of him until he was begging for me to put it in my mouth. I spit on his dick and rubbed my saliva around the head and down the sides of his thickness. Slowly I slid on top of him and rode him. We both let out moans of pleasure. Jarvis was wonderfully built and his dick should be bronzed and put in a jar for all men to aspire to.

"You given my pussy away?" he asked pumping into me.

"Never," I lied.

"Stone can't fuck you like this?"

"In his dreams," I smiled.

I grinded my pussy hard against Jarvis's pelvis making sure that my clitoris was being worked on too. He was pumping into me like a man who was digging for gold. Every thrust was deep and hard.

"Damn, girl, you feel so fuckin' good." He whispered.

"You do too, Jarvis, fuck me just like that. I want to cum all over your dick, baby. Don't stop Boo, don't stop." I told him.

Jarvis and I were matching each other stroke for stroke. I could feel my orgasm rising. It started deep within my pussy walls and then began to slowly ascend to my stomach. I grabbed Jarvis's hands and put them on my breasts.

"Ummm, Jarvis, that's it, baby." I instructed.

Jarvis was wearing my pussy out. I felt him thrusting faster, which normally meant he was about to cum too. I grabbed his hands and placed them above his head. I held on to them as I continued to fuck him. I felt my orgasm coming. It's coming!

"Ooohhhh...ooohhh shit... Jarvis, I'm cumin'...Oh, Jarvis, BAABBBYYY!!!!" I screamed.

My orgasm hit me like an electric rod. It came from deep within my pussy and spilled over into my belly. I sang Jarvis's name in octaves I've never hit before. I was still bucking wildly on top of him when I felt him grab my ass tightly as he poured his seed into my wetness. I collapsed on top of my man.

Jarvis held me tightly for a few minutes before he said "Let's get another hit."

"Let's do it," I smiled.

We bonded on another kind of level. A level that after awhile, would cause me greatly. But at that moment, I just didn't give a fuck.

Chapter Seventeen

I was in the supermarket geaking. I wanted another hit the moment I selected a shopping cart and pushed it down the aisle. Why eat when for real, I wasn't even hungry?

"I heard that Jarvis whooped that ass." I whipped my head around and Dubbs was standing behind me. He'd taken me briefly out of my desires.

"What the fuck are you talkin' 'bout now, Dubbs?" I asked.

"You, baby. I heard that Jarvis found out you was workin' for Stone and beat that ass." He jeered.

"Jarvis ain't crazy enough to put his hands on me!" I lied.

"Well maybe the next time you and him are in there fightin' like two champion boxers, you may think 'bout goin' in the bedroom so we can't hear y'all in the hallway! Although Jarvis was yellin' loud enough for everybody in the Heights to hear no matter what room ya'll were in. I heard every fuckin' word he said to you 'bout workin' for Stone and oh yeah...fuckin' Stone." Dubbs snickered.

"You know what, fuck you, Dubbs! Fuck you!" I shouted.

"That's what I want, Kaneesha. Stop bullshittin' and give me some of that good pussy you been givin' Stone." He snipped.

Dubbs's head snapped back when my hand slammed across his face. He grabbed my arms and pushed me and the shopping cart up against the can goods. They toppled over at my feet. Other shoppers whispered and walked the other way assuming me and Dubbs were having a domestic dispute.

"No no, baby girl. You can't slap me around like you do Jarvis." He whispered in my ear.

Dubbs pressed his body to mine, and I felt his dick swell against my leg as he continued to mash me against the shelves. He was grinding on me and licked the side of my face.

"You's the one I want. And one day I'ma give you what you

need." He continued.

"Hey take that outside!" a bald headed white man yelled down the isle. Dubbs let me go.

"Your days are numbered, Dubbs. You ain't gettin' away with this shit!" I yelled.

"Watch what you say, Kaneesha. Your days might be numbered, too." He replied and then he ran out the door.

"Are you okay miss? Do you need the police?" The bald white man asked.

I snatched my purse out of the shopping cart and ran out the door. It was time to see Stone.

I decided to call Reds first and talk to her when I got home.

"Reds, Dubbs just put his hands on me at the market. I'm sick of him and I need this shit to stop! He don't know who he fuckin' wit."

"Calm down. Are you alright?"

"No! Why won't he leave me alone?"

"You know his ass is crazy."

"Well so am I. I think it's time for me to tell Stone. He said he was gonna do somethin' to him anyway. I don't even know why he still walkin' around."

"Girl, Stone ain't killin' nobody for you. That's just somethin' he said to make you feel good. He ain't killin' unless somethin's in it for him. I told you that along time ago."

"If he knew he was fuckin' for me, I know he would do somethin'."

"Look, all Stone thinkin' 'bout is his money? When was the last time you talked to him?"

"I can't remember."

"Exactly so unless you still fuckin' him, you gonna have to beat this battle on your own."

"I'ma tell Stone."

"If you do, get ready for whatever may happen. Including your involvement in a murder."

"What are you saying?"

"I'm saying you should think twice before you go running to him anything. That's all."

"Well what do I do?"

"Maybe we can think of someway to get him ourselves, Kaneesha."

"I'm listening."

"I'll be over in an hour," She said hanging up.

I sat down briefly to collect myself. I could tell Jarvis about Dubbs, but knowing him, he would go over there and kill his ass. And I didn't want that to be on Jarvis' back. I would just have to wait to see what Reds and I could come up with.

In the meantime, Lil Man left with my dad for the weekend and I washed the dishes and cleaned the kitchen. Suddenly I had the urge to smoke again and I was happy Reds was on her way because maybe she'd be willing to share.

Reds knocked at the door an hour later and stopped me from scrubbing the kitchen floor. I answered it and let her in. She had gotten a little bigger but not very much. She waddled in and sat down at the kitchen table.

"Get me some city punch." she said.

I grabbed a bottle of water from the fridge and gave it to her. We sat down at the table and were just about to get into our conversation when Jarvis came out the bedroom. He was grinning and shit like a Chester cat. He pulled a miniature nottyhead bottle from his pocket.

"Hey, Reds," Jarvis smiled.

For some reason, I was threatened by their past friendship. Because Jarvis and I had done the ultimate.

"Hi, Jarvis." Reds responded not looking directly at him. "How have you been?"

"Good. You?"

"I'm fine," She said rubbing her belly.

"Drink this and then rinse it out so I can make you a pipe."

He said to me ignoring her.

Reds looked at Jarvis, then at me, and then back at Jarvis.

"A pipe? Did you say a pipe? A pipe for who?" Reds asked.

I was about to say something when Jarvis handed me his pipe and lit the ashes. I didn't hesitate to take a pull. I hit the rock and no more needed to be said. I took the bottle from him and poured the nottyhead in a glass, and rinsed out the bottle so Jarvis could fix it up for me. Reds was shocked.

Her mouth was agape as she watched Jarvis and me.

"Kaneesha, you smoking now?" She asked.

"Well, I take a hit off the pipe once in a while." I said.

"Girl, let me find out! Shit, then ya'll won't mind me pulling out my gear!" She asked excitedly.

"No, Reds. Get your shit." Jarvis said.

We were all seated at the table with pipes ready. Jarvis began to cook his product first.

We were smoking away when Reds said, "I miss you, Jarvis. We used to be real close."

I blew smoke out of my mouth and handed the pipe to Jarvis.

"What you talkin' 'bout girl? I saw you the other day." He continued as being high gave him the freedom to be real.

For some reason, I was a little alert.

"You ain't tell me you saw Reds. I mean, I don't care, but why you ain't said nothin'?"

"'Cause she told me what you said. But it's okay now. We ain't gotta go behind your back and fake. You one of us."

"Yeah," Reds said reaching over to me. She pouted her lips and I knew what that meant. I opened my mouth and inhaled the smoke that came out of hers. "You one of us now. What's mine is yours and what's yours," she said looking at Jarvis, "is mine."

I wasn't sure what that meant, but for right now, I didn't care.

Two hours had passed while we sat at the table and got high and higher. I had to pull myself up just to go to the bathroom. Once inside, I looked at myself in the mirror. My eyes were dilated twice their size causing me to have this spaced out look. I couldn't stop grinding my jaws and I had slight hand tremors.

"What is going on with me? I can't believe I took it so far."

"But you got this," I thought I heard someone say. "You ain't like Reds and the rest of them crack hoes. You stronger than this."

I turned around but no one was there. Splashing water in my face, I looked at myself in the mirror again believing that the voices although not real, were right.

I opened the door of the bathroom and decided to stop off in my bedroom to take off my jeans and put on sweatpants. I was bending over looking in the closet when I abruptly stopped. The hairs on my neck and arms stood up. I tiptoed out of the closet and went to the bedroom door.

I didn't move...just listened. I immediately went back into the closet and got my holster but my gun was gone. Where had it gone ? It wasn't even mine and I was supposed to give it back to Stone. And then Jarvis came to my mind. When we got high today, I didn't bother asking where he got the money from, now I knew.

I grabbed a bat instead. My heart beat heavily in my chest as I stepped out into the hallway. I heard one voice in particular. As I moved down the hall the voice got louder. I came into view of the living room, to find Stone and his Replacement Killas in my house. When Stone saw me, he narrowed his eyes. He had Jarvis on the floor and the Replacement Killas had Reds hemmed up against the wall.

"Do you know why I'm here?" Stone asked me.

"I don't have the gun!" I yelled. "It's gone, please don't hurt them."

"That's only one portion of your problem," he said. "I have anotha beef wit you and your man."

"What is it? I'm sure it's just a mistake."

"No mistake. Jarvis here stole from me. Didn't you, Jarvis!" Stone shouted, bent down and punched Jarvis in the face. "You tink you could take food from my family?! You must be wicked crazy mon to tink that you could do that! Nobody fucks over Stone. Nobody!" Stone shouted.

Stone came over to where I was standing. I couldn't do anything but look stupid. The Replacement Killa's did exactly what their name stood for...Kill, and I knew it. Stone approached me and I stepped away from the table where we smoked moments earlier. I didn't want him thinking I was smoking and I definitely didn't want him thinking it was his shit. But his eyes scanned the table. His eyes damned near popped out his head when he saw the remnants of our session. He snatched up a pipe in his hand and turned and looked at Reds, Jarvis and finally me. He stepped to me with the pipes in hand.

"So this where my crack went? Jarvis stole my shit so you mothefucka's could get high on my dime? I count three pipes. I look around the room and I count one, two, tree' mutherfuckas." He yelled pointing to each one of us. "That includes you."

I shook my head no.

"Oh yes, Kaneesha," he said rubbing his hand over the side of my face. "So, you smokin' this shit too now huh?" Stone pushed me down into the chair and got in my face.

"What did I tell you 'bout this shit huh? You remember our conversation right?" he snarled in my face. "Right before I let you suck my dick do you remember what I said?"

I looked at Jarvis who appeared too high and scared to hear him.

When I didn't answer, he grabbed me around the neck.

"You, pussyclot! You fuckin', Bumbleclot! I should take all of you out. This is vexin' me good." He shouted.

"I didn't take your shit, Stone and please leave Kaneesha alone! She ain't got shit to do with this!" Jarvis shouted.

Stone snapped his head over his shoulder, released his grip

off my neck and went back over to where Jarvis was.

"Stand him up," he told his men.

Stone got in Jarvis's face but Jarvis didn't flinch or back down.

"You dare stand there and tell me a fuckin' lie to my face, Jarvis?" Stone sneered.

"I didn't steal shit from you, Stone." Jarvis defiantly stated.

Stone burst out laughing.

"You really are a fucking bloodclot." Stone yelled.

"But I should have," Jarvis said. "You fucked my girl and then expect me to have respect for you." Jarvis had a maniacal look on his face. "Yeah I know about all the times you kept me busy just so you could fuck her. Dubbs told me about the time he saw you leaving out of my apartment. I even know why you got me strung out on this shit." He laughed. "But, you didn't expect my hold on her to be so strong now did you? You didn't thing I could get her on this shit. Well I did. If I couldn't have her, you weren't going to either. I know you'd never wife a bitch on crack now would you?"

My eyes grew wide and I was deeply hurt.

"Please, Jarvis. Don't make him angry." Reds said.

"Shut up, crack whore! Your days wit me are ova!"

Reds sobbed but said nothing else.

With the swiftness of a Ninja, Stone reached behind his back and took out a small black baton and struck Jarvis in the shoulder causing Jarvis to fall on one knee. Jarvis reached out to throw a punch and when he did, Stone struck him again and again in the face and body. Reds turned her head away as Stone continued to wail on Jarvis with the baton.

"Stone, stop it right now! Stop it!" I said running up to him with the bat.

The Replacement Killas immediately pointed their laser weapons in the middle of my head. Reds ran over and stood next to me. I dropped the bat and knew this would not end well.

I had done the ultimate betrayal by attempting to hurt

Stone but I also wondered if there was any truth in Jarvis's statement. The Replacement Killas were pointing their lasers between my forehead and Reds. If I knew Reds, her Dessert Eagle was somewhere on her and she just couldn't get to it. Stone stopped beating Jarvis who was now laying' on the floor in a bloodied heap. My heart leaped in my chest as I watched my man lying there helpless. God please help us. I was mad at him but I so desperately loved him. Stone moved away from Jarvis and stood in front of me.

Reds reached for her gun and aimed at him. He stopped in his tracks.

"You seem to be forgetting all the lessons and conversations we had. Haven't you?" Stone asked her.

"Stone, you're scaring me. I just don't want to die. I don't want anybody too."

"Yes, I understand. However, what did I say to your bloodclot ass about pullin' a weapon and not using it? Don't you remember that lesson?" he said slowly walking closer to us.

"Get back, Stone! You're gonna make me do something that I don't wanna do. Please stay where you are!" She begged.

Stone appealed to her plea.

"Reds, you do know that you all could be dead right now...don't you? I'm the one saving your sorry wicked ass life." He said moving forward again.

We backed up and Reds kept her aim on the weapon.

"Stone, you know I got mad love for you, please don't make me choose." She told him tears running down her face.

"I won't kill you today but I turn my back on you all. Jarvis owes me sixteen hundred dollars and I want my mutherfuckin' money in a few days! If I don't get my money soon, a bounty will be enforced for all three of you." He pointed his finger at Reds and said through clenched teeth, "You were my best girl. Now I have to let you go. You no longer work for me. And you, Kaneesha, you could have been my queen. I would have done any ting for you. *Any ting*. But now you're dead to me, too! Jarvis better get me my fuckin' money!" Stone walked back over to

Jarvis and kicked him twice again. Once to the head and once to the stomach

"Piece of pussyclot shit!" he yelled.

"Stone, leave him be! You're killin' him! Please!" I begged again cryin' now.

He stopped and watched me crawl over to Jarvis. He was badly beaten. I felt for a pulse and couldn't find one. I felt again and a slight thump against my finger said Jarvis was alive but barely. He would have to get to the emergency room now. Stone kneeled down beside me.

"I sure hope your loyalty to him was worth it," Stone said.

Stone gave a signal with his hand. The Replacement Killas opened the door for Stone. I watched him leave out first and the Replacement Killas backed out of the door behind him guns still pointed at us. When the door closed, Reds immediately locked it and came over to help me with Jarvis.

"Girl, we gotta get him to the hospital. His breathing is shallow." I said.

"We gotta call an ambulance." Reds said.

"No, we can't have no ambulance around here. If they take Jarvis down the steps like this, everyone will be looking to see who the ambulance is for. It will certainly jump some shit off." I said.

"Kaneesha, we ain't got no fuckin' choice! How the fuck we gonna get Jarvis down the steps. We can't move him. He's not even woke. Fuck that, I'm callin' the mutherfuckin' ambulance right now! We ain't got time to be wastin'!" She yelled as she dialed 911.

"Shit, I gotta clean up this shit!" I shouted pointing to the coke and the pipes that were thrown about the table.

I left Jarvis's side and quickly began snatching everything off the table and throwing it into Reds' purple bag. Reds gave the 911 operator the address.

And when the operator asked what was the problem was she said, "He'd fallen and was unconscious."

A blind man could tell that was a lie, but for now, it would have to do.

She knew not to tell them Jarvis was beaten. It would have summoned a police escort along with the ambulance and after a night like this one, we didn't want any of that.

Jarvis lay in the critical care area on life support. Stone had beat Jarvis into a coma. I was questioned by the hospital nurses about Jarvis's beating and I told them that I came home to find him in that condition. One of the nurses wanted to call the police.

"If you call the police you put me and my son in danger." I stepped to her and said. "Please keep this between us. For now. Give him a chance to get well and he'll deal with this with the authorities."

"What kind of danger?" she inquired not caring about my pleas.

I was not up for her questioning right now.

"Just mind your fuckin' business. No fuckin' police! Okay?!" I snapped.

"Your funeral," She said as she walked away.

Later, the doctor gave me his prognosis. Jarvis suffered a pleural infusion which was a collapsed lung, several broken ribs, a broken wrist, some internal bleeding that had to be stopped, some swelling on the brain and multiple contusions.

Reds held me in her arms and we both cried as the doctor told us that Jarvis was barely alive and that the next forty-eight hours would be critical as Jarvis would hang between life and death.

Through it all she was as distraught as me, go figure.

Chapter Eighteen

I called my father and asked him to keep Hysear for a couple more days because to be honest, he was getting on my nerves. All I wanted to do was get high and think about what was going on with my life.

I told my Dad that Jarvis was robbed coming home from work and when I got off the telephone, my body was shaking. I was a mess and I was lying to my father. I couldn't function and I was scared for my life. Stone wanted sixteen hundred dollars and he wanted it yesterday. I also realized Stone kept his word about shit. And if the money didn't appear a bounty would be placed over our heads.

I called Reds needing to talk and to get some things off of my mind. Who am I fooling? I wanted to get high too.

A half hour later, Reds arrived and she had ready rock. We got our pipes out and got ready to blast. Reds began cutting it up.

"Why do you think Jarvis doesn't believe I didn't fuck Stone?"

"Because you did fuck Stone."

"I know...but why doesn't he believe me?"

"Who knows. If you think I said something I didn't. He probably believed you did even though you kept denying it."

"Maybe."

"On some otha shit, do you remember Manny?" She asked me as she stopped cutting.

"Yeah, I remember Manny. Why?" I replied rubbing my arms.

Lately the urges had become harder to deny and I went into physical distress.

"Cause I talked to him the other day."

"So?"

"He wanted to know about you," she said.

"Why he wanna talk 'bout me, Reds? What the fuck is that about?" I snapped.

"Bitch, chill with the tone. Manny is willing to put us on for a couple of packages." She said. "And since you been puttin' in less and less on our smoke lately, we need his ass. Plus I'ma 'bout to run dry since Stone not fuckin' wit me no more."

"So you blamin' me?"

"No, I'm just statin' the facts. We need money."

"Okay, so what we gotta do for these packages and what type of package are you referring to? Stop being the Riddler and come at me straight." I said.

"Manny likes you and wants to get with you." She said flat out. "So we ain't gotta do much."

"Reds, you talkin' 'bout hoein'?" I asked.

"Girl, it ain't hoein'. The man is willin' to give up some cane and money for some time spent with *you*." She said.

"Reds, I ain't no hoe and I damn sure ain't gonna start actin' like one. I ain't tryin' to spend time with no man right now unless he can give me sixteen hundred dollars straight up in cold hard cash. If he can't do that, then he can keep walkin' the fuck on." I replied.

"Okay. It's your call. Just remember that Manny may be our only option."

I waved my hand at Reds and said forget it. She put the pipe to her lips.

"Reds." I softy said. She put her pipe down and looked at me.

"I already know what you thinkin', Kaneesha. But I don't know what to do about the money." She said.

"But Jarvis said he didn't steal that package. And I believe him, Reds. Maybe if I can talk to Stone again, he'll believe me."

"Kaneesha, I been knowin' Stone longer than you, and at this point, all he want is his money."

"I still don't believe it."

"Look, Jarvis is smokin' now. Hell, we all are. This shit here we're doing is habit formin'. It can make you do all kinds of crazy shit when you need another hit and ain't got one. He was always down Me-Me's all the time gettin' high, I'm sure he wasn't goin' to work which meant he probably ain't have no money. Now like I said before, I don't know where Jarvis got his crack from, but he always had some and always had nice sizes. If Stone did real inventory, I'm sure he'd discover he stole much more." Reds stated.

"At this point, Reds I don't know what the fuck is going on. All I know is that we gotta find someway to get some money to Stone, for all of our sakes."

"I got your back on this too, Kaneesha. We in this shit together!" She said slapping me five.

We picked up our pipes and started smoking. When Reds and I finished we were feenin' for more. Reds had started looking in the carpet for her make-believe rock. I also looked a couple of times, but then I caught myself. Out of habit and because of the psychoactive nature of smoking coke, we had delusions that we might have dropped some on the ground. That caused the smoker to look continuously on the ground and especially in carpet for anything that resembled a rock. I can't tell you how incredibly stupid we must look to an outsider. To the smoker, this was a common side effect.

"Kaneesha, where is Jarvis's pipe?" She asked.

"In the bedroom in the drawer. Why?" I questioned.

"Go get it so I can look at it." She told me.

"Why, you got your own shit? What you want with his pipe?"

"Bitch, just go get the pipe and bring it here. I want to check it for something."

I scooted my chair away from the table and went to get Jarvis's pipe. I came back and handed it to Reds. She looked at it and smiled.

"Kaneesha, how long Jarvis been smoking on this pipe?"

"I don't know maybe two months or more. Why something wrong with it? It's works just fine to him." I said taking his pipe from Reds' hands and putting it back on the mirror in front of me.

I didn't know what she wanted but if she wanted to keep his pipe, that shit was a no go.

"Neesh, he ever clean it?" Reds asked.

"Not that I know of. I didn't know that you were supposed to clean it."

Reds exhaled and shook her head.

"Girl, you mean Jarvis ain't turned you on to Freddy."

"Freddy, what the fuck is Freddy?" I questioned.

"Sometimes Freddy is better than the rock itself."

"Reds, I don't know what the fuck you're talking about. So stop asking me questions and tell me what the fuck is Freddy." I demanded.

"It's the residue from all the coke that collects in your pipe girl." Reds explained.

"How the hell do you get that shit out, with soap and water?" I asked half serious.

"No, crazy ass, you don't wash it out with soap. You clean it with alcohol. I'm 'bout to do mine." Reds said.

Reds reached into her Crown Royal bag and took out a thirty-five millimeter canister. She took the aluminum foil off her pipe. She took the alcohol and poured just a pinch in the bottle and then put her finger over the opening and shook the pipe up and down with the alcohol in it.

"Move that stuff off the mirror." she said. I pushed stuff off the mirror.

Reds poured the alcohol out on the mirror. She took a match and lit the alcohol.

"What the fuck you doing, girl?" I shrieked at her not sure what the hell was going on as the flame got bigger.

"I'm gettin' us some Freddy." she laughed.

Reds picked up the mirror while it was still flaming and tilted it down and then to the left and to the right. This caused the alcohol to run and burn out faster. After the flame died out, Reds put the mirror on the table. What was left after was a white film. Reds picked up her pipe and went to the sink and washed it out. She came back to the table and put fresh foil on the opening.

"So what the hell is this?" I asked bewildered. "I ain't never seen no shit like that before!" I told her honestly.

"Just fix your pipe." Reds told me.

She took the razor blade and scrapped the white film of residue off the mirror and made a small pile of white chips when she was done. She took some of the chips and put them on her ashes and lit them.

"Go ahead and put some on yours cause after you hit this, we gonna Freddy mine next."

I took some of the chips and put them on my pipe. I was a little leery about smoking this shit. I have never done that before nor have I ever seen Jarvis do this. But when I did, I was instantly beamed the fuck up. That shit was off the meter. I loved it.

"Damn, Reds, how come you didn't tell me about this shit before and why the fuck is it called Freddy?" I asked.

"It's called Freddy like Freddy Kruger. You know cause Freddy Kruger only get's you in your dreams. They call the residue from Freddy because it has a dreamlike effect. It's not the real thing." She explained.

I burst out laughing.

"Reds, I done heard it all, but I'm glad I did!"

We smoked what was left and hoped the high would last long. It didn't.

"Oh shit, I need to call my job."

"You still employed?"

"Yeah. They put me on probation a couple weeks ago, but I still be calling off. They need me."

"I heard that."

" I'ma tell them I won't be in for the next couple of days because of Jarvis."

I opened up my cell phone and placed the call. The phone rang twice and the manager Gerald picked it up on the third ring. I took a deep breath before I spoke.

"Hi, Gerald this is Kaneesha. I'm calling because I need to take several days off. Jarvis was robbed and beaten and he's in the hospital in a coma. So I need to be with him." I said high as a fucking kite and wishing I had some more crack.

"Kaneesha, if you don't come in today, you're fired." Gerald told me in a cool monotone voice.

"Gerald, I can't come in today. Didn't you just hear what I said? Jarvis is in the hospital...in a coma and I need to be with him." I pleaded.

Gerald must have put his hand over the phone because I heard talking but it was muffled. He came back to the phone and told me to hold on. Several minutes later, he was back on the phone.

"Kaneesha, I pulled your record and I'm looking at it now." He paused and I could hear paper being shuffled. "Kaneesha, you have called off a total of fifteen times within the past two months. You were put on probation with a stipulation of not calling off within a thirty-day period. If you don't come into work today, turn in your uniform. Do I make myself clear?" He sternly warned me.

"Well this bitch ain't comin' to work! So I guess I'm fuckin' fired then.!"

"Bring back our uniforms. That's the only way you're going to get your final paycheck." And with that said, Gerald hung the phone up in my ear.

I snapped my phone shut and sat on the couch shaking my head.

"So you just fired yourself?" Reds asked.

"Yeah, I guess I did. Fuck it, I'll find another job." I said trying to convince myself.

"Well I'm bouncin'. I'm high as shit and the baby is kickin' my ass right now. I'll be glad to get the little motherfucker out of me." Reds said.

"I sure hope this your last one."

"Neesha, don't get mad at me cause you got fired. Bye."

I hurriedly walked her to *and* out the front door. I reflected on what was going on in my life. Jarvis and I both were jobless...I had no more money stashed from working with Stone...I was now smoking crack and Jarvis was accused of taking a package from Stone. Now he's in the hospital fighting for his life. If. I didn't find the money soon, my days would be numbered.

And for some reason, Dubb's threat to me the day he accosted me in the supermarket came back to haunt me. Now that Stone was no longer an option of protecting me, I really wondered what would become of this Dubbs situation and me.

Thoughts of death kept grabbing at me. And if I didn't find the money for Jarvis, I would have to make preparations for my son. There was nowhere to run. How I wish I could take back the day I got in Stone's truck. But I can't.

Chapter Nineteen

This was one of the rare Fridays that Tok had off. He sat down at the bar and ordered a Red Stripe. When the beer was handed to him he snatched it and greedily drank it down without stopping. The barmaid stood gawking at the fine six foot five muscular man. His Dolce and Gabbana shades sat on a clean-shaven face. His locks were twisted behind his back into one large braid and secured with a Jamaican bandana.

He pointed to the bottle and the Barmaid retrieved another. She placed it down in front of him and went to serve the next customer. Tok picked the bottle up and turned around to take in his surroundings. Several women were sitting at table directly to his left and they all just openly stared at him. Tok didn't like American women. He found them to be abrasive and very disrespectful, especially to their men.

But he continued surveying the room. When he found nothing to catch his eyes, he decided to pay for his beers, take a piss and leave. Tok had just finished pissing in the stall when someone walked into the bathroom talking on their cell phone. He stopped what he was doing to listen. The person walked into a stall and closed the door..

"No man. I told you that I got that package for you. Man I told you I was going to get his ass. That mutherfucka didn't even know I hit their shit until the next day. The mutherfucka that got pinched was Jarvis. Yeah, Jarvis! Stone thinks it's one of his own men who got the bag. I got that mutherfucka as a matter of fact, I killed two birds with one Stone so to say." The voice laughed. Tok moved by mistake startling Dubbs. "Wait, let me look out here for minute."

The stall door opened and Dubbs peeked out, quickly looking under neighboring stalls. Tok stood on the toilet and peeked in between the crack in the stall door. When he did, he saw Dubbs looking around the bathroom. When Dubbs didn't see anyone, he went back into the stall and continued his conversation.

"Well I heard that there's a bounty on that punk Jarvis' and his skank ass girlfriend. That bitch thought she was so 007 cuz she was working for Stone. Now that bitch is shaking in her mutherfuckin' thong and Stone is out of some of product. He better be glad that was the only package that was there. I wished I could have hit that motherfucker for all his shit! Yeah, call me when you have the money. I gotta go. Be in touch soon." Dubbs snapped his phone shut and opened the stall door.

He looked around again and when he didn't see anyone, he left. Tok got down off the toilet seat zipped up his pants and flushed. He walked out the stall door and out the bathroom. When he got in his Escalade, he pressed the button to make his call.

When Stone answered the call Tok, who was also a Replacement Killa, said, "Stone, meet me at the location. I have some information you need today. And it's gonna change a lot of things."

Chapter Twenty

Jarvis came out of his coma on the sixth day of his hospital stay. I was with him when he opened his eyes. The swelling in his brain was gone down and his collapsed lung was back to normal. Jarvis was still in bad shape but the worst of it was over. The doctor said Jarvis would probably be in the hospital another two weeks.

We talked about him getting better and I told him not to concentrate on anything else. He wanted to talk about Stone but I refused. I left him each night with the promise of returning the next day. He looked scared and I couldn't blame him. I had the same thoughts that at any minute, Stone would send one of the Replacement Killa's over here and it would all be over. Living in this type of fear was getting to me. I had no desire to look for work and barely took care of myself now.

My dad came to visit Jarvis in the hospital and then followed me home. The conversation between us was intense to say the least.

"You're losing weight."

"I'm fine, dad."

"Why? Are you smaller?"

"I've been small. You're just imagining things."

"Daughter, I know you. You're getting skinnier." He paused and swallowed hard. I could tell that whatever he was about to ask me was difficult for him. "Are you on drugs?"

"No, dad, I'm not on drugs." I lied.

"Well what's going on with you and look at this house? It's a mess! I know you're spending your time at the hospital, but Jarvis is going to be fine and will be home soon. So what's really going on?" He asked. "And why does Hysear think he lives with me?"

As my father is talking to me, all I thought about was getting high.

"Look, dad. I...I'ma be real with you, Jarvis and I both lost our jobs. They fired me because I needed to take off to be with him and they weren't feeling that." I explained.

"So why was Jarvis fired?"

"I don't know, Dad. Jarvis never did get a chance to tell me that." I said truthfully.

Exasperated my father let out a long sigh and I hated lying to him like this but I had no choice.

"So what do you plan to do, Kaneesha? You and Jarvis need to find some work. How the hell you gonna pay your rent? You know my place ain't big enough for everyone. Damn, Kaneesha, this is just not the time to be losing no damn jobs." My father shouted.

"Daddy, stop it!" I screamed covering my ears. My body was going through pangs and my tolerance for chastising was low. "I've got enough over my head right now! Please, just do me this favor and keep Hysear with you for the next two weeks while I look for work and help Jarvis get back on his feet. Please, daddy. Can you do that for me? Please!" I cried.

My father grabbed me and held me tightly.

"Shh. Shh. It's okay, baby girl. I'm sorry. It's gonna be okay." He soothingly said as he rubbed my back.

He let me go and pulled my chin up so that our eyes met.

"You take all the time you need. You know Hysear is my only grandchild and I love spending time with him. Just get a couple of his games and some clothes together so I can take with me."

Thankful for his generous hospitality, in record time, I gathered up Hysear's clothes and his Wii game system with most of his games and handed them to my dad.

"Come see Hysear during the week when you get it together. Kaneesha, I still say you've lost some noticeable weight. I truly hope you ain't out here doing no drugs or nothing like that."

"Daddy, I'm not doing drugs of any kind. I wouldn't lie to

you. Now please stop worrying about me. I'm fine. Now go ahead so you can pick Lil Man up from school. Tell him I'll be over to see him later this week. I'll call him tonight."

"I will."

My dad was just about to leave when I realized I ain't have any money.

"Dad, uh...you know I ain't got a job right now. Can you give me a few dollars to tie me over? I just wanna get on my feet."

"Why you keep shaking and moving? You seem anxious."

"What?" I said trying to stop.

"You're jittery. Why?"

"Dad, are you gonna give me the money or not?!" I screamed.

His head dropped and sorrow washed over him. But as always, he came to my rescue.

"I love you dad," I said kissing his face tucking the money within my bra, my breasts momentarily peeking through because I didn't have on a bra.

"And I love my daughter," he said sadly, "and when you see her, tell her I miss her dearly. And her son does too."

I didn't respond.

I just watched him walk out the door and place some calls for my next high.

Chapter Twenty-One

I jumped up to hear my phone ringing. I grabbed it off the nightstand and looked at the number. It was Reds. It startled me because I didn't remember falling asleep. The last thing I remember was watching an episode of *Meet the Browns* and I must have dosed off.

"What's up?" I groggily asked.

"Put some clothes on. I just got a text that Manny's down Me-Me's." She told me.

"Reds, who's gonna be down there? Cause Me-Me keeps company with a strange crew. The last couple times we been down there, I felt a little uncomfortable." I said.

"Well you on crack now so your crew is her crew."

I was so angry my face turned warm. I hated being reminded of my predicament. And for some reason, I didn't feel like I was addicted. I thought I could control it.

"Look, I might be on crack but I'm not *crackish*. Now who gonna be down there?"

Reds had taken me down to Me-Me's and introduced me before. Me-Me seemed pretty cool and we all got high together a few times. A couple days ago, when we were down there, Me-Me told me she heard about Jarvis and wished him well. When she said that, I wondered who told Me-Me that Jarvis was in the hospital to begin with because the only people who knew were my Dad and Reds, so I thought.

"Just friends, nobody to be worried about."

"Reds, let me ask you a question? Did you say anything to Me-Me about Jarvis?"

"No, why?"

"Cause she told me to tell Jarvis to get better. She knew about him being in the hospital and why he was there." I said.

"Did Me-Me say how she knew?" Reds asked.

"No." I replied. Reds blew her breath out. "Well I don't know then. Don't worry about that, Kaneesha. It ain't like the man wasn't carried out of there in a stretcher. Girl get your clothes on." She said.

"Okay."

"I'll be over in a few."

I got out of the bed and took a birdbath when I heard a knock at the door. When I peeped out the peephole, I saw it was Reds. She was looking around. I opened the door and she hurried in.

"Come on, girl." Reds urged.

"Let me get my bag and I'll be right there." I said running to the closet to get my coat.

I went to the bedroom and got my purse. In my purse was my new Crown Royal Bag. I officially got me one so I was in the clan with Reds and we rolled out to Me-Me's.

When we got there, there were two other girls that I had never seen before sitting at the table along with Me-Me and Tommy. The two girls were throwing mean daggers at me when we walked in. I also saw Tommy standing by the table. Tommy was another neighborhood crack queen. I had gotten high with Tommy twice while I was with Reds.

Reds and I took a seat on the couch in the living room. I wasn't sitting at the table with these two unknown bitches and I was not feeling them at all. Me-Me had gone to the back of the apartment. I heard a voice coming down the hall and saw Me-Me reappear in front of Manny. I had seen Manny around but never talked to him or been officially introduced. The last time I saw him was in the hotel room the night Stone came in to get us

He came out into the living area where everyone was. He didn't see me until he cut the corner off to the kitchen.

He smiled.

I didn't.

I just looked the other way. Tommy jumped up off the couch like she had fire under her ass.

"Manny." she crooned. "How you doing with your fine ass?" Tommy asked all up in the man's face. "I didn't know you would be here!"

"Shit neither did we!" The girls at the table piped in.

"It gonna be a party now!" One of the girls said.

Manny looked around the table.

"Yeah, I told Me-Me to call my girls and I was gonna treat ya'll." He looked over at Reds.

"How you doing, Reds?" he asked.

Reds smile deepened and she said, "I'm fine."

"What's up with this lovely thing sitting over there on the couch, acting like she don't want to be here? I remember you from the hotel room." He said as if he didn't tell Reds not too long ago that he wanted to fuck me.

Tommy interrupted and said, "Yeah, that's Kaneesha. She cool and all, but what you got for us, daddy?"

"I wanna hear from her mouth," Manny said looking at me.

"If she acting like she don't wanna be here, maybe she shouldn't. Shit when did she become part of our clan?" One of the unknown girls said throwing shade at me again. "I heard she snort, so why she even here?"

"What you say your name is again?" Manny asked pointing at me.

"Her name's Kaneesha." Tommy replied.

"Tommy, I can talk and I do hear ya'll. If Manny wants to know about me then he should ask me himself!" I shot back.

I heard one of the girls at the table suck her teeth. Tommy looked over at me and threw me a look. I gave her one back and Manny broke the tension in the air.

"Before we do anything in here, I want all my girls to come give me a hug."

Manny held out his arms and every last one of them bitches jumped up out their seats and Me-Me ass came running out the kitchen like she was Flo Jo or some shit. Even Reds gave that nigga a hug. I couldn't believe that they were hugging this man like he was some damn prince and shit. Fuck this shit. Let me get my ass up out of here. I ain't bought to kiss his ass for no crack.

I got up and started towards the door. Manny saw where I was going and broke away from the arms of all his bitches. Every one of them looked at me evilly.

"Reds, I'm goin' home. I'll catch you another time." I was trying my best to get to that door before Manny's ass reached me but no such fucking luck.

"Whoa, little lady, where you going? I thought you wanted to party." He said blocking the door.

"No, I don't. I'm goin' home." I told him.

"Shit, let her go, Manny. If she don't wanna be here, let her ass go. We ready to party!" one of the girls said.

I snapped my head around. I had just about enough of her fat-ass mouth.

"Who the fuck is you talkin' 'bout? You don't know me! Stop tellin' me that I need to take my ass home! I didn't come down here to see you no way!" I was mad now. "And if you say one more thing I'ma have both of my feet in your ass."

I saw Tommy's eyes get big and Reds got up and stepped to the side. She knew that I was getting ready to get stupid up in here. She quickly tried to diffuse the situation by stepping in front of me.

"Hey, ya'll, come on. This is my girl Kaneesha. We just tryin' to get in the party mode. Ya'll know that Kaneesha don't hang out like that with us. So why ya'll trippin'? She just a little uncomfortable with this that's all." Reds said.

"Well, if you uncomfortable in here, why don't you just take your ass home like you was fixin' to do? We ain't stoppin' you!" One of the girls said.

I jumped for her but Manny stepped in between the two girls and me. He turned around and extended his hand towards the two girls.

"Kaneesha, this is Cheryl and Tracy." He said looking at me.

"I don't give a fuck." I said.

"And we don't give a fuck either."

"Calm down. Didn't we all come to have a good time?" He asked.

I didn't say shit. Fuck them bitches. They about to get sliced the fuck up. I had my hand on my knife in my purse just in case a bitch broke bad.

"Look, I don't want no shit up in here. Now I called Me-Me and told her to tell you Tommy, Cheryl, Tracy and Reds to come on down and hang out with me for a while and I guess Ms. Kaneesha just lucked up to be in the right place at the right time. I want all ya'll to shut the fuck up with that dumb shit and get yourself ready to do what the fuck ya'll know I want ya'll to do. I don't want to hear no more shit out of anyone here or I'm packing up my shit and going across town to my other spot. Ya'll got that?" Manny said looking each woman in the face.

They all shook their heads and said yes. Then Manny turned to me.

"I'll talk to you later on. For now, take a seat at the table while I take care of business in the back." He looked at Cheryl and Tracy.

"Ya'll go on to the back." he commanded.

They mean mugged me again. I mouthed the words fuck you to both of them and Manny saw me. He winked at m and I turned my head. They got their purses and went down the hall to Me-Me's spare room. When they were gone, Tommy slapped me on the arm.

"Girl, what the hell is you trying to do? I thought you were getting ready to fight up in here. You almost caused that man to pack his shit up and go!"

"Yeah, Neesha, I don't know what attitude you got but you needed to check that shit at the door. And I ain't having no fighting and shit going on in my house." Me-Me said giving me a hard look.

"Chill out with that shit y'all. Them bitches is hatin' on Kaneesha for no reason." Reds interjected.

"You know them girls didn't know me and they didn't have no

business talking shit like that about me." I said to Me-Me.

"Yeah, they was wrong, but don't let them fuck you outta your high." Tommy commented.

I looked at Tommy and rolled my eyes.

"Why do ya'll act like that around him? Ya'll act like he's some type of God or something. Shit, he's a common drug dealer who likes throwing around his money and coke to get women." I said.

Me-Me leaned down in my face.

"Girl, Manny is known all over the eastern seaboard. And when he comes in town to party, he does just that. He don't party with everyone. We are his chosen select girls and when he calls, we drops our shit and come running cause we all know that we will get broke the fuck off. And I ain't about to pass up the money or no coke. Shiiiit...If you don't know, you better ask somebody. Every girl right now wishes they was down here at my house laying up with Manny. Shit, girl, you better recognize." Meme high-fived Tommy.

"You ain't never lied." Tommy said.

I briefly looked at them and for a moment, I felt out of place. What is this, a Crack Head Convention? They act like they involved in a cult or something.

"Well, I don't know Manny like that and I ain't trying to get to know a nigga on that level. Besides, that's Reds man." I said pointing to Reds.

Tommy smirked and Me-Me burst out laughing.

"Girl, Manny ain't Reds' man. Reds ought to be fuckin' grateful that he even looks her way with her pregnant ass." Me-Me said.

"Fuck you, Tommy?" Reds said. "You ought to be grateful that Manny just lets you suck his dick with your toothless triflin' ass." Reds spat back to Tommy.

"Whatever, Reds. I ain't fixin' to argue with your ass today. Shit, I'm waitin' to get my high on." Tommy and Reds parted ways.

Reds went down the hall to the bathroom and Tommy came

back over to where me and Me-Me were sitting. I looked at Tommy and Me-Me.

"How long Reds been smokin' this shit anyway?" I asked Me-Me.

"Shit, I don't know." Me-Me replied.

"Why ya'll ain't try to help her get off this shit while she pregnant. Ain't ya'll her friends?" I asked.

Me-Me and Tommy both threw their hands on their hips.

"Bitch, I know you ain't talkin' cause you be wit' her now more than me and Me-Me. Why ain't you trying to help a bitch?" Tommy said.

"Fuck you, Tommy. I got enough to deal wit' on my plate. I can't be responsible for Reds habit too." I snapped back. "Besides, I tried to get into her business 'bout that shit when we first started hangin'. She shut me right down. I just figured ya'll would have more influence since you known her longer." I continued,

"Stop assuming that we didn't try to talk to Reds ourselves. She told us to mind our fucking business!" MeMe chimed in. "So that's what the fuck we intend to do."

Manny reappeared at the kitchen table where we were all sitting. He put a mirror on the table that had about a gram of coke on it.

"Divide the coke up between yall."

Me-Me started dividing the powder and I made sure she wasn't given herself more.

Before he left, he tapped me on the shoulder and said, "Can I see you in the kitchen?"

Both Tommy and Me-Me cocked their heads and gave me the, "girl you better get your ass up" look. I slowly got out the chair and followed him into the kitchen. Manny reached out and stroked my face. I reared back.

"Don't be afraid, I don't bite. I just wanted to speak with you in private for a minute. You know I'm surprised to see you down here among the likes of them. You don't look like the type to smoke. And I definitely was surprised to see you with Stone at the hotel. You too pretty for this shit. So, why you down here for real?" he asked.

"What?" I asked looking at him like he lost his fuckin' mind. "I like a good high like everybody else."

"This ain't you or your style. The first time I laid eyes on you was at the Elks club, you was wit' Jarvis. You was one of the finest things up in the club. Then I seen you another time at the mall. You had a little boy with you. The next time was when you rolled up in the hotel with Stone and Reds. Never had I once seen you on the street or down here getting high. So I'ma ask you again, why you down here with these crack queens, now?"

"First of all, I don't know you like that to be telling you my business and second, what I do ain't your business. Tommy and Me-Me are my friends and I came down here on the invite of Reds." I said sarcastically.

"Don't get hype, lil mama. I was just asking that's all. But if you comin' to play, you gotta pay."

"What's that supposed to mean?" I asked.

"It means that all my bitches know what I want. They back there in the bedroom for a reason. You feel me?"

"I thought you was Reds' friend." I said backing up further away from him.

He began to laugh loudly.

"Girl, Manny don't belong to no bitch. Ain't enough women in any of these bitches for me to even consider them as my main lady. Shit, you must be crazy. And Reds, shit, she just feeds a need cause of what she serves and how well she serves it." he said.

"Yeah, well you can count me out. As a matter of fact Mr. Manny, I'm on my way out the door right now."

"You ain't gotta leave."

"What you want I can't give."

"Look, why don't you make sure don't nobody come to the door and if they do, you tell them to get away. Hear?" He handed me a baggie of powder. "See...now you're earning your keep."

I took the prized package and turned around.

"No thank you or nothing, huh?" Manny said.

I turned back to face him and couldn't help but notice that the man was fine as shit.

I pursed my lips and said, "Thank you, Manny."

"You welcome, pretty mama." He said winking at me.

He walked out the kitchen and pointed to Me-Me and Tommy. They got up like robots and followed him down the hall. He already had Tracy and Cheryl back there, damn! Reds came back in the kitchen and I pulled out what Manny gave me. It was sweet. It had to be at least a fifty-cent piece.

"Manny gave you that?" Reds asked.

"Yeah, nice ain't it."

"Yeah, girl. Hurry up and cook up a piece. Shit I need a hit." Reds said.

We both copped a seat at the table and I broke out my purple bag and went to work. About a hour later, we was mellow, sitting on the couch trying to watch some TV. I don't know what the fuck I was thinking about cause you can't watch shit high, but I was doing my best to stay focused. I kept looking around and getting up and walking around. Reds was laughing at me cause I even peeked out Me-Me's curtains a few times thinking someone was outside her door.

I noticed that sometimes I would become paranoid although I'm sure it just the gloom of Stone's threats. I was gonna have to put that paranoia shit in check. But at the moment, I heard a noise coming from down the hallway from Me-Me's bedroom area. Tommy and Cheryl were coming down the hall talking loudly. The closer they got the more it sounded like an argument. Tommy came over to the kitchen table and took a seat. She had her purple bag with her.

"Shit, Cheryl, didn't I tell your ass not be so fuckin' greedy? You know how the fuck Manny get. Why you have to go and take more than he was tryinna give you? Now he put your ass out and mine too. I don't know why the fuck I had to leave. Shit, I was sucking his dick just like he asked me too. And then your bold ass gonna pick another rock and try to light it. Girl, was you out your mind?" Tommy asked.

"Fuck you, Tommy. Had you been sucking his dick and not been so worried about who was smoking, your ass would still be in the bedroom too. So shut the fuck up." Cheryl pointed out.

"Fuck you, Cheryl!" Tommy hissed back.

Cheryl rolled her eyes and Tommy sat down on the couch beside me. I sniffed the air and made a face.

"Damn, Tommy, you smelling, girl. You need to go wash your face." I said to her wiggling my nose.

Her mouth was white all around her lips and I could smell her dick sucking breath on her face.

"Fuck that! What you got to smoke?" she asked me.

I know this hooker didn't just ask me what the fuck I had to smoke.

"Wait, hold up! Didn't Manny just leave you some shit out here on the mirror? What the fuck?! What you do with your shit? And don't say that you smoked it cause I know that's a lie."

"So, Manny didn't give you anything? She asked me again ignoring my question.

"Why you all up in my shit? I questioned her.

Cheryl was sitting at the kitchen table all this time listening to Tommy and me before she decided to add her fucking two cents.

"What I wanna know is why you was left out of the party in the back? Shit, all of us had to go back there and work for our packages. Why is you special?" She asked me.

I slowly said, "You're Cheryl right?

"Yeah, I'm Cheryl." She hissed.

"Cheryl, I don't know you and I can't figure out why you got such a nasty attitude with me. But for the record, I am not one of Manny's bitches! You can be his bitch all you want, and hoe for him, but I'm nobody's bitch." I said setting her straight.

Cheryl jumped up from the table.

"What the fuck you mean hoeing? Ain't no body hoeing for

shit. And bitch, you don't know me either, I'll whoop your little skinny ass." She said coming up to my face.

Jarvis always said never let a nigga step to you first. You swing first, and that's exactly what the fuck I did. I balled my fist up and punched the shit out of Cheryl and my blow landed dead on her chin. She was stunned. I don't think she thought I was bold enough to hit her in the face. She quickly regained her composure and swung back connecting with my lips. I felt the stinging sensation and knew that one of my lips was busted. Fuck this. Before I could get my Mike Tyson on, Cheryl popped my ass again this time upside my head.

"Yeah, bitch, come on! Come on bitch !" she shouted.

Cheryl planted her feet and was sticking and moving like a prized fighter. Shit, this bitch was no fucking joke. I tried to move away from another punch but was caught on the left side of my temple by her heavy hand. I staggered into the table and then into Me-Me's china cabinet bringing down several glasses and plates with a loud crashing sound to the floor.

I'm confused. I don't even know what we're fighting for. But at this time, it didn't matter. I swung back and landed a punch on Cheryl's lips. She automatically counterpunched and I was thrown off balance. She threw three more blows to my face. Cheryl was whooping my ass. I needed to get this bitch off me before she beat me to death in here. Before I could get my next action into play, Cheryl lunged forward into me. I grabbed her as her momentum propelled both of us to the middle of the living room. Both of us couldn't break the fall as we fell backwards into the coffee table shattering it into pieces. I tried with all my might to push Cheryl's ass off me but I couldn't get the leverage I needed. I could hear Tommy screaming in the background and felt Reds pulling at me.

Then I heard other voices come into range. I heard Me-Me screaming at the top of her lungs. Eventually Manny grabbed Cheryl off of me. Tommy and Reds helped me up out of the frame of the broken table. My nose was bleeding, my lip was bleeding, and I was cut all over my arms. My head was pounding something fierce and I was winded. Cheryl tried to grab at me again until Manny pushed her down on the couch.

"What the fuck happened in here!?" Manny shouted to Cheryl.

"Look at my fuckin' house! Look at my fuckin' house! Look at this shit! What the fuck did you two bitches do? Oh my God! Just look at my shit!" Me -Me was hysterically crying and shouting at Cheryl and me.

Tracey came running into the living room to see what all the commotion was about and Reds spoke up.

"Cheryl came out her mouth wrong to Neesha. Neesha said some shit back to Cheryl and words turned into a fight." Reds helped me to stand up straight.

I could hardly move. Me-Me went over to the couch where Manny had pushed Cheryl down. She pointed her finger at Cheryl.

"What the fuck did you say? Why you always got to be starting shit every fuckin' time you come down here? You always got something to say about somebody. Cheryl your ass is going to pay for fuckin' up my shit!" Me-Me screamed at her.

Cheryl stood up in Me-Me's face.

"I ain't payin' for shit. That little bitch right there hit me first. She needs to be payin'! Don't no mutherfuckin' body call me no hoe to my face and think they gonna walk away like that. Fuuuuccck that shit! And since that little bitch thought she could, I had to show her she was wroooong! " Cheryl flipped.

Manny stepped in between Me-Me and Cheryl.

"Look, Cheryl, I'ma give Me-Me some money for her shit and then you will be indebted to me cause I know that your ass started this shit." Manny said.

"Fuck her, Manny. I..." Cheryl stopped in mid-sentence.

With base in his voice and an evil look Manny walked over to Cheryl and said, "Shut the fuck up, bitch! You say anything else out that mothefuckin' smart ass mouth of yours and I'll beat your ass myself! Now sit the fuck down and don't fuckin' move." Manny commanded.

Manny the King of the Crack Heads had spoken. She didn't say another damn thing and sat her ass back down on the couch. He came over to me, looked at my face and shook his head.

"Reds, take her to the bathroom and clean her up," Manny said.

Just as I was walking past her, Cheryl reached out for me again but my ass had enough of her shit. I don't know how, but I reached across Red's back and snatched the pewter candleholder off of the table and swung it hard, straight across Cheryl's face. It connected with a mighty thud and the bitch went down.

Everyone stopped and waited to see if she was going to move. Suddenly she was screaming at the top of her lungs as several of her teeth fell out of her mouth and onto Me-Me's blue carpet. Blood was free flowing from her mouth, down her chin and all over her clothes. Cheryl tried to talk but couldn't. Her Jaw was broke. I snatched myself free from Tommy and Reds's grip and stood over Cheryl.

"If you had kept your mouth shut and your fucking hands to yourself this shit would not have happened. But you didn't! And this is what the fuck you get!" I yelled.

I swung the candleholder again, striking Cheryl in the stomach. She doubled over in pain and no one came to her aid. They all watched me as I hock spit on Cheryl. I picked my purple bag up off the ground, found my coat and keys and looked back at everyone. Then I opened the door and walked out. I slammed the door so hard, I heard something fall and break on the inside. Fuck them bitches! Reds took a few minutes but then walked out behind me. She helped me limp back to my apartment. Once inside, she found some alcohol and peroxide to clean up my cuts.

"Damn, Kaneesha, that was a gangsta move you put down on Cheryl. I bet she won't be talkin' shit no more." Reds snickered.

"It could have been worse." I said flinching from her dabbing alcohol on my arm.

"Why you say that?"

"Cause she coulda been dead. If I had my defender she woulda gotten dealt with."

"I'm sorry. When me and Jarvis sold it, I couldn't believe you gave it to him."

The room was spinning and I pushed her hand away.

"What the fuck you mean when me and Jarvis sold it?"

"We sold it...for some money for a package. He ain't tell you? You smoked it with us and everything."

"Fuck no! And since you my friend, why you just telling me? Stone was gonna kill me for that gun."

"Stone ain't botherin' you," she joked.

I didn't smile.

"Look, you gotta take that up with Jarvis. I'm your friend and I'm telling you now so it's obvious I thought it was cool. You know I wouldn't have done no shit like that."

"You gotta lot of shit with you, Reds."

"Don't we all?"

When Reds phone rang, she held it up and showed me the message.

"Do you think that shit's real?" I questioned, my heart racing.

"Stone don't say nothin' he don't mean." She replied.

"You sure that's Stone's number?" I quizzed.

"Look at it again, Kaneesha, you tell me. Don't nobody fuck wit' Stones' personal phone but him. So yeah, this is from Stone." She affirmed.

We both read the message a third time and slapped each other a high five. The text read, *'the dogs were sent home. No worries, clean slate!'*

We knew that meant that the contracts on our heads were lifted. I wondered what happened to change Stones mind. Did his shit turn up or did the real thieves resurface? At this point, I ain't give a fuck as long as he wasn't coming for our heads.

"Damn, Reds. I hated living in fear of my life like that."

"So did I. When I sold my Eagle, I felt powerless and defenseless." She said.

"You sold yours too?"

"Yep."

"Well, I'ma buy me another one and sleep with it under my pillow."

"I feel you," she sighed. "After all the adventure, I'm ready to blast. What 'bout you, Neesh? You feel alright to cook some?" She asked.

"Shit yeah! And we got some good news too! Fire it up!" I said.

Chapter Twenty-Two

With the bounty revoked, I felt free. Reds and I smoked up both packages that Manny gave us. We didn't stop smoking until the next morning. I couldn't get any higher but kept smoking anyway. I was so zombified after that, I couldn't even think straight. Reds complained about her stomach and said she was having cramps. So after awhile, I told Reds she needed to go home and get some rest.

I couldn't get any sleep so I waited until I came down off my high so I could go to the hospital to see Jarvis. Several hours later, I was dressed and ready to go. The swelling in my face had gone down some from my fight with Cheryl, and I covered the other bruises with make up. When I walked out my apartment and snatched the eviction notice off the door, I kept it moving. Notice or no notice, I was on cloud nine. For the first time in a long time, I walked out the door without being paranoid that my life could end any minute. On my way out, I stopped in the stairwell to check a text message I was sending. I read it over to make sure it read correctly.

I don't know what happened to make you change your mind, but I am eternally grateful. The fear was killing me slowly. Oh and my Defender was stolen and I can't return it. I know that you are still upset with me, but you will always be my King.

I was satisfied with the text and sent it. I watched the little envelope twirl up in the corner of the screen and then the confirmation came across letting me know that my message was delivered.

As I walked down the steps, I thought about Stone. I had not heard or seen from him. I still miss him and I don't understand why. I shook his memory from my head and got in the car. But the moment I closed my door, thoughts of him were still there.

There's not use at me dreaming.
I'm a crack head, and I'll never again have his heart.

Jarvis was sitting up in the chair in his room when I arrived. It was good to see him. I hadn't been to the hospital in three days. I had called and spoken with him but he wasn't happy about me not coming. I lied to him and told him I had been out job hunting but I knew he knew it was all a lie. I spent my free time with Reds getting high. Shit, what was I going to do with Jarvis, when he was stuck in the hospital?

Before I went inside, I fixed my hair with my hands, and pulled up my pants. Then I rolled them down at the waist a few times because they kept falling down. When I felt I looked good, I strutted inside like I was the finest thing in the world because in my mind, I was.

When he saw me walk through the door, he smiled. And I went over to him and gave him a kiss on the forehead.

"Hey, babe. How you feeling today?" I asked sitting on the edge of his bed.

"I'm good. I'm moving around much better than before. But my ribs still hurt. The doctor said I should be able to go home in a day or two. What the hell happened to your face?" Jarvis yelled. "Did Stones' boys do that shit?" he questioned angrily.

"Hell no, Jarvis. If they had, I'd be stretched out downstairs in the morgue not walkin' around with little bruises like these and shit! I got into it with some bitch 'round the way. Nothing major, I got her ass good though."

"So that's why you ain't been to check on a nigga? Cause you out there fightin' and shit?" Jarvis asked.

"No, I been out looking for work, Jarvis. I told you that. Shit, I just pulled the eviction notice off of the door today. If we don't come up with some money quick, our asses are out on the streets...again! On a good note, listen baby, check this out!" I paused hoping to give him some good news. "Stone found out who stole his package. It wasn't you."

"I know it wasn't me." He frowned. "You didn't believe me?"

"No...I mean yes. It's just that, you have been acting sorta weird lately."

"I'm many things but I'm not a thief, Kaneesha."

"Well how would you explain your goin' behind my back and selling my gun?" I said putting my hands on my hips.

He got quiet, looked down and then back up at me, "I was really sick, Kaneesha. I needed a fix. I'm sorry. And I took the gun because I didn't want you to have it. I was worried about you."

"Sure. And that's why you take my best friend with you?"

"Your best friend? When did ya'll get there?"

"When I realized she's realer with me than you are. She was the one who told me ya'll were hanging out. You never told me even after I told you to stay away from her."

"Nothing is going on between me and Reds."

"It's not the point, you made me give up Stone and I did it."

His forehead creased and his eyes narrowed. "I made you give up Stone? I made you give up Stone?! What are you saying?"

"I didn't mean it that way. I meant to say, you made me give up working for Stone and I did it."

"And so did I. I gave up working for him and hanging with Reds. I just needed her help to move the gun. You're gonna learn soon enough that there's an oath to being on crack. Your loyalty lies with the drug, not with people."

"So what do you mean?"

"I mean...do you have anything on you now? 'Cause I need a fix."

His truth hurt.

I looked up at him, smiled and said, "Naw. I ain't got nothin'." I lied deciding to keep the rock in my pocket for myself.

If he took the oath, then so did I, and in my book it means every man's for himself.

Two days later Jarvis was safely home. He was still in pain and walking slowly. All he wanted was a blast. I was Jonesing too and I needed one desperately. Jarvis went to the back to lie down. He wanted to take a pain pill but I told him he would be crazy to do that, especially if he was gonna blast off later. He may fuck around and kill himself. I told him to try to rest, and that I would see if I could go out and get us some rock.

"Kaneesha, I got twenty dollars in my wallet. You can use that."

"Why were you holdin'? You knew we ain't have nothin'."

"Well I'm tellin' you now. Remember the oath?"

"You serious about that shit ain't you?"

"Just go see if Baggs is out there anywhere."

I quickly found Jarvis's wallet and snatched out the twenty-dollar bill.

"I'll be right back!" I said and hauled ass out the door.

I walked around to the other side of the circle from where I lived, when I saw Baggs leaning against a white mustang. I didn't wanna just walk up on him 'cause I didn't know who was in the car. I don't need everyone in my business. Instead I waited to get his attention. He was laughing when he happened to turn his head around and see me.

I waved my hand in the air for him to come over. But he waved his hand back for me to come over to him. I exhaled and walked toward Baggs. I stopped, meeting him halfway. I wasn't going any further. Frustrated, he told whoever was in the car that he would be right back.

"What's up, Kaneesha?" he asked grinning at me all hard. Baggs had gold grills in his mouth and looked fucking ridiculous.

"You got anything?"

He arched his eyebrows, scrunched up his face and then rubbed his thin beard.

"Wow."

"I'm not tryin' to hear your shit, Baggs. You want a customer or not?"

"With that attitude you must be gettin' weight."

"All I got is twenty. I just need a twenty cent piece of either coke or ready rock." I told him.

"So you smokin' now?"

"Fuck...Baggs! It ain't for me, it's for Jarvis." I lied.

"Oh, how he doing?" He asked looking me over.

"He's okay."

Baggs pulled me by the arm and walked me further away from where we were standing.

"Listen, Kaneesha, Dubbs been runnin' around tellin' everyone about ya'lls business." Baggs told me.

"What business is that?"

"He said that Jarvis stole some shit from Stone and that Stone came up in there and beat him. He said you were working for Stone too and fuckin' him behind Jarvis's back." He explained. "Now I understand you gotta do what you gotta do, but is that true?" He asked rubbing is dick.

I stood there in a daze. "Look, I don't know what he told you but its all lies. So he just running his mouth about shit he don't know about. Look, I gotta go. Can I have my shit?"

He jogged over to an abandoned car at the corner and reached behind the back tire. When he came back to me, he handed me a little vial of ready rock. I gave him my money.

"Thanks, man. I needed...I mean, Jarvis needed this."

"No problem."

"So look, Baggs. Is that offer still open? For you to work in our place? We kinda need the money now."

He scanned me over and said, "Naw. I'm good with that. But maybe I can put you to work somewhere else." He said licking his lips.

"That's...okay," I said embarrassed. "Later."

"Later, Kaneesha."

When I left him, I took my pipe out of my pocket, went on the side of the building and blasted away. I allowed the euphoria to take over me. I didn't think about the repercussions of smoking without Jarvus until the rock was all gone.

"Oh my God! What am I gonna tell Jarvis?"

Looking down on the ground, I took a bottle, and breathed out two times. Then I crashed it against the side of my face. When I felt a piece of glass sticking out of my skin, I left it in, barely able to endure the pain on my walk home.

Ready to put on a performance I ran in and said, "Baby, I been robbed!"

"What?" He said looking into my hands. "Stop playin'. Give me the rock."

"I don't have it, look at me. They hit me over my head with the bottle and took my rock."

"Where your pipe?"

"Huh?"

"Your pipe...where is it?"

"Come on, Jarvis. I ain't got time for that shit." I said walking past him.

The moment I hit the corner, Jarvis hit me so hard in my face, I forgot what month it was. With the strength he had left, he got over top of me.

"Listen, bitch and listen good. You take your broke ass out there and get me my rock. I been in this shit too long to be fooled by your rookie ass. Don't fuck wit' me, I'm not playing. Don't come back in here without it. You hear me?"

I couldn't believe it.

Jarvis had hurt me over a rock and didn't care.

I pulled myself together, got up and went outside. It took me two hours but I got Jarvis his rock with a little extra. Let's just say by the end of the night I made Jarvis and Baggs two satisfied men.

Chapter Twenty-Three

Lil Man was back home getting on my nerves. It was great having him gone for a couple weeks because it gave me some chill time but now he was back. Home life was okay and we still had our apartment. I wasn't sure how long this would last because the final eviction notice came yesterday.

The trust was almost gone between Jarvis and me. I thought he was trying to get over on me, and the thought I was trying to get over on him. To make matters worse, we had not been successful in finding work. But truth be told, we let those opportunities to search for a job slip away day after day. We were too busy getting high with Reds.

In order to keep up with our habit and keep some food in the house for Hysear, because we ate less and less, we sold our DVD players, the stereo, CD's, DVD's, my computer, some of my jewelry and the little flat screen television that was in the kitchen. No matter how bad our Jones got, we vowed never to touch Hysear's things and we tried to keep our promise.

It was bad enough that he was looking at me funny and complaining about the smell in the house and why Jarvis and me were always in the bedroom. At first I told him we were sick but he never believed me. So when that didn't work, I told him to stay out of grown folks business.

Reds told me to go reapply for welfare and I did but was told that the first check wouldn't come for another thirty days. And then it still would not be enough to pay for the back rent. When I told the rental office about our situation they told me that they couldn't help me unless I came up with eight hundred dollars within the next week.

Needless to say, eviction time came around hard and fast.

It was raining the day that we were going to be put out. What we had not already sold was left in the apartment and put out in the rain. The notice for the eviction was posted on the door earlier that day. Jarvis and I tried again to talk to the rental office but they weren't having it. The skinny-ass white woman told us that she had given us more than enough time to try to get our money together and that there was nothing she would do to stop the process.

The sheriff would be at our apartment later that day. Jarvis and I sat down on the end of the bed. I could not hold back my tears any longer. Wasn't no sense in acting like we wasn't getting ready to get put out cause we were. Jarvis tried consoling me but the more he consoled me the harder I cried. Lil Man was in school and did not know that we were being evicted so I went over to my neighbor and friend Pepper's house.

Pepper and I were cool neighbors from the day that I moved in. We even hung out together and snorted coke with each other sometimes. Her son DJ played with Hysear all the time. I broke down and told Pepper about the eviction and asked her to meet Hysear at the school bus stop while she was picking up her son. She agreed to take him to her house.

I knew he was going to ask questions especially since he would see all of our shit sitting out on the fucking sidewalk. I couldn't believe that we had let our shit get to this point. No jobs, no money, no place to lay our heads or to wash our asses. This was just crazy.

Jarvis had found some boxes and had begun to pack up the bedroom. I left and went to Lil Man's room. I closed the door and looked around. How was I going to tell him that we no longer lived here? I unplugged his Wii and gathered up all his games.

As I was bagging up all his things, I thought about what would happen to him. I didn't even know where we were going. He would have no use for these things and I decided to buy him another Wii and more games later when we had another place to stay.

It took me fifteen minutes to exchange my son's toys for crack. Because we couldn't afford any gas, I walked in the rain. Guilt rested on me when I was halfway home and I tried to find Baggs to get the game system back, but he was gone. My betrayal was too heavy to bear. So I crawled in my car, and smoked one of the twenty piece rocks he gave me for it.

As I inhaled, I felt invincible. In this moment I didn't have a son or responsibilities. I could do and be anything I wanted and what I wanted was to get high. But when I exhaled and inhaled and exhaled again until it was all gone, my reality was waiting. I had sold my son's game, the only thing he had in this world, for a rock.

I pulled myself together and went back in the house. I looked under the kitchen sink and found the box of trash bags and walked back to Hysear's room. I pulled one out and put Hysear's clothes in them. I cried the whole time I was in his room putting stuff in trash bags.

I was just about done packing up Lil Man's room when I heard the loud, hard knock at the door. I already knew it was Five-0 with the damn eviction crew. He was ready to serve us.

I straightened up my back, squared my shoulders and wiped my eyes dry. I refused to let this mutherfucka see me cry. By the time I turned around to go to the door, Jarvis was already opening it. The Sheriff walked in with papers in hand.

"I'm Sheriff Walker. Are you Jarvis Thompson?" He asked.

I saw the attitude on Jarvis's face.

"Yeah, I'm Jarvis Thompson." He reluctantly stated.

"I have an eviction notice for you. You must clear out of the premises now." He told us.

"Now?" We both shouted.

"Yes, now!" He said.

I wanted to faint. He didn't crack a smile as he handed Jarvis the eviction papers. I needed to see if I could buy some time. I didn't want my son to come home and see them putting our stuff out. If he was at Pepper's before they started then she would keep him inside the apartment until after the eviction.

"Officer Walker, please, I have a son and don't want him to come home to see this. Can you give us maybe two hours to pack up our clothes and other personal items before they start to take the furniture out?" I pleaded.

"No, ma'am, the moving crew is outside the door waiting to do their job." He informed. "You have wasted enough of these people's times with your lies and promise to pays. Out now."

Jarvis looked defeated. He walked over to door turned the handle. I walked up behind him and snatched his hand off the knob. He turned around to face me.

"Jarvis, where the fuck are we supposed to go and what are we supposed to do with our stuff?" I half screamed and half cried.

"Kaneesha, I don't know what to tell you, baby. You think I wanted this to happen? We fucked up, that's all there is to it. We both fucked up. Right now, I can't be cryin' like some bitch. I gotta think of where I'ma put our stuff and then I gotta find us somewhere to stay for a minute. I need your help, Kaneesha. You gonna have to suck this shit up and move the fuck on. Do you hear me? I ain't got time for you to be breaking down now. We knew this shit was coming and we knew the day. It ain't like it was with Mr. Levine. It was no surprise. So come on and help me take this shit downstairs to the bottom of the steps." He told me.

I picked up the mutherfuckin' bags and followed him down the stairs. Jarvis gave me a hard look then he softened his eyes.

"Kaneesha, I'ma get us a place okay? We just need to get past this shit first. I already got a job lined up. I didn't want to tell you anything until I knew it for sure...okay? But baby right now, you're going to have to be strong. And you may even have to do what you have to do to tie us over."

"Do what I have to do?"

"Yes. We'll talk about it later. For now, let's go."

I was tired at this point from everything. Mentally, I was drained. Physically, I was exhausted. Emotionally, I was lifeless. Jarvis and I continued to walk bag after bag of our shit down the steps. The rain had cleared up and it was sunny. The weather made me feel a little better about our stuff being out on the sidewalk. At least the shit wouldn't get wet for the moment.

I noticed that some of the nosey-ass neighbors were outside, standing around and pretending that they were talking to one another. Shit, half them mutherfuckas didn't even speak to each other on the regular. But now their asses was out there talking up a storm. Nosey fuckers. They were there to watch the sheriff put us out. I was on my last bag when Jarvis came back into the apartment. He was huffing and puffing when he walked through the door. He closed it behind him and looked around at the rest of the stuff. Suddenly he snapped his fingers and a grin came across his face.

"Okay, Jarvis, what the hell you thinkin' 'bout doin'?" I asked him as I sat the heavy-ass bag back down on the floor and leaned against the wall.

"Kaneesha, you know the apartment downstairs below is abandoned right?"

"Yeah and?" I said dumbfounded.

"So after they put everything out and they leave, we gonna break open the lock on the door and put our stuff in there." I looked at Jarvis like he was just fucking stupid.

"What, are you crazy? How you know that place ain't dangerous or rat and roach infested? That's why they got them boards all around the windows and shit, Jarvis. I would rather put my shit in the back of the dumpster first before I put my shit in that nasty ass place. I heard that shit been boarded up for over two years, Jarvis. Come on, man."

"Kaneesha, when are you gonna release your holier than though attitude? You not better than everybody, Kaneesha. We ain't got nowhere to go. I've already been down there and it ain't what you think. It's clean and safe. There's even running water and electricity."

"How you know?"

"I use to get high down there sometimes before I started going to Me-Me's house. Ain't nothing wrong with that apartment. They boarded up the windows cause the kids threw rocks at them and broke them out. Other than that, the place is fine. I fixed the lock a certain way to get in it. Once you get in you can lock it just like a regular door." He told me.

Feeling like he was right about my judgmental attitude, I said, "Fuck it, let me see it!"

"No, we can't right now. Too many damn people out there. I don't want nobody knowing that's what we 'bout to do. We just gonna take the rest of our shit down them steps and wait for the moving crew to come back and bring out the furniture. I want you to stay downstairs with the stuff. I know how to get in. What I'ma do is sneak back up the steps and go in and make sure it's just like I saw it a few months ago. Okay?"

"Jarvis, please be careful."

He kissed me on the forehead and said, "Okay."

I picked up the bag that I had put down on the floor, took a deep breath and swung the damn thing over my shoulder. I proceeded down the steps. When I got downstairs, I put it down on the sidewalk with the rest of the bags. I heard our apartment door close above me and knew that Jarvis had come out to sneak into the abandoned apartment. But the Sheriff was coming back with his henchmen. Damn!

I ran back towards the first floor and gently tapped on the door. I whispered as loud as I could to Jarvis. Seconds later, he crept out the door and gently closed it behind him. We both ran back to the front of the apartment building, waiting for the moving crew and the sheriff. The sheriff approached us and asked us if we had gotten what we needed from the place. We told him yes. He nodded to the other three men and they went up the steps. After about an hour, all the furniture was sitting out on the sidewalk. The sheriff got in his car and left as the moving crew headed back towards the office.

It was about four-thirty when my home in 32-C Heights came to an end. Fuck it! I sat down on the couch and took in what the fuck just happened. Here I was sitting outside, on the sidewalk, on my couch, with my boyfriend and all of the rest of my belongings at four-thirty in the afternoon.

"Don't Worry Be Happy". I heard someone outside singing.

What the fuck? I turned around to see a couple of my neighbors singing to us. Then I heard another voice join in and sing along, then another voice joined in. Before we knew it, they were all out there singing "Don't Worry Be Happy." A couple of them came over and hugged us and told us it was going to be all right. After the singing session, folks moved on. That was weird but in a strange way, it made me feel better. When the coast was clear, Jarvis ran back to the abandoned apartment and opened the door.

He came back to the steps and motioned with hands for me to come on. I looked around before I went down the back of the first floor. Jarvis pulled me into the apartment the moment he saw me. I walked in. Jarvis had a flashlight. I looked around. He was right the apartment was clean. He walked me from room to room. There was really nothing wrong with it.

"Okay, so we gonna do this?" I asked him.

"Hell yes. Go on and get some of the bags and start to bring them up here."

I ran back down to the front of the building and picked up some of the lighter bags. The faster we got those in the place, the better. Jarvis was right behind me. We carried bag after bag inside. We even moved our furniture inside. An hour later, Jarvis and I had moved all of our shit into our new rent-free apartment.

He said he was going to find Baggs and see if he would loan him some money to get a new lock for the door. That way we would have keys.

"No!" I screamed. "I mean, not right now."

"Why?"

"Uh...just wait."

I didn't want him finding out that I not only sold Hysear's game, but that I also smoked and left him out. I think when it came to the Crack head oath, about every man being for himself, that he didn't want it to apply to him.

"I can't. We need money now."

I relented and hoped Baggs would keep my secret. We went outside and brought in our mattress. Then we put it on the bedroom floor. I found a lamp and plugged it in. Light flooded the room. With the boards up at the window, it was pitch black in here. I didn't want to put lights up all over the place 'cause I didn't know if you could see it through the cracks in the boards. So Jarvis used his flashlight.

I found some sheets and a blanket in our bag, and I made the mattress up. All the big furniture was placed in the living room. We pushed everything in the corner and put the couch and coffee table out in the open to use. After we were done, we sat on the couch to catch our breath. We didn't say anything for a long time. I felt like I was in a twilight zone or a bad dream.

But this shit was real and we were assed out.

Chapter Twenty-Four

The time had come to confront Hysear. I couldn't bring myself to tell my son that his mother had let them get evicted and that I sold his Wii. I decided against mentioning the Wii.

I turned on the cold water, splashed some on my face and looked in the mirror at my image. I couldn't help myself as I burst out crying, dropping to my on the cold floor. I cried for not being strong enough to resist the urge of the drug. I cried for my son...my wonderful beautiful little boy. He didn't deserve this. He counted on me and Jarvis for his survival and look what the fuck he got in return.

An hour later after my crying fit, I pulled myself up off the cold floor and washed my face. It was time to pay the piper. I had to go to Pepper's house and talk to Hysear. I had no idea of how to approach this. I walked out to the living area and looked at what was left of our miserable lives. Everything we owned was now sitting in this boarded up apartment. Moments later, I solemnly made my way up the stairs to Pepper's place.

I smoothed out my clothes and looked down at myself before I put my hand on the knocker. As I waited for the door to open, I began to pray.

God, I know you probably don't want to hear from me right now, but if there was ever a time that I needed you to help me, this would be one of those times. I know I done fucked up God, but right now, you would be my only saving grace for my child. Please help me to find a way out of this soon God, please. Please do it for Hysear God. For Hysear.

The door opened.

"Hey Pepper, where's Hysear?" I asked in a shaky voice.

She moved to the left side of the door and waved me in. I

came in and stood in the doorway embarrassed. Pepper closed the door and went to DJ's room. I began to fidget from one foot to the other. Minutes later, I heard small feet running from down the hall. Before I could get myself together, Hysear appeared. Eyes bright, smile shining from ear to ear and his book bag famously dragging behind him. His coat was thrown over his shoulders and he ran straight to me.

"Hey, Mommy. Pepper said you wanted to talk to me. Are you going out? If so, can I stay here with DJ and play in his room? Is that what you wanted to talk to me about?" he said pulling the book bag up on his other shoulder.

"No, son."

"Mommy, I need to take my stuff home. And I'm hungry. Can we go home now then? I got some hard math homework to do and I'm going to need your help."

I looked at Hysear as if I was seeing my child for the first time. I put my arm around my son's shoulder and looked down into his face. I kneeled down to his level. I took his soft little hands into mine and looked his yes. Hysear knew something was wrong. Before I could say anything, he dropped his book bag and coat on the floor and threw both of his arms around my neck and hugged me.

"Mommy, it's okay." My heart was breaking into millions of pieces.

This was probably the hardest thing I ever had to tell my son. I hugged him tighter than pulled back from the embrace.

"Hysear, listen to me son. Some things have changed. We don't live across the hall anymore. Mommy and Jarvis didn't have enough money to pay for the rent and so they told us we had to move." I watched Hysear's eyes widen.

I waited for his response.

"Why can't we go home, Mommy?"

"Hysear, I just told you because we didn't have enough money to pay the rent and the rental office said we had to move so we did."

"Well, let's go to our new house then. Where is it, mommy?"

"Hysear, we don't have a new home yet. Mommy and Jarvis are working on it. We don't know where we will live yet." I told him.

"Well, where did you put all our stuff? Where is my bed and my Wii and Playstation 3?"

"We put the Wii and Playstation up in a safe place. I didn't want anybody to steal it," I said as more tears welled in the corners of my eyes. "And do you remember the apartment that was underneath us that has the boards on it?"

"Yeah?"

"We put our stuff in there so no one would steal it." Several moments of dead air hung between my son and me. I was melting into the floor waiting for his response.

"How did you get in there? Ain't it spooky?"

"No, it's not spooky in there. And Jarvis and I didn't have a choice. We had to put our stuff somewhere so people wouldn't steal it. But listen to me, Hysear, right now we have to sleep down there, Lil Man. We don't have any other place to go."

"Sleep down there?" Hysear yelled. He was clearly shaken at this revelation.

"Yeah, we are going to have to stay in there for a couple of days until Jarvis and I can figure out what to do next."

"I don't want to stay down there. I'm scared, Mommy, I'm scared." Hysear began to wail.

There was nothing I could do but pull my little boy into my arms and hold him tightly. Hysear pulled away from me and looked me in the face.

"Mommy?" He said as he wiped away the tears from his eyes "Are you sure that the place ain't spooky?"

"Yes, Hysear. I'm sure. If it was, I wouldn't be there."

"Why can't I stay here with Pepper?" Hysear asked.

"Because Pepper already has two children to take care of and besides, you're not Pepper's responsibility, Hysear. You're mine." I told him.

I couldn't believe that I just made that fucked-up statement. *Responsibility*. What the hell did I know about that word? Shit, just look at what my responsibility had done.

"Hysear, just think of it as camping out."

I didn't have anything else to tell him.

"Like camping? Okay, Mommy. Can I go down there and see it?" He asked.

"Not yet, Jarvis went to get a lock for the door. When he comes back I will come and get you and then we will take you down there okay?"

With much hesitation, my son slowly shook his head. I could see the fright in his eyes at the prospect of going down stairs to an abandoned apartment. It was probably one of the worse things that could ever happen to a child.

"Hysear, listen to me. You can't tell anyone about this. If you do, they will call social services and come and take you away from me. Do you hear me?" I said turning my son to face me.

In a monotone voice that sounded like it was full of hurt, anger and confusion, Hysear uttered, "Yes Mommy."

"Hysear, go and get Pepper for me."

He took off running down the hallway towards the bedrooms. Moments later, Pepper appeared.

"Pepper, may I please impose on you once more? Would it be okay if Hysear stayed with you just for tonight? Jarvis & I temporarily moved our stuff into the abandoned apartment downstairs. I don't want him coming down there until I can get some stuff ready for him."

"Of course he can stay, girl. Just get him some school clothes and I'll send him to school from here."

"Pepper, thanks so much. Right now, I just don't know what to do. I'm so sorry about this!" I felt I was goin to cry again.

Pepper immediately took me into her arms to console me. I was so ashamed of my actions.

"Pepper, thanks for everything. I don't know what I would do without a good neighbor like you." I confessed.

"Girl, Hysear is like a son to me. I won't see anything happen to him. But you are grown and your decisions and actions rest solely on your own shoulders. Now, I'm not going to give you a lecture and because I love you like a sister, I'ma tell you this. Maybe you need to think about leaving Jarvis. Everyone knows Jarvis was out there on the pipe. So it was only a matter of time before you got caught up too.

"Kaneesha, for God's sake, get it together. If you don't, somebody might call social services on you and Hysear will be gone. Don't let that happen to him. And think about this, if Jarvis is not willing to let go of smokin' crack and you are, then you need to drop his ass like a bad habit. Fuck that shit, Kaneesha. I really hate seein' you in this state right now." She reached out to hug me again. I fell into her arms and cried one more time.

"Thank you."

Feeling it wasn't enough she said, "Kaneesha, I will gladly help you find a program to help you get off this shit. But either way, something has to give." Pepper continued.

"I'm fine Pepper, just a little bad luck right now. Jarvis and I will find some jobs soon and then get another place to live. But right now, we are where we are. At least we're not sleeping in the streets. Look, I'ma go and find Lil Man some clothes." I said moving towards the door.

"Well it's Wednesday, he might as well stay with us for the rest of the week." She said.

I told her thank you and hurried off to get his clothes. I got back downstairs to the bottom floor and looked around to make sure no one saw me before I went into the apartment. I carefully opened the door and went in. It was pitch inside. I began to feel my way back towards the area that Jarvis and I had set up our living space. Along the way, I tripped and banged my knees and legs several times on shit. Eventually I found the lamp and turned it on. I need to find Lil Man some clothes for school but right now, I just want to lie down and sulk. I lay down on the mattresses that were on the floor and began to pray.

Within ten minutes I wanted to get high and had no idea how.

I jumped straight up to my feet. I was scared. Oh shit...who the hell is in here with me? I grabbed the flashlight and my baseball bat.

"Jarvis?" I said softly.

I walked out of the bedroom and into the living area and I heard the noise again. My heart beat rapidly. I shined the light into the living room but didn't see anyone. But I had the bat ready on my shoulder for a swing attack if a mutherfucka was up in here. Suddenly the door opened and two figures came into view. Someone was at the front door. I backed myself up against the wall and waited.

"Man, come on. It's cool. Don't nobody know we here."

It was Jarvis's voice but I didn't know who was with him. They were walking towards me. I turned on the flashlight and shined it in their faces.

"Fuck, Kaneesha, you almost gave me a got-damn heart attack! What the fuck you doing?" Jarvis yelled.

"I was scared! Who's with you?" I shined the light towards the other person. It was Baggs. There was no sense in asking Jarvis why Baggs was there.

"Hey, Kaneesha!" Baggs said.

Every time I saw him I felt guilty. First I sucked his dick and let him cum in my mouth for Jarvis's rock, and then I sold him Hysear's Wii system.

"Hey." I said blandly.

"I'm just helpin' out. You know, lendin' a hand," he said winking at me without Jarvis noticing.

"Oh...well hurry up, I was trying to get some sleep."

Jarvis busied himself with taking the lock out of it's packaging so I used this time to appeal to him to give me Hysear's game station back.

I moved him closer to me and farther from Jarvis. "Look, do you still have the game? The Wii?" He nodded. "I made a mistake," I whispered, "a big one. Can you please give it back? I'll pay you when I get the money."

"Can't do that," he whispered back.

"What ya'll talkin' about?" Jarvis asked although he wasn't looking in our direction."

"Nothin," I said. "Just thanking him for helping."

Jarvis was too busy with the lock to care at this point. He was really acting like this was our crib, all in the hallway with the locks and shit. "Please, Baggs. I really need it back. My son is already hurt at our new living conditions and that game means a lot to him."

"You shoulda thought of that before you gave it to me."

"Please...he'll die if he finds out it's gone."

He looked me up and down licked his lips and said, "Meet me tonight, and you can work it off."

"What? What about Jarvis? It'll be weird if I left out tonight."

"Either work it off or find another one. It's up to you."

"I'll meet you in the back of the building, at 7:00 o'clock."

"I'll see you then," he said joining Jarvis.

This thing with Baggs was getting out of hand, but what was I to do?

Baggs and Jarvis went to work on the lock and I put the bat down and began to look for some clothes for Hysear. I grabbed the bag and headed upstairs to Pepper's.

As I was going out, Jarvis said, "Don't be too long."

I knew exactly what that meant and my craving immediately kicked into high gear. He must've gotten a hook up from Baggs. Suddenly I thought it unfair that Jarvis got breaks off the strength of their friendship, while Baggs made me do unquestionable acts for my high. Still, I hot tailed it up the stairs. When Pepper answered the door, I didn't go in.

"Hey, Pepper. Jarvis is waiting on me downstairs so we could change the lock on the door. I'm here to bring his clothes."

I quickly ended our conversation and took off like a shot out of a gun downstairs. When I got to the apartment I opened the door and walked in. The familiar smell hit my nose and Jarvis was puffing up a storm. Jarvis had my pipe sitting on the mirror and Baggs pushed me a piece of rock.

"For you," He smiled while looking at me seductively. Jarvis was engrossed with his glass dick.

"Thanks," I said grabbing it from him.

"It's all good, you can add this to the balance," he whispered.

Chapter Twenty-Five

Jarvis and I spent the first few nights in the abandoned apartment not getting much rest. We were scared that someone would try to break in or the rental office would find out we were here and put us out again. And, Hysear, was due to move into the abandoned apartment with us come the weekend.

I had to prepare myself for this shock to Hysear's system. Jarvis got up early this morning and took a shower. The water was cold as there was no hot water in the apartment. He was going to the job he had found at another restaurant in the mall. I found him some clothes in one of the many trash bags and ironed them. He dressed, kissed me and headed out to work. Meanwhile, I was resigned to stay in the apartment.

It was too early to go down to Reds house cause her mother was still there. Besides, Reds needed her sleep. Lately she was having stomach pains. I told her she needed to go to the doctors for prenatal care but of course she didn't do it. She was being taken care of medically by the state but like me, she was too busy getting high.

I shuddered from the chill that was running rampant throughout the apartment. It was cold November weather and I thought about the coming holidays that lay ahead for us. Would we be able to get out of our current situation before Christmas? If we didn't, what would we do about gifts for Hysear? What about a tree? What about Christmas dinner? How was this going to affect Hysear?

I didn't want to think about it so I pushed those thoughts from my mind. I had no direction at all in my life right now. I was just existing. I plugged in the TV, but it only got four stations so I turned on the clock radio and listened to 92-Q. I needed to do something to pass the time away. I decided to start going through the bags of clothes and separate mine from Jarvis and Hysear's. This way when we moved we wouldn't have to search for shit.

When I finished with the clothes I was tired. But I wasn't just tired from that task, I was burnt out. I needed help, I needed guidance. I sat down on the side of the mattress and hung my head in self-pity and prayed.

Jesus. I need a miracle from heaven right now. Lord, if ever I needed you it would surely by at this time. Right now I don't know but one prayer, so God I'm sending it up. Our father who art in heaven, hollowed be thy name. Thy kingdom come, thy will be done, on earth as it is in Heaven. Give us this day our daily bread. And forgive us trespassers as we forgive those who trespass against us. And lead us not into temptation but deliver us from evil. For thine is the kingdom, and the power and the glory. Forever and Ever. Amen.

I was on my knees. Tears were falling effortlessly from my eyes. My soul was in pain. My heart ached so bad I that I actually had pain throughout my chest. I looked around at the apartment and at everything that I owned. I was crushed, defeated, helpless, and unworthy of life. For the first time in my life, I didn't know what to do, what to feel, what to think, how to act or what to say. My son deserved better. He didn't need a mother who couldn't provide for him. My addiction had taken over my common sense and my ability to think straight and do the right things for me and my son, there was no other choice, I wasn't fit to live.

I found some paper and a pen and began composing my letters. I wrote my dad first.

My Dear Father:

I am writing this letter because Hysear is now left in your care. Please tell him that I love him very much. I love you too, Daddy. I don't know what else to do at this point in my life. I have made such a mess of things. Hysear doesn't deserve this type of life and I can't give him anything better right now. You are his grandfather and I know that you will do everything in your power to raise your grandson right. I'm not a very good mother. Please don't be mad at me. But at this moment, this is the only thing that I can do that will make things right. I love you Daddy. Please take care of my little boy. Tell him I love him and always will.

Love,
Your daughter, Kaneesha.

Next, I wrote Jarvis a simple letter.

Jarvis,

I can't do this anymore. I feel less than a woman, less than mother, less than a human being. Help my father take care of Hysear. I love you all.

Love,
Kaneesha.

I thought about the box that I had packed away. I frantically searched for it around the cold apartment. I found it and tore it open. I found what I was looking for. I was enchanted by the shiny silver blade and how radiantly it shined even in the dim light seeping through boarded windows and the apartment's only lamp. I turned the knife over and over in my hand. I ran my fingers along the side and down the handle. I didn't have one fingerprint on it. She was clean and I was getting ready to make a damn mess by slicing my wrists.

Now where do I do it? I took the letters that I had written and put them on top of the dresser. Each was folded in half and addressed. I remember seeing Scarface and the man getting cut up with the chainsaw in the bathroom behind the shower curtain. I found the bag with the bathroom stuff in it and took out the shower curtain. I need to hang it so that it would stop all the blood from going all over the place. I found two nails that were sticking out of the wood of one of the boarded windows. I hung the shower curtain by its holes on the board. It was a perfect fucking fit. I moved furniture out of the way and grabbed a kitchen chair. I brought it over to the window and set it in the middle of the shower curtain that was on the floor. I sat down. I asked God to forgive me. I asked my father to forgive me, and I asked my son to forgive and love me forever. I asked Jarvis to forgive me. I picked up the knife and I put it against my wrist. I silently said a prayer ran the knife across my wrist. The pain was excruciating although I hadn't really punctured my skin.

I dropped the knife, and it fell onto the floor. I threw up. Balled up in a fetal position, vomit escaped my stomach until I had no fluids left in my body. It turns out the shower curtain came in handy after all. I wasn't meant to die right now. I gripped my wrist and cried out loud, not caring who heard me.

I stayed that way until Jarvis came in to find me in a state of delirium. When I finally came to my fucking senses, it was a day later. Jarvis said he was scared and if I hadn't come around when I did, he was going to call my father and an ambulance and take my crazy ass straight to the nut house. Jarvis sat vigil by my side while I spaced out. He said I wouldn't talk at all. I just looked out into space as if I was looking for something. He said he couldn't believe it himself when he walked in to find me on the floor with the gun. He just knew I was dead. After I was back to normal, Jarvis was so mad at me that he wouldn't talk to me. I was callous about my life. But trust me when I say, I was at my wits end.

Chapter Twenty-Six

Hysear came down to stay with us for the first time. He cried as he walked into the cold apartment. I took him to the bedroom showed him where we're going to be sleeping and spending most of our time. My son was distraught. I talked to Hysear and tried to tell him that we were doing the best we could with what we had. Hysear wasn't trying to hear what I had to say. He just wanted to know when we were going to get out of the 'creepy' apartment. Jarvis would bring food home at night that he stole from his job. He would also bring sterno cans that we could use to heat the food with. The TV channels we were able to get were better than nothing. It gave Hysear some comfort. Reds had also given me an electric blanket to help us stay warm.

The first of December was approaching fast. It was cold as shit now. We didn't have any heat, so we stayed huddled together for warmth under the electric blanket along with several other blankets. We slept in thick socks, sweatpants, and hoodies. I got up in the morning and heated water as best I could and to wash Hysear with it. I dressed him and then walked him to the door to make sure no one saw him coming out of the apartment. When he came home from school, he would wait for me down at the bottom of the landing and I would go and get him. We were about a week into this routine and Hysear was adjusting. I was still getting high with Reds in the morning after Hysear went to school and when Jarvis went to work.

This particular night the conversation that Jarvis and I shared would change some shit between us. Jarvis was home from work. He was tired and worn out and had even lost weight. He didn't smile anymore and when you looked in his eyes, there was nothing there. Any signs of life had vanished.

Jarvis seemed almost robotic now. He sat down on the mattress and pulled out some leftovers that he managed to steal, herb chicken, rice pilaf, and green beans. He even had two pieces of cake.

We didn't talk much. We just didn't have much to say.

"How's Lil Man doin' wit' this?" Jarvis asked. He continued to take stuff out the bag.

"He's not doin' too bad but he can't live here like this long. We have got to do something soon." I said.

"Yeah, I know, Kaneesha. This shit is breakin' me. I'll think of somethin', Okay? Your father still doesn't know does he?" He questioned.

"Are you still breathin'?" I asked him.

He chuckled momentarily. That was the first time I had heard him laugh in weeks. My dad assumed we were staying with friends. There was no way I could tell him that I was living in this predicament. I lied so much to him about what I wasn't doing that I couldn't bear to face him and tell him the truth now. As long as we weren't in a shelter or on the streets, I felt like we were okay for the moment. My father would most certainly try to kill Jarvis for letting this happen to his family.

"Do you want me to wake Hysear up? Did he eat today?" Jarvis asked looking over at Lil Man.

"Yeah, Reds brought us down a whole case of Oodles of Noodles and some hotdogs." I replied.

"When she gonna have that baby? He asked.

"I don't know but she damn sure ain't gettin' no bigger."

"Yeah, I noticed."

Jarvis was stirring the food with a plastic fork. He stopped stirring and put the fork down on the side of the paper plate and he fixed his look on me.

"Kaneesha, I'm goin' to my brother's house this weekend. I'm goin' to see what's happenin' at home." He told me.

"What you mean, you goin' to see what's happenin' at home? Are you goin' take me and Lil Man with you?" Jarvis folded his hands behind his head and leaned against the dresser.

"Kaneesha, it would be easier for me to go alone this weekend and see what's up. I'm just goin' to see if my brother and cousins might have some room. Maybe I can talk to them about movin' us up there. Or at least get a few dollars from one of them while I'm there. I just need to go home this weekend and see what I can work out." Jarvis said.

I didn't know what say so I didn't say shit. Dead air hung between us for a moment. He fixed me a plate and handed it to me. I picked through the food my appetite had disappeared.

"Aren't you going' to eat? Shit, Kaneesha, you know I had to steal this food for us." he pointed out.

"Yeah, I know, Jarvis." I said. I put the plate on the mattress.

"What's wrong, Neesh?" He asked.

"How you just figure you gonna leave me and Hysear here for the weekend? Don't you think that maybe we want to get the fuck outta here for a few days too? Shit, I wouldn't mind soakin' my ass in some hot water or layin' down on a bed or even the damn floor as long as there's heat in the house. Why can't we go with you?"

"Alright, alright, Neesh. Stop fuckin' wildin'. Shit, I'll call tomorrow from work and see who's goin' be home. We'll catch the bus there Okay?" he said noticeably frustrated.

"Yeah, that's fine with me." I quipped.

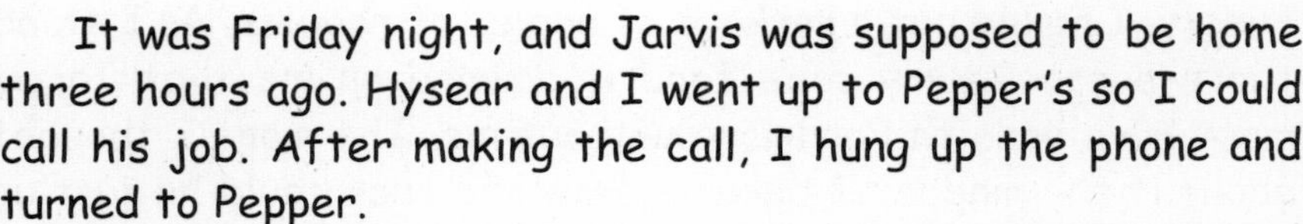

It was Friday night, and Jarvis was supposed to be home three hours ago. Hysear and I went up to Pepper's so I could call his job. After making the call, I hung up the phone and turned to Pepper.

"They said that Jarvis didn't come in to work today." I said solemnly.

Pepper looked at me in puzzlement.

"You sure that's what they said?" Pepper questioned.

"Pep, the nigga didn't go to work. Where the fuck is he?" I

said out loud.

"Kaneesha, you don't think that he's out somewhere gettin' high do you?"

"I don't know, Pepper. He did get paid today." I said.

Pepper thought for a moment.

"Umh, that's not like Jarvis, girl." Pepper tried to sound convincing.

"I don't know, Pepper. Shit, I don't know who the fuck neither one of us are any more." I admitted.

"How *are* ya'll doin', besides the obvious?" Pepper asked sincerely.

"I ain't tryin' to be a smart ass, Pep, but how the hell do you think we doin'? My life is fucked up right now and I got my son out here wit' me like this. Listen, I'm gone. Thanks for lettin' me use your phone. If you hear from Jarvis, you know where to find me." I turned to make my way to her front door.

"I got you, girl. And I'm so sorry." She reached out to hug me.

"I'll be fine. I'm a survivor literally." I said as I turned in to give her a brief hug.

Neither Jarvis nor I had told anyone about my suicide attempt so she didn't know of my true feelings

I went back down to my cold, abandoned apartment. That day turned to afternoon that turned to evening that turned to night that turned back to another morning. Jarvis had not come home at all. Hysear was up early on this Saturday morning. I turned on the TV so he could watch cartoons. He was hungry. I pulled out a package of oodles of noodles. As I stood there preparing my son's food it dawned on me that Jarvis must have gone to Baltimore without me. The more I thought about it the madder I became. How the fuck could he just up and leave and not say anything about going?

The noodles were hot and ready for the seasonings. I was sick of these mutherfuckas but that was all we had to eat. I poured them into a bowl and took them to Hysear. He snatched the bowl out of my hand and began to eat while watching Tom and Jerry. All I heard as I sat down on the mattress beside him was the fork hitting the bowl with every forkful that he scooped out.

I pulled my knees up to my chest, put my head down on my knees and shed tears. I didn't want Hysear to hear my crying but at any moment I knew that I was about to wail. Before I could get myself up and out of the room to cry in peace, I let out a loud scream. Hysear dropped his bowl of noodles on the mattress. He looked over at me wide eyed and scared. I couldn't do anything but fold myself over and scream into the mattress. I screamed, kicked, punched, and screamed some more. I hadn't noticed that Hysear's arms and hands were holding me. He had somehow managed to lift up my head and put it on his chest to comfort me. I cried hard and long into my son's arms.

"It's okay, Mommy. It's okay. Don't cry, Mommy. Don't cry. I love you, Mommy. We are going to be okay." I heard him continue to say.

I felt Hysear's soft little fingers stroking my face gently while he rocked me in his little arms.

"Mommy, stop crying." Hysear pleaded.

"I can't, Hysear, I can't. I don't know what to do right now." I sobbed into his arms.

With conviction my son turned my face to his.

"Yes, you do Mommy, you know what to do!" He said.

I sat up and stopped my crying and looked at my precious gift from heaven.

"Mommy, I prayed before I went to sleep last night." He said. I wiped the last tear from my eyes. "You did?" I asked.

"Yes, I did mommy." He paused. "Aren't you going to ask me what happened?" I knew what he was asking.

"And what did God say?" I replied

"He told me that he was taking care of you and for me not to worry. God said he was protecting you, mommy." Hysear smiled.

"Protecting me?" I quizzed.

"Yes, protecting you!" he reiterated.

"Did God say from what?" I was curious.

"No, he just told me that I was a good boy and that you were a good mother and for you to stop saying that you weren't." Hysear continued.

My mouth fell open and I didn't know what to say. I didn't want to believe what my son had just told me so I questioned him again.

"Hysear, are you making this up? God didn't really say that. God doesn't talk to you like that, Hysear. You're telling stories." I told my baby.

"Yes, he does. When I'm sleep sometimes God will talk to me in my sleep." He said sincerely.

"Hysear, you're dreaming." I retorted.

Hysear became upset. "Mommy, that's not right. God talks to me and he said that you probably would say that."

"Okay, sweetie. If God said he is protecting me then I believe it." I told him.

A smile came across his face. He reached up for me again and hugged me. I held him with all my might.

"Mommy, I...can't breathe." He said in a smothered tone.

I slowly opened my arms just enough to give him air and then wrapped them back around him again tightly. It felt good to hear his laughter against my chest. As we sat there laughing, there was a knock at the door. I told Hysear to remain quiet. I grabbed the bat and tiptoed to the front door. I peeked out and saw it was Pepper so I opened it and let her in. She came in and looked around. This was the first time that she had stepped foot inside the apartment.

"Damn, Neesh, it's cold as shit in here." She said as we both watched her breath condensate and float through the air. She then peeped the bat.

"Yeah, we're keenly aware of this. Pep, what's up?" I wanted to know why she was there. I didn't want her seeing my condition and looking down on me.

"Jarvis called my house."

"And what did he say? Where is he?" I asked excitedly.

"He's at his cousin's in Cherry Hill."

"Umph, umph, umph. I knew it I knew he took his sorry ass to Baltimore. That mutherfucka!" I yelled.

"I'm sorry, Neesh, I really am."

"He say anything else?" I asked.

"Yeah, he's going to call you tomorrow around noon. So why don't you and Hysear come up and spend the day with us and have Sunday dinner." She offered.

"That's all the fuck he said. He didn't say he was coming home?" I asked.

"No, he didn't say anything like that." she replied sadly.

He had done what I thought. He left my son and me down here in this abandoned apartment with no food, no money, no heat, no nothing. He didn't even have the balls to tell me that he was going. He lied about going to work and now this nigga wanna call over to Peppers and tell her to give me a message. That mutherfucka! How could he do such a thing? Ain't this a bitch!

"Thanks for the info." I said.

"What about dinner? For Hysear if you don't want to come?" she asked looking upon him with pity.

"We're fine." I took her by the arm and started leading her toward the door.

"Damn, girl, don't worry, I'm leaving. You ain't gotta push me—I'm gone." And Pepper was out the door.

I heard her heavy footsteps as she went up the stairs to her warm apartment. I closed and leaned against that cold-ass door for several minutes trying to come to terms with what Jarvis had pulled. Hysear and I spent the remainder of the day under the covers watching programs on the four channels that we could get a picture from, trying to keep the warmth with our own bodies.

On Sunday, me and Hysear hot tailed to Pepper's house. I

wanted to make sure my ass was there for this phone call that Jarvis was supposed to make. Hysear was ecstatic to be in a warm house and especially happy to know that he was staying for dinner. He and DJ ran around like they had lost their minds. Pepper let them do just about anything that they wanted. She didn't mind the ruckus that these two caused. They were hard players. Knocking down shit, falling over shit and breaking shit...but Pepper didn't care. She said they were boys and most of the shit in her house was replaceable or she got it hot so there was no real loss.

Pepper and I were talking when the phone rang.

Pepper threw me a look and said, "Hold on."

She walked back to me and handed me the phone. I hesitated but took it out of her hands and placed the warm receiver against my ear.

"Hey, Kaneesha." Jarvis said.

"Hello, Jarvis." I coldly spat back.

"I'm sorry, Neesh but I needed to do what I had to do."

"So you lied about going to work and then you snuck off like a thief in the night

"I said I was sorry."

"Fuck that shit, Jarvis! What the hell does sorry mean any fuckin' more?" I shouted into the phone.

"Kaneesha, I didn't call to hear this shit! Now I need you to hear me!"

"What?" I continued to scream into the phone.

"Listen, Kaneesha. I'm goin' stay here for a couple of days to see 'bout a good job to get us a place." Jarvis told me.

"You're what?!" I screamed. A long pause punctuated my question.

"I said I'm stayin' in Baltimore. I need to find a better job here. I got family who can help me get on my feet."

"Jarvis, you sneaky mutherfucka. How the hell you gonna do me and Lil Man like this? You just gonna leave us down here?!" I started crying. Before he could answer, I screamed into the receiver again. "Say something! Stop acting like you don't know what the fuck to say! Talk to me!" I pleaded.

"I will if you let me. Right now, I'm tired of dealing with the shit we in. I'm the man of the house. I need to find a way to get us out of this so let me do that. I need to be here to do that!" he declared.

"Why did you do it this way, Jarvis? What are we supposed to do in the meantime? Lil Man & I have nothin' now. We need you. I need you." I cried.

"Kaneesha, I ain't trynna argue wit' you. I said I was doin' this for us. Now, I gotta go. I'll call you later this week to check on you." He told me.

"No don't fuckin' call me! I hate you, Jarvis! I fuckin' hate you. Don't come back for me. We don't need your ass. We'll be just fine without you!" I screamed and cried into the phone again. By this time Lil Man had eased next to me and I was unaware.

"I'm sorry, Kaneesha, I know you mad and you don't understand how I feel but this is something that I must do for me, for you and Lil Man. And for what it's worth, I love you."

One final time I said, "Jarvis...if you leave me...if you leave us...I'ma die. Please don't stay away. I'm not strong enough to do this alone."

"I'll be back when I can." He said softly.

I banged the phone down. Fuck him and his love! I threw myself down onto Pepper's couch and had a crying fit. She let me cry as she went to the kitchen to finish dinner and Lil Man walked away. She must have known when it was time to let a bitch have her moment. And trust me, I was having mine.

Chapter Twenty-Seven

Loud banging on the door startled me. Shit, who the hell is this at 8:30 in the morning. I looked out the peephole and saw Reds standing there. I hurriedly opened the door to let her in.

"Hey, Neesh, Lil Man gone to school yet?" She asked.

"Yeah, girl he gone." I told her excitedly.

"I came over to get you. Manny's at my house" She informed.

"Manny?" I questioned.

"Yeah, he wanted me to come over and get you so he could treat us."

"Really?" I asked.

"Yeah, now put your clothes on and come on. I'll be at the house."

"You ain't gonna wait for me?" I said as I tried to get myself together in a hurry.

"No, he's at my house alone, shit, I need to get back just in case he decides to leave. I don't want him leaving without him breaking me off with something."

"Go on! I'm coming!" I told her.

Reds left, and I ran back to freshen up as much as possible. After I cleaned up, I put on some jeans and a sweatshirt. I grabbed my purse that had my purple bag, cigarettes and keys in it. And when I walked out, I noticed Dubbs standing at the top of the landing. I wondered if he saw exactly where I came from and what was he up to now?

"Where's Manny?" I asked after Reds let me in.

"Go back to the room. Manny's in there waiting on you."

"Girl, I ain't going to no bedroom with no Manny. Shit, I

ain't that desperate for no coke."

"You just don't get it do you?"

"Get what?"

"Even now you trying to have respect where there should be none. You are living in an abandoned apartment with no money and no coke. Manny has the money and the coke. Now if you don't wanna get high, go home, it's up to you."

She was right and it was tough to hear. "What does he want?"

"Girl, if you go in the back with him he'll break us each off at least a fifty-cent piece." She said.

"Each or do we have to share?" I asked her.

Reds looked at me and shook her head.

"No girl, he's gonna give us our own packages."

"Reds, I don't know girl."

"Kaneesha, I'ma be straight up. If you suck his dick, he'll hook us up. I was gonna do it but he wasn't fuckin' wit' me. So what you gonna do?"

"I ain't suckin' no damn dick for no blast! Fuck that Reds!" I shouted. She pulled me closer to into the kitchen area.

"Shhhhhhh! Damn, you loud. Shit, you know how many other girls would be jumpin' up and down just to spend *any* amount of time with him? He got bank and got plenty of rock. Now, he said if he could party alone with you and if you acted right he was goin' treat us lovely and I ain't tryin' to pass this up. Besides you owe Manny for what happened down Me-Me's." Reds stated.

"Owe him? How the fuck you figure I owe him?" I shouted to her.

"Girl, Manny paid for the shit you and Cheryl broke and then he told Cheryl and Tracy that if they fucked with you in any way their asses was his. Why you think them bitches ain't bank you behind that shit? You knocked the bitch teeth out! Manny handled that shit."

"Okay but why the fuck does he want me? Ain't you supposed to be fuckin' Manny yourself? " I asked.

"Girl, I just said he ain't fuckin' wit' me and we never fucked. He just like to get his dick sucked while he hit the blunt." She laughed.

I had to laugh at that shit too.

Before I could reply, the bedroom door flew open and Manny was standing out in the hallway. He had a homemade pipe in his hand. He stopped in front of me and pushed the pipe in my mouth. Before I knew it, he lit the match and I had instinctively inhaled my beloved smoke. When I let it out, I was done. All I heard was Manny tell Reds to lock the door, not to answer it and not to disturb us. How the fuck I get inside the room so quick was beyond me. Next thing I know, I was in the bedroom with Manny.

"Sit down." He said patting a spot on the bed next to him.

I sat down on the bed.

"Here." He said handing me the pipe. "Fix you another hit."

Manny got up to close all the blinds and turn the light off. There was only light illuminating from a lit candle. He only wore a pair of boxers and a wife beater. Damn, he is fine to be in his early thirties. When he smiled he showed all thirty-two of his pearly white teeth. I could tell he worked out too the way his muscles budged from his chest and thighs. He was a quiet type of dude though, one who dressed in the latest fashions but drove a regular car so not to draw too much attention to himself. I heard he had a modest house out in Baltimore County that was worth a million dollars that he paid for in cash.

I realized I must have looked crazy, caught up in my thoughts so I got up and walked over to the dresser and put my pipe down. I went to reach for a rock when he stopped me.

"I want you on your knees. Now get on 'em!" He commanded.

I just stood there momentarily frozen. This wasn't the same Manny that I had talked to down Me-Me's. This nigga was throwing shade and I wasn't feelin' this shit at all. But my Jones had kicked in. Manny knew what he was doing when he came out into the kitchen and made me hit the pipe right then and there. He knew once the first hit was taken, I was pretty much going to do anything to get the next blast. So...I dropped to my knees.

"Go on and suck this dick like I know you want to do." He said while he blew smoke out his mouth from his blunt.

I looked up at him from down on my knees.

"Suck it, girl. What the fuck you doing?"

Manny's personality had changed. He was becoming aggressive. I picked up Manny's semi hard dick in my hands. I brought his dick closer to my face and got ready to put it in my mouth. I stopped.

"Girl, what you doin'?" he asked.

"I can't do this shit, Manny. I'm leaving."

I turned to walk away when Manny reached out and grabbed me from behind. He grabbed me so hard that I fell backwards onto the bed. He jumped on top of me and straddled me. He had me pinned under him. I was scared and all I wanted to do now was get the fuck out of there. I tried to get up but he pushed me down. He put his hand over my mouth. He looked down at me and his eyes were as big as saucers.

"Kaneesha, I ain't tryin' to hurt you. But when you came back here in this room, you already knew what the fuck was up."

He slowly pulled his hand away from my mouth but he continued to straddle me. I was scared to speak but I found my voice.

"Manny, I got a man and this is wrong."

"You gotta man? Really? From what I've been told that nigga up and rolled out on you."

"Oh so you supposed to be better? You got me up in here tryin' to treat me like a hoe!" I yelled. Manny let out a smirk of a laugh.

"Yeah, I hear you, Kaneesha." He slowly got off me. I sat up on the bed. He walked over to the dresser.

"Go head, take a hit." He said.

I got up and walked towards him. He handed me the pipe and a small rock.

"Sit down." he said.

I sat back down on the bed and lit the rock and watch it melt into the ashes. I was beamed up. Manny stood near the bed and just looked on as I got higher and higher. The effects of the rock had me feeling good. All my troubles and problems were no longer my focus. For that moment I felt nothing but bliss. I looked at Manny and a feeling of sexual prowess overcame me. I stood up and guided him to the bed then pushed him down on it. I climbed on top of him and reached down into his boxers and grabbed his dick. I put it in my mouth and slowly began to suck him. He was not as big as Jarvis or Stone but he was had a nice size to him.

"It's much better when you don't take it," I said before sucking him with all I could.

I could hear him moaning. I looked up and saw he had his eyes closed and his head thrown back. He put his hands on both sides of my head so he could fuck my mouth harder. Manny was pumping in and out of my mouth like he was possessed. Spit had begun to spill over the sides of my mouth as I tried to keep him steady and at a distance to keep him from gagging. He grabbed my head with a force and pushed his dick down as far in my throat as he could.

"That's it...Kaneesha, baby...that's it girl...suck this dick. Ummm...Yeah, that's it...shit! Ahhhh, that's it!" He never let go of my head and never let up the pressure.

I felt Manny's ass tighten. He let out a loud moan as he held my head and emptied out his cum into my mouth.

"Kaneesha, baby, damn!" Was all Manny could say.

He pulled me down onto the bed next to him and just looked at me. He looked like he wanted to say something but must have decided not to. He just got up off the bed and went to the dresser.

I was ready to go. All of a sudden I felt bad like I did something wrong. All I wanted was my package so I could go the fuck back to my dungeon and get high on my own. I decided to ask Manny for my shit so I could go leave.

"What you in a hurry for?" Manny asked.

"No, Manny I really feel like being on my own now." I said.

"Alright, that's cool. I can dig that."

Manny's leather jacket was at the head of the bed. He grabbed it and reached into his inside pocket. He pulled out a plastic baggie. My mouth fell open. I had never seen that much coke in one plastic baggie in my life. Even Baggs shit would look like a sandwich bag compared to the one that was starring me in the face right now. Manny unrolled the very large bag and opened it.

"Reach into my pants pocket and get the money out."

He said as he nodded his head towards his pants lying on the floor by my feet. I bent down and picked them up. I reached into the right pocket and pulled out a roll of money. I held it up in front of him so he could see. Manny told me to take the clip off the stack. I did and let the money unfold.

"Take a fifty dollar bill out of there."

I looked through the stack of hundreds and twenties and found a fifty.

He put the coke in the fifty and said, "That's yours."

I looked on the fifty and saw that I had well over a gram of beautiful white granules. I carefully folded up the sides and then the middle to make a pouch and put it in my bra. He rolled up that large ass bag of coke and put it back in his jacket pocket. He put clothes back on. I handed him the roll of money and he put it in his pocket.

He was smiling.

"What are you smiling at?" I asked him.

"You."

"Why me?"

"'Cause you good peoples, Kaneesha. You okay with me."

"What does that mean, Manny?"

"Just know this, I trust you, Kaneesha, and you proved it today. Okay. It's not like I was putting you to a test but I did see that you wanted me to know that you could be trusted and I like that

"Thanks," I said not knowing if it was warranted.

"Well what's the shit between you and Dubbs?"

"Why are you askin' me 'bout Dubbs? I don't deal wit' Dubbs in any way. As a matter of fact, I can't stand that bastard." I confessed.

"Yeah, he kinda feels the same way 'bout you and Reds. What did y'all do to him?"

"We didn't do shit to that fake ass smurf! That motherfucker got mad when Stone put Jarvis on and didn't put him on. And then he and Reds had some words."

"So why is he mad at you then?" Manny inquired.

"Because I won't fuck his short ass! And I really don't want to get into to all this with you Manny. So this conversation about Dubbs and Stone is dead." I spat.

"Aight, aight, I feel you. Just make sure you watch him. That nigga got larceny in his heart. Just keep your eyes opened."

I nodded my head.

I sat down at the table with Reds and cooked my coke. When it was ready, I prepared my pipe and took a pull. All of a sudden my head began to spin and I was feeling lightheaded. This was some new shit. I had never felt like this before. My heart began to beat harder and faster and I clutched at my chest and stood up. Eventually I dropped the pipe on the table. That's when Reds knew I was serious because she jumped up.

"What the fuck! Oh shit! Girl, please tell me you ain't fixin' to have no heart attack up in here. Shit, Kaneesha! Shit!"

I couldn't say shit. My breathing was irregular and I felt heat rising within my body. Reds came around to my side and held onto me. She was shouting in my ear but her words were garbled and she sounded far away. I began to feel faint and grabbed onto the table for support. I was sweating and my left arm was numb.

"Kaneesha, girl, keep walkin'! Come on keep walkin'!" she was screaming at me.

I was being lead around the living room by Reds. She was

rubbing my back and pushing me at the same time. But I needed to sit down and close my eyes. I stopped and stood briefly before I just fell down onto the couch. My head began to roll from side to side as I tried to catch my breath. I closed my eyes and was just about to drift to some place when I felt a sharp pain across my face. Reds had slapped me and then slapped me again. I opened my eyes and tried to yell at her but my words were barely audible.

I heard distant voices in the background and felt someone pulling me up from the couch. They took me to the bathroom and put me in the tub of cold water and I instantly opened my eyes. I felt water being poured over my head and again another slap. If this bitch slaps me one more time, I'ma whoop her red ass.

I felt water running down the side of my neck and back and I felt someone bathing me under my arms and on my chest. The water was cold as shit. Red's voice was becoming clearer.

"Is she comin' to? Please say she's comin' to!" Reds screamed.

"Calm down, Reds, I think you got to her in time. She's comin' around. Kaneesha, can you hear me, Kaneesha baby, come on girl, talk to me?!" The familiar voice said.

I opened my eyes and focused in. It was Manny.

"Manny" I whispered. "What happened? Why you got me in this water. I'm cold. Get me out of here!" I yelled at him.

"Girl, slow your ass down. Shit, I thought your crazy ass was gonna die up in this bitch! You scared the shit out of me!" Reds interjected as she and Manny lifted me out the tub of brutally cold water.

I stood there shivering. Manny pulled the towel off the towel rack and wrapped me in it. He led me by the arm out of the bathroom and back to Reds' room. I didn't know what to say. Manny helped me sit down on the bed. He knelt down in front of me and took my hands in his.

"Kaneesha, you almost overdosed. You scared us to death."

"I'm fine," I told him.

Reds came into the bathroom and handed me the rest of my coke wrapped up in the fifty.

"Girl, don't do nothin' else until tomorrow." She said handing it to me. "Let your body rest today."

"Listen to the pregnant crack queen. How you gonna tell me to let my body rest and you carryin' a living being in there? You should be the one resting your body. Shit, that little bastard gonna come out of there with his own damn pipe. Talkin' 'bout beam me up Scotty." I laughed. Reds looked like she was mad but then she burst out laughing.

"I'ma let you have that one because we almost lost you. But go home, Kaneesha! I'll see you tomorrow.

I stood up and Manny looked me over.

"Want me to take you home?"

"Yes...I mean...no!" I screamed not wanting him to see where I lived. "I'll be fine."

"Just let me know," He said handing me his phone number which he must've already had prepared. "Call me to say you're okay."

We looked at each other and gave each other a hard long hug. I appreciated the care but I needed to get away. The only thing on my mind was cooking my next batch and getting my next hit!

Chapter Twenty-Eight

Hysear was off to school. It was getting harder day-by-day to stay in the apartment. Hysear was not happy any more and his grades were reflecting it. I checked with Social Services about the check and was told there was some delay because they had to verify my mailing address. And until I had an address that could be verified, I was not getting a check. Reds came down to see me and we were blasting away as usual.

"Kaneesha, why don't you call Stone?" I instantly chocked on the smoke in my mouth.

"Call Stone? Girl, that man ain't trynna hear from me. And what the fuck am I goin' tell him? *Hi Stone this Kaneesha. I'm on crack and I let me and my son get evicted. I'm living an in abandoned apartment and now I'm sucking dicks for my next hit."* I said in a high-pitched voice.

"Yeah, I guess you're right, Kaneesha. We should be grateful enough for him pulling the bounty off our heads."

"Me too, but you know what, there was a time when I doubted Jarvis. That's probably one of the reasons he abandoned me. I ain't support him enough."

I looked at Reds.

"What?" she said raising her hands. "I have no comment. Only you know why your man walked out on you. What I would want to know is why someone would set up Jarvis."

"Girl, I don't know. Why do nagger's do ignorant shit period?"

I met Hysear at the bus stop. He slowly walked down the steps of the bus. He looked beat down.

"What wrong, son?" I asked.

Hysear didn't say anything.

"Hysear, did you hear me? What is wrong?"

His voice was barely audible. "Mommy, are you smoking crack?"

With a look of shock and embarrassment, I stared down at my son bewildered and for a brief moment, I couldn't say anything.

"Hysear!" He slowly looked up at me with big tears running down his face"Where did you hear this? Who the hell told you that lie?"

"Some of the kids around here said that. They said they saw Jarvis going to the crack house all the time and that you was a crack whore. Some of my friends say that you and Jarvis are crack addicts." I snatched Hysear by the arms and pulled him closer to me.

"You listen to me, young man...I'm nobody's crack whore!" He looked down at the floor. I picked his face up in my hands. "Hysear, which kids told you this bullshit?" I asked as if blaming them would make my problem go away.

"Kenny, Sam and Yvette. Their mothers told them that and they be teasing me on the bus all the time." Hysear told me.

"Hysear, why didn't you tell me this?"

"Cause I know it's not true and I didn't want you or Jarvis to get mad. I know Jarvis would have went down there and beat them up."

I continued to talk to my son and convince him that his mom and stepfather were not crack addicts. We got to the dungeon and Hysear began to cry again. He stood outside the door.

"Hysear what's wrong now, baby?"

"I don't like living here, mommy. It's too cold, and it's dark. I can't play my games and I can't take a bath any more. Call Pap Pap and tell him to come get me. Please, mommy call Pap Pap!" he pleaded.

Hysear was crying uncontrollably now. I guess it was time for him to have his crying fit. I took for granted that I could pull the veil over his eyes about the situation. My heart was breaking and I knew that it was the right thing to do by calling my Dad. I calmed Hysear down then we went up to Peppers and made the phone call.

"Hi, Daddy."

My father's tone was low and monotone. "I have been waiting for you to call me. Where is my grandson?"

"He's fine, daddy. He's with me."

"And where exactly is with you? I came to the apartment and know you're not staying there anymore. I can't even call you."

"With friends for now." I lied.

There was a pause.

"Pack up your shit! You're moving in with me! Tell me where you're staying so I can come get you." My father said angrily.

"Daddy, listen, I don't want to move in with you. I just need you to take Hysear for a while."

"What the hell you mean you're not movin' in with me? Yes you are! Now get your shit together and tell me where you are!" He insisted.

"Dad, listen to me. I don't want to move in with you. I just need you to come and get Hysear. Can you do that for me daddy?" I pleaded.

"Kaneesha Lynn Watkins, I'm not about to let you stay in those streets. Now you get your shit and I'm comin' to get ya'll!" He yelled through the phone.

"No! I'm sick, daddy. Do you understand what I'm sayin'? I'm sick and don't want to be around you like this."

My father paused over the phone again. "Tell me where to pick him up." He said and I told him where we were.

"Have my grandson ready. I will be there within the hour.

My father came to pick him up.

"I'm disappointed in you."

Out of everything that has happened to me, nothing made me feel worse than those words leaving my father's mouth.

"I'm sorry."

He left in a huff without saying another word.

Hysear seemed relieved and didn't bother looking back at me as he walked out of Pepper's door.

It would be the last time I saw him before I approached the worse time of my life.

Chapter Twenty-Nine

A month had gone by and I was officially out there now. What I once vehemently denied to my son had come to fruition. I was a crack addict and a crack whore. With Hysear gone, and Jarvis in the wind, Reds and I were inseparable.

Reds was showing me the ropes on how to get the high I wanted...*every time*. She knew just about all the big time drug dealers who had the long money. She had hooked me up with several of the major dealers around town. I was now sucking dicks and laying on my back in exchange for my precious drug. Very seldom did she ever spend her time on the bag boys or drug runners. She still looked good so could get away with it.

Whenever the big dogs came into "The Heights" the first thing they did was call her up and she would come get me. I packed a bag with stuff that I would need to freshen up to be presentable to whoever was down her house. When I got to Reds', I took a quick shower and prepared for whoever was coming over. It was Wednesday and Reds came over to get me to meet one of our regular dealers, but she was complaining about her stomach. We got to her house and Reds double over in pain. The last time she did this shit she was having a baby.

"Girl, what the fuck is wrong wit' you?" I asked concerned.

"I don't know, Kaneesha. My stomach's hurting like shit." She cried.

"Here, sit down, Reds." I said as I lead her over to the couch.

I propped her feet up and sat down beside her. I began to rub her belly.

"Reds, you sure you ain't about to have this baby early again? Maybe all this crack shit ain't good." I said calmly.

"Naw, Neesh, I think I might have gas. Stop worryin'. Just get my pipe. I wanna blast the rest of my rock."

I never thought twice about getting Reds her pipe 'cause she smoked for all her pregnancies. So she knew what was going on with her body more than me. She got busy doing her thang while I was in the kitchen cooking mine.

"UGGGGG! Owwwww! Kaneesha! Kaneesha!" Reds screamed out.

I dropped my spoon and ran out to the living room to find Reds on the floor balled up screaming in pain.

"Reds! Girl, what's wrong?! What's wrong, Reds?" She grabbed my hands.

"Kaneesha, I think the baby's coming." Reds continued to yell.

"What?! Reds, you can't be havin' no baby right now! Girl, it ain't time." I yelled back.

"Goddamn it, Kaneesha, this baby ain't waitin'. I gotta push. Help me get out of these pants." Reds instructed.

"Right now!? You gettin' ready to have this baby right here!? Oh shit!! Reds, I gotta call the ambulance. I ain't deliverin' no baby!" I yelled.

Pain must have shot through Reds' body because she hollered in agony. She was not at nine months or even eight months pregnant so this was not good.

"Kaneesha, I need to get these pants off and push this mutherfucka outta me right now! I can't wait! Help me, please!" She begged.

I grabbed Reds pants by the legs and pulled them down under her little belly and casted them aside. Reds was bleeding. I was scared as shit now.

"Reds, I gotta call the ambulance. You bleedin' girl. I gotta call somebody

"Hurry up then! I'm hurtin', Kaneesha!" Reds cried.

I ran to the kitchen and damned near ripped the phone out of the wall. I hurriedly dialed the famous 911 numbers and told the operator what was going on. She told me to go back over to Reds and keep her calm. She also told me not to hang up. Reds was moaning and writhed in pain on the couch. I tried to sooth her by talking to her but I know she wasn't paying me any attention. Suddenly she let out a blood-curdling scream. I dropped the phone and reached out to hold her. She was panting and sweating. Her face was contorted in what was probably pain. She reached up towards me.

"Kaneesha, I gotta push. Help me please!" She whispered.

"No, 911 said not to push until the ambulance get here! Reds, you gonna have to hold on for a few more minutes! Please girl. Just hold on!" I was crying now with Reds.

"I can't!" She said and with that Reds began grunting and pushing.

I snatched up the phone and told the operator what was going on. She kept telling me to tell Reds not to push.

"Fuck that! She pushin'. I can't stop her!" I yelled into the phone.

"What the fuck do I do now!?"

I listened to the instructions the operator was giving me. I positioned myself down between Reds legs and opened them. When I did, I almost passed out from all the blood and tissue matter that was discharging from Reds' vagina. She was grabbing the sides of the couch as she continued to bare down and push. I dropped the phone again and ran to grab several towels and put them in front of Reds' opening.

"Kaneeeeesha!" Reds sobbed. "This shit hurts! Oh my God, Kaneesha!" She continued to yell.

She grabbed my hand and squeezed it as she bore down again with another push. When my foot hit the phone, I remembered that I had dropped it. I put it back to my ear.

"Hello, hello!" I said hoping the operator was there.

"Yes, I'm still here!" The operator said.

"What's going on, is she still pushing?" She asked me.

"Yes and there's so much blood!"

The operator said the ambulance was less than ten minutes away. I heard another blood curdling scream from Reds. I threw the phone down on the couch and repositioned myself between her legs. The towels were soaked in blood and then I saw the head of the baby sticking out of Reds' vagina.

"The baby's head is out! Push, Reds, Push!" I shouted.

I looked up and Reds eyes were closed. I jumped up and stood over her - Reds was out cold. I gently shook her. She didn't move. I shook her again and called her name several times. Still Red did not move. I ran back to look between her legs. The baby was still stuck in the same position. Only the head was sticking out of her vagina. I didn't know whether I should just start pulling or not. Where the fuck is the ambulance?! I found the phone.

"Hello, Hello!" I yelled and again.

"I'm still here."

"She's out cold."

"Make sure she's still breathing. Keep her legs apart. She's probably in shock."

"In shock? What the hell does that mean? Shit, she looks like she's dead and she got a baby hanging halfway out her ass! Where the hell is the goddamned ambulance? I don't know what else to do!"

I felt like I was going to pass the fuck out at any minute now my damn self. I don't know what the hell the operator was saying any more. She began to sound like the teacher on the Charlie Brown cartoon...Whaaaa.Whaaaa..Whaaaa.

With no more time to spare, the paramedics showed up and stabilized Reds and then took her outta of there quick, fast and in a hurry.

What an ordeal! They were unable to save the baby. Reds had to stay in the hospital for three days but wasn't really coherent or able to speak until the third day. And trust me, I was here everyday.

"You doing okay, girl? Shit you scared the fuck outta my ass. I thought you was dead up in that bitch!" I said as I hugged Reds.

She laughed. "Girl, I ain't dying no time soon."

"I'm sorry that you lost your little girl, Reds." I told her sincerely.

"Kaneesha, I ain't trippin' off this shit. It wasn't meant to be." Reds said.

"Yeah, but you lost your baby Reds. Ain't you feeling some kinda way 'bout that?" I asked.

"Kaneesha, I'm out here smokin' crack. Don't that tell you somethin'? Do you honestly think I thought twice about the baby?" She said. "You know that."

"Did you even talk to the father?" I asked and Reds belted out a laugh.

"I ain't talkin' 'bout that."

"Why not?"

"'Cause I'm not, Neesha! I don't care about it okay? And who I was and am fuckin' is my mutherfuckin' shit to deal wit' not yours! It don't matter no way. But the man I wanted to be his father, is dead." Reds updated.

"Dead, what the fuck happened?" I inquired.

"He went to Baltimore to get a package and was set up by one of his own people. They rolled up on him while he was sittin' in the car and blew his brains out."

"Damn, Reds, that's fucked up." I said.

"Dontay was my boy. He was the one that I would have wanted as the father but he wasn't. I know who the daddy is and trust me, he ain't no good."

"I'm sorry to hear about him going out like that." I told her.

"Me too." She said.

I hugged my girl again. "Okay, if you're cool wit' it then it's all good."

"You seen Manny?" Reds asked me.

"Girl, you know that man ain't come through the Heights without hittin' me up. Shit we was at the hotel for the past two days." I giggled. "It was much better than bein' in that lonely apartment."

"Well, they lettin' me out this bitch today so we need to get at our boy so we can celebrate my release." Reds said. "And you know what I need."

"Yep, that ain't nothin' but a word." I grinned.

"Kaneesha, go find the doctor. I need to know when the fuck they gonna sign my papers to let me the fuck outta here." She said.

I didn't need any further coaxing. I hit the corner in search of the nurses' station so we can go celebrate with Manny properly.

Later that evening Reds and me were comfortably inside her apartment getting ready to blast. I could not get in touch with Manny so we had to settle for copin' a rock on our own.

We smoked a twenty-cent piece. The product was not good at all because it was stepped on and the result was the rock came back small and with no power in it. We were disappointed at spending our last twenty dollars only to be teased by that sorry ass coke.

"I can't believe that we got stiffed for that package. I ought to take my knife and go cut a mutherfucka up for this shit." Reds said.

"Yeah, I'm feelin' the same way Reds. That was money wasted. Who the fuck you cop that from?" I asked.

"Girl, Terrence's ass. He was the only mutherfucka out in the circle. I couldn't find Baggs."

We heard a knock at Red's door and she looked out her peephole and back to me.

"Girl, its Benny." She whispered.

I knew who Benny was. I had met him once and seen him a couple times while I was out with Reds.

Benny was from Nigeria. He was well known around the Baltimore area and he frequented Annapolis a lot because he had family in the area. He was strong in his slinging game. Although he didn't really need to sling because his family owned an aviation company back in Africa. He was supposed to be coming to the states to acquisition new business partners for his family's business but he liked the easy money that he could get from the dope game. He eventually sent for his son to come to America too.

"Open the door." I whispered back.

Benny walked in and behind him was a young boy. He couldn't have been older than sixteen.

"Reds, baby girl. How you doing?" Benny asked.

"I'm fine, Benny." Reds replied. He looked over at me and smiled.

"Hey there, Kaneesha, I was hoping you would be here!" Benny spoke.

"Hi, Benny." I said wondering what he meant by hoping I was there.

"Who's this?" Reds asked.

"This is my son, Jaquan." Jaquan nodded his head at us.

Benny told his son to sit on the couch because he had some business to attend to with us. Benny walked straight over to me and pulled me aside.

"It's my son's birthday today. I want him to get special treatment." Benny stated with an underlined look in his eyes.

"What exactly do you mean by special treatment?" I said.

"He's a virgin." Benny said smiling widely.

"Oooh. How old is he?" I asked.

"He's sixteen." Benny said.

"I could go to jail messing with that boy." I said cutting my eyes over at Jaquan.

"You ain't going nowhere. Besides, he said he wanted you."

"Wants me? He doesn't even know me," I said.

"Ah, he has seen you many times before and I know you could use some of these." Benny went into his jacket pocket and pulled out a bag of rocks. I didn't need any more motivation after that.

"Give me a minute or two then send him back." I said.

I went to the back room and waited for Jaquan. Minutes later, he walked in. He was medium height, but taller than me and thin. He looked like his father with the same wide nose and square jaw line. He was sporting locks and they were freshly done. He wore a pair of sagging designer jeans and shirt. He had on a pair of Nike boots. The cologne he wore had a fresh but yet woodsy smell. Something similar to Polo but not quite. I knew that strong-ass Polo cologne a mile away. Overall, he was a nice-looking young man. I motioned for him to come further into the room. He obliged and I closed the door. He didn't seem to know what to do.

"You scared?" I asked him.

"Naw." He said, but his eyes told a different story.

"Good." I said. "Come here." He came closer to me.

I took his arms and placed them around my waist.

"Kiss me." I said.

He awkwardly brought his mouth down to mine and accidentally bumped my lips with his teeth.

"Sorry." he said.

"It's okay. You just have to be loose and go with the flow. Okay?" I assured him.

"Okay." He was clearly nervous as shit.

"Feel me." I said. He didn't know what that meant. I took one of his hands and placed it on my breast.

"Rub it slowly."

Slowly he began to rub my left breast.

"That's it. Just like that." He seemed to like that as he started to knead it.

He placed his free hand on my right breast and did the same as he was with the left. I stretched my neck and gently kissed him on the lips. He kissed me back hesitantly. I pulled him closer to me. This time I kissed him in pecks. He was still rubbing my breasts and began to grip them firmly. I actually had a virgin boy. I became excited at the prospect of being the one to take his virginity. I stopped kissing him and took my shirt off. I took his hand and showed him how to unsnap my bra using his one hand. When it fell off to reveal my bare breasts, I heard him suck in air.

He immediately started rubbing them again. This time, he

bent down and pressed his lips against mine on his own. I opened my mouth and inserted my tongue into his. He pulled back at first but I put my hand around his neck and pulled his mouth back to mine. He let me tongue him for a moment, then he joined me. After several attempts at French kissing, he got it. He pulled me closer to him this time. I felt his penis grow against my leg. For a sixteen year old, he felt large. I reached my hand down to his pants and squeezed his dick and he accidentally bit my tongue. I pulled back and giggled.

"Sorry." He said embarrassed.

"It's okay. Relax. Ain't nothin' to be nervous about." I assured him.

I unbuckled his pants and let them fall to the floor. As soon as the pants fell, his long thick dick sprang forward through the hole in his boxers. I dropped to my knees and positioned myself to break him in. I took hold of his thickness and brought my mouth to the tip of his head and licked it. I felt him shiver.

For some reason, I enjoyed it more than I should have. Maybe I was finding some pleasure in taking someone else's innocence, as Jarvis had taken mine when he turned me onto crack.

I slowly enveloped his thick head in my mouth. I sucked his dick like it was candy and I used my hands to help pump him in and out of my mouth. I made sure I kept it nice and wet with my saliva. Jaquan was squealing like a baby pig. He didn't know what to do or how to receive a blowjob. He was actually backing up from me. I grabbed him around the ass and held him in place while I continued to give him head. I knew he was about to explode because of the sounds he was making. I pumped my hands a little faster and pumped his dick in and out of my mouth with the same rhythm. He started to moan loud and long. I felt Jaquan grab my head and go rigid. His cum filled my mouth. I got up and went to the bathroom room to clean up. When I got back, Jaquan was dressed.

"I've never felt anything like that before," he said in a

thick African accent. "I enjoyed it a lot."

He opened the door and walked out. Moments later, his father came into the room. He handed me a package.

"My son says you were good. He can't stop smiling!"

"Well, he was a great student." I replied.

"Maybe next time we'll bring some rubbers and you can take his full virginity."

"No, that's for someone special. That's an act that should be done with his first girlfriend. Not me." I told him.

"I like that. That says a lot about you, Ms. Neesha." Benny said.

He reached into his pants pocket and pulled out a couple of bills and laid the money on the on the dresser. He winked at me and then left the bedroom. I went over and pocketed the two hundred dollars that I counted. When I walked out and to the kitchen, I found Reds by herself.

"Benny gone?" I asked.

"Yeah, he seemed happy with what you did with his son. You must have fucked him good." Reds laughed.

"Girl, I ain't fuck that little boy. I just gave that nigga his first head. Shit, the way he was squealing in there, I thought the nigga was trying to give birth busting that nut." We fell out laughing.

"Benny break you off, Reds?" I asked.

"Yeah, he gave me a package."

"What the hell we waitin' on?"

"Shit, that ain't nothin' but a word." Reds said.

We both reached for our purple bags again.

Chapter Thirty

My life over the next few weeks was a routine of getting up just to get high. Reds and me was really running wild now—especially since she was no longer pregnant. I had changed so much over the past couple months. I was harder and had taken on a "fuck it" type of attitude. As long as I got my rock and by any means necessary, I was happy.

I put the key in the abandoned apartment door to let myself in. I had just scored a couple rocks and some dough. When I turned the door handle and walked in, I reached down in the corner of the door and found the flashlight. I turned it on and walked to the area of the apartment that I had made my living quarters.

I was immediately snatched and thrown against the wall. Before I could react, I was struck in the face. Dazed I tried to put my hands up to deflect the next blow that I saw being delivered to my face. I managed to block it. My attacker and I arm-wrestled before I could kick him. He fell backwards and I tried to run but he lunged and clipped me at the ankles, bringing me crashing to the floor on my stomach.

Air violently left my body and I couldn't breathe. My attacker pounced on my back and began choking me from behind. I needed to get some leverage. I elbowed him several times in his side and then pushed up with all my might, like I did with Luchi, and my attacker fell off my back. I tried crawling away but couldn't get away fast enough. He tried grabbing at my legs again as I windmill kicked him. Suddenly the attacker pulled out a gun and I could see its silver reflection. It was pointed at me.

"Make another move and I'll kill you." The voice said.

I lay still on the floor and he kneeled down beside me, took duct tape that he already cut and hung from the dresser, and put it over my mouth. He put the gun to my head and I got a chance to see the familiar scratches on the weapon. It was mine. Jarvis and Reds had sold my gun and somehow it ended up in his hands.

"That's it don't fuckin' move." He said again.

I remembered that my bat was on the floor beside the bed. But I was in the dark living room too far away to get to it. The only light that was in the apartment was the night-light plugged into the hallway near the bathroom.

My attacker tried grabbing my arms but I put up a fight and he struck me with the butt of his gun causing me to lose consciousness for a moment. He wrapped my wrists in duct tape, too. I was now completely at his mercy. He ripped my shirt open and snatched off my bra and my breasts were revealed. It was cold so my nipples immediately became erect.

"Damn, look at them beautiful things." He said.

He gruffly smelled my neck and then moved down to my breasts and bit them so hard I thought he drew blood. He laid the gun on the floor beside him again and I felt my sweat pants being tugged down. When he accomplished getting them off, he opened his coat up and unbuckled his pants. His dick sprung out. He stood up over me stroking himself as he looked down on me. Then I felt a warm liquid on my chest and realized he was pissing on me. When he was done he positioned himself over me on his knees and tried nudging my legs apart.

"Bitch, open up so I can get that pussy! Open up your legs before I shoot them motherfuckers open." He hissed grabbing his gun and pointing it at me again. He nudged them open with his knee and then shoved his finger in my pussy.

"Oh yeah. This oughta be good." He said.

He stuck the head of his dick in the entrance to my pussy and pushed and pushed until he was completely inside of me. He moved in and out of me slowly, moaning and grunting as he did. He began to speed up his pumping and grabbed my breasts with such force that I thought he was going to rip them off my chest.

"Yeah, Kaneesha. I told you I was going to get this pussy. Didn't I?" he grunted in my ear as he banged in and out of my pussy harder. My eyes wanted to pop out of my head and I finally recognized the voice. The ski mask that Dubbs wore protected his true identity but I knew it was him.

"Turn the fuck over! I want that phat ass!" He whispered as he roughly turned me on my stomach.

With my hands being duct taped I could not fight Dubbs off me. I felt him part my ass cheeks then reposition himself behind me. He slowly pushed himself in my ass and then with one strong stroke he forced himself in. I screamed through the duct tape and he wrapped his hand around my neck.

He whispered in my ear. "I'm fuckin' you like the whore you are. I've seen you goin' down to the crack houses giving other mutherfucka's your pussy. Why you ain't come to me? I got money. I coulda took care of you." He said humping in and out my ass.

"You thought you was goin' give everyone else some of this and not me?" he strengthened his chokehold.

"You think Stone is the only mutherfucka good enough to get this, huh? You could have been my sidepiece but you thought I wasn't good enough and wasn't ballin' like Stone. Well where is your Stone now, bitch?" He screamed in my ear as he continued to violently ram himself in my ass.

The pain was excruciating. Dubbs was sodomizing me and choking me at the same time.

"Yeah, Kaneesha, this some good ass. You like this dick? Well let me give it to you real good then." He said and rammed himself in me repeatedly. "Ahh...yeah.....ahh...yeah...that's it....yeah, bitch! I'm gettin' ready to bust this nut...ahhhhh-hh......shiiiittt!" Dubbs hollered as he choked me to the point of passing out.

For what seemed like hours, Dubbs fucked me in every hole on my body. When he was done, he beat me and then duct taped my legs together.

"I told you your days were numbered, bitch!" He said as he

got himself together and left out the door.

I felt the cold winter wind as it rolled through the apartment after Dubbs left. I lay there shivering, wet, bleeding, butt naked and bound. I drifted in and out of consciousness.

Reds hid against the wall as she watched the figure come out of Kaneesha's apartment. She saw the figure take off his skullcap, then flee down the back steps and disappear into the night before she could see his face. She tiptoed to the door and waited. She listened for any movement. Building up the courage, she pulled her knife out of her bra and turned the door handle. Reds was familiar with the layout of the apartment so she knew a flashlight was supposed to be at the door. When she reached down and couldn't find it, she reached in her purse and took out her lighter. She flicked it and slowly tiptoed further into the room. When Reds came around the corner she screamed at what she saw.

Chapter Thirty-One

I awoke in a warm bed in a strange place. I sat up and looked around. And then I heard his voice coming from the corner.

"You up?" Stone asked.

He came over and sat on the bed and examined my face.

"And you're healing up." I opened my mouth to speak and couldn't find my voice.

He reached for the bottle of water that was on the nightstand, opened it and placed the opening to my mouth. The coolness felt good going down my throat.

"You okay?"

"Yeah...yes. I...I think so."

"You know before you opened your eyes, I didn't even know tink it was you. You've lost so much weight and you don't look the same. That shit is really taken you for a ride."

"Stone, please. I'm not tryin' to hear this right now."

"Well you're goin' to hear it. If I waste my time picking you up, you will hear all of it." He paused. "You're a disgrace. It doesn't warrant the pain he put you in, but you still let yourself go and I'm sad for you."

I couldn't believe he was in front of me because I thought I'd never see him again but I wasn't feeling the third degree. While I was contemplating his presence, a smile spread across my face when Reds came through the door. She smiled widely and hugged me gently.

"Neesha, oh my God, girl, I'm glad to see you up! You hungry? I'ma fix you some soup."

"Slow down, Reds. She's just been through some wicked shit. Give her a minute to adjust." Stone said in a weak voice.

"How did I get here?" I asked.

"I came down to get you and I saw someone leave your

apartment. He had on a skullcap so I couldn't make out who it was and then I came in and found you. I called Stone and told him what happened." Stone sat closer to me.

"Kaneesha, do you know..." I cut him off.

"Dubbs!" I said. Both Reds and Stone stopped in their tracks. Time stood still.

"How do you know it was Dubbs? I couldn't tell who it was with the ski mask on." Reds asked me.

I looked over to Stone and reached up for him to take my hand. He grabbed it and looked me directly in my eyes.

"Dubbs did this to me. There is no mistaking it. He had the gun I use to carry," I assured Stone. "The one you gave me. My defender. I know you wanted it back but I couldn't give it to you."

I wasn't about to tell Stone that Reds sold my weapon. If I had he'd be in her shit. I just wanted him to know he had it and it wasn't me.

Stone stood up and went to the door.

"Kaneesha, Dubbs will be taken care of! Mark my words. I want him first!"

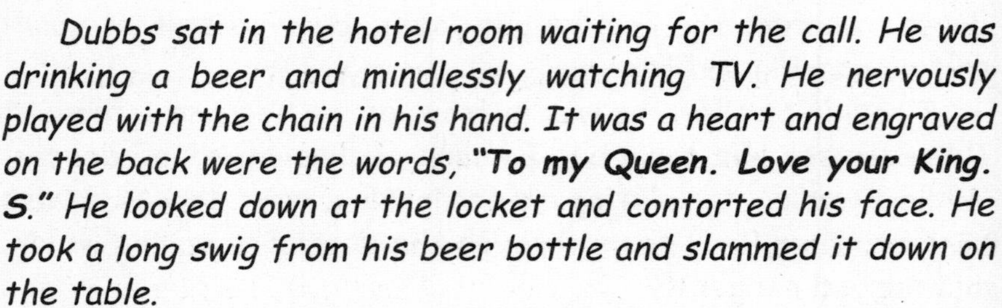

*Dubbs sat in the hotel room waiting for the call. He was drinking a beer and mindlessly watching TV. He nervously played with the chain in his hand. It was a heart and engraved on the back were the words, **"To my Queen. Love your King. S."** He looked down at the locket and contorted his face. He took a long swig from his beer bottle and slammed it down on the table.*

"Bet that bitch is feeling like a queen now especially after I gave her the royal treatment. That stuck up bitch got served. Yep, I stuck her right up her ass!" Dubbs said laughing out loud at his own joke.

He played back the night he raped Kaneesha and pulled the chain off from around her neck. As far as he was concerned, she got what she deserved. He looked down at his swollen dick.

Damn, I want some more of that pussy. How can I fuck her again? He thought.

Her and Reds were always together and after the rape, he doubted she would be in her apartment alone again. He thought he saw Reds the night he raped Kaneesha but he left in a hurry for fear of being seen. He had to lay low for a minute. Word was Kaneesha hadn't gone to the police but someone placed a bounty on his head and if he had to guess who it was, he would've guessed the Jamaican called it.

Dubbs took another long swig from the beer. He wanted Reds so bad he was almost tempted to leave the sanctuary of his hiding spot to roll up on her and beat her down. Dubbs wanted her to pay for stepping to him in the Nordstrom and making him look foolish in front of everyone. He needed to think of a way to kill two birdies with one stone. An evil smile played across his face.

He snapped open his phone and scrolled down his address book until he found the name he was looking for. He hit the button and call was placed. When the man answered the phone Dubbs told him that he had a proposition for him. Dubbs went on to lay out his proposition. The man accepted. Finally, he was going to get retribution for how Reds and Kaneesha played him.

I stayed with Stone for two days and then went back to my cold apartment. I was terrified at first, but learned that Dubbs had not been seen around lately. I just hoped he didn't show back up for me. Stone had no idea that I had been evicted and I was not about to tell him that. I was ashamed of what had happened to my family and me. He assumed that Dubbs had taken me into the abandoned apartment to rape me and I left him with his assumptions.

He told me he would be in touch but I doubted it. He wanted to put some things in motion, whatever that meant. He said he didn't want any fuck ups. For some reason, he seemed to have a vested interest in finding Dubbs. It didn't seem like it had nothing to do with me. He could have easily sent the Replacement Killa's, but I told Stone killing Dubbs was too easy. I wanted to make Dubbs hurt like he hurt me. Stone agreed and said he would put some "Feelers" on Dubbs because he was sure he skipped town.

When I finally got the chance, I questioned him about the bounty that was revoked on us. He wouldn't say anymore other than Jarvis was. I told Stone that Jarvis was in Baltimore visiting family. He said he wanted to see Jarvis the minute he got back in town. I didn't offer any more information on Jarvis and me or our situation. It didn't matter now anyway. My feelings for Stone were hardened by what he did to Jarvis, Reds and me.

I thought about Manny. Manny was different from the other dealers that I had been with. He wasn't soft in any form of the word but Manny had a heart and I liked that about him. My thoughts of him turned to thoughts of what had happened over the last six months of my life. I sat on the edge of the mattress, pulled my knees up under my chin and shivered. I pulled the electric blanket that Reds had given me around my body.

I sat taking what had now become my life in, and I didn't' like it. My shit went from having a son and a man, to losing everything and everyone. And in order to get crack or money for my crack, I was trading the most precious commodity that I had - my body. What kind of sick shit was this?

I drifted off to sleep but was awakened by a nightmare. I sat straight up in the bed breathing heavily. I felt for the bat to ensure that it was still beside me under the covers. A series of soft knocks at the door made me stand up. I knew it was Reds so I unlocked the door and she waltzed in.

"Damn, bitch, it's cold in here. How the fuck you stand this shit?" She asked.

"I've gotten used to it I guess."

"Well shit, Manny's waitin' on you so come on!"

"Before we leave, what happened with that gun? My defender? I didn't know you and Jarvis sold it to Dubbs."

"What? Is that what you think?"

"Well he had it."

"Kaneesha, I put Jarvis onto where to go to get some money for it. I gave him a few names in exchange for a portion of the crack. He was the one who made the sell. But I never...not once mentioned Dubbs' name."

I believed her but after being raped, it was hard to trust.

We got to Reds' house and Manny was waiting for me in the bedroom and he already had rocks up on the dresser. She sure knew how to keep a bitch high. He put one on the pipe and handed the pipe to me. I took a hit and waited for the euphoria. When I let the smoke out of my mouth, Manny grabbed me and kissed me. He kissed me like he was my man.

That nigga ain't ever kissed me and I was a little taken aback by this gesture. He put his arms around me gently, pulled me in to his chest, and hugged me tightly. I didn't know what to make of this affectionate side of Manny. Shit, maybe his ass is psychotic now. I pulled back out of his arms and he was looking at me like he was in love or some shit.

"Manny, what's wrong? Why you looking at me like that?"

He paused and then pursed his lips.

"You're beautiful, Kaneesha, and I just can't stand to see you out here like this." he said.

I was tired of niggas always giving me their opinion. I put my hand on my hip.

"Manny, if you're so concerned, then help me out. Shit, I need a place to live. You gonna get me an apartment and pay for it? I need a job. You got one of those? I need a car to get to work—that piece of shit I had died months ago. I need a fuckin' good man for me and my son. Can you help me with that?" I asked with much attitude. I paused a little longer and said, "I didn't think so."

"Kaneesha, I didn't expect you to say all that. But if you

truly want my help, then you got to stop smokin' this shit. I'm willing to help you find a job. I'll even come and take you on some job interviews. But you gotta stop smokin'. You gotta get clean."

"But you're the main one giving it to me."

"Because it's the only time I get to see you."

"Real talk—if I stop smokin', you gonna help me?" I asked seriously.

"Neesha, I've always had a thing for you. I used to look for you around the neighborhood and watch you, just to see you smile. You have such a beautiful smile. I would see you at the club with Jarvis and always say he was a lucky man. You always kept yourself looking nice, before you got caught up in this world. You wore nice clothes and shoes and your hair was always done. I can't believe Jarvis left you out here like this. That shit ain't cool!" Manny told me.

He was killing my high with this conversation. I didn't come down here to get philosophical and shit. This nigga know he ain't helping me do a damn thing. But let's test the waters.

"Okay, Manny, let's say I get clean. What are you going to do for me since you got a thing for me? Put your money where your mouth is. What 'cha gonna do?"

"I'll help you find a job like I said. I'll even give you some money to keep yourself up. Just get clean. You and Reds both need to get off this shit. This game is crazy and you two are my girls. I just don't want you two to get hooked up in the wrong crowd with this shit. This shit could be the death of y'all."

"Stop talking like that, Manny. You're scaring me. I ain't dying from this shit. Hell, I learned how to smoke so I don't have them episodes like I used to. So stop talkin' that

"Kaneesha, I wasn't talkin' 'bout the way you smoke. I'm talkin' 'bout the people you runnin' wit'. Watch your back." Manny warned.

I had just had a similar conversation with myself less than several hours ago and now here he goes. I even dreamed about death. I just don't know who died and how because I couldn't remember the dream. Just the feeling of death.

My high was ruined now. I don't know what happened or what came over me but I didn't want to be in the room with Manny any longer. I stood up.

"Where you goin'?"

"Home, Manny."

"Good, Kaneesha. I'm 'bout to get up outta here myself after I leave Reds her package. Here's one for you."

"Wow...what happened to all that stop smoking talk?"

"This will be the last package that you will ever get from me. From this point on, I'm cuttin' you loose. I don't want you actin' like a hoe for this shit. You better than that, and I ain't goin' treat you like that no more either. Take this as a partin' gift from me." Manny pulled my right hand up and placed the package in it and kissed me on the forehead.

"Get clean, Kaneesha. Do it for your son and for me." Manny gathered up his coat and his leather satchel and walked out the bedroom door.

"I'm about to go," I told Reds on my way out too.

"First Manny leaves and now you. Everything okay?"

"Yeah."

"Okay...I love you, Neesh." Reds told me.

"I love you too, girl."

I got back into the apartment and leaned against the door. The more I thought about what Manny said, the more I wanted to stop this cycle. I had to face the truth. I had turned into one of them zombie, crack-head hoes. I didn't like the title of what I had become, but the title was exactly what I was. It wasn't the title that I didn't like. It was me that I didn't like.

Chapter Thirty-Two

I awoke the next morning shivering my ass off. I had to get outta here. I decided to go down and hang out with Reds. When I got there, she was washing dishes. I immediately picked up the dishtowel and started drying them. We talked for a few when Reds snapped her fingers.

"Girl, I knew there was somethin' I meant to tell you—we got invited to a party on Saturday." She said with excitement.

"Who's, where and how?"

She playfully hit me with the dishrag. "Damn girl, who is you, *Murder She Wrote*?"

"I saw Manny and he said that one of his boys was giving a party over at the Elks lodge and he invited both of us. He said that an after party would take place at his cousin's house out on the waterfront."

"That's cool. But how we gonna get there? I ain't 'bout to catch no bus to no club. And you know the bus stop runnin' at ten fuckin' o'clock anyway. So is Manny comin' to get us?"

"No, but he left something for you." She stopped washing dishes, rubbed her wet hands on her pants and went to her bedroom. She came back with an envelope in her hand.

"Here. He said make sure you do the right thing."

She handed me the envelope and I tore it open and looked inside. There was a note and some money. I counted the money, three hundred dollars. I unfolded the note and read it.

Neesha,

Take this money and buy something pretty. Get your hair done. Save some for a cab to the club. I will see you and Reds there. Look like you used to.

M

I looked up at Reds.

"Did he leave you something?"

"Girl, you know Manny did. You know he do us right." I showed her the money.

"I got the same amount you did. So we might as well go shopping and get our stuff. You can bring it down here and put it in my closet. After my mother leave for her night job, you can come on down and take a shower and get dressed here. Okay?" Reds told me.

"Yeah, girl. That's fine wit' me. Shit, hurry up wit' the dishes. We got some shopping to do."

Reds and I caught the bus to Annapolis Mall and shopped like we had a million dollars. My clothing size had changed from a size six in my waist to a size zero. I didn't feel sexy having lost so much weight but I made do.

I couldn't tell you how good it felt to shop when I haven't in a long time. I hadn't been to the mall in over six months. I felt like a B.A.P. - Black American Princess. When we got back to Reds' place, we laid out our clothes and accessories on the bed. We even bought a cheap pair of shoes at Payless. I hadn't worn high heels in ages so I had to walk around Reds' apartment to reacquaint myself with stiletto walking.

We squealed and giggled like two high school girls going to the prom. I couldn't wait to dress up and go out. I also made up in my mind that I was not going to get beamed. I would stick to my drink for the night. However, it was Friday and Reds and I had money left over. Needless to say our promise didn't last long.

We each pitched in twenty-five dollar and bought a fifty-cent piece from Baggs. I hadn't seen Baggs for a minute. Rumor was he caught a case and had been in jail. He must have made bail. It wasn't my business to ask and honestly I didn't care. I really didn't have any words for Baggs. He didn't have many for me either.

Reds and I did the package. She were tempted to spend some more money but I told her no. We need to try to have some sort of control over this shit. She didn't agree with me and told me to stay in the house and she would be right back. About thirty minutes later, Reds came back with two guys trailing behind her. I watched them walk in. They stood talking among themselves but were looking at me hard. The look they was throwing made the hairs on the back of my neck stand up so bad, that I got up from the table and walked into the kitchen. I heard Reds telling them to have a seat in the living room. Before I could say a word, she grabbed me by the arm, led me to her bedroom and shut the door.

"Girl, I got a way for us to get high the rest of the night for free." Reds said.

"Reds, who the hell are those boys out there?"

"They cool. I've seen them before. They slinging for Terrence. You've seen them around too, Neesha. Remember?"

"Yeah, maybe I have, but what do they want?"

"Girl, what you think they want?" Reds laughed.

"Reds, I don't know them mutherfuckas. Shit, you know we don't deal with bag boys or runners. They ain't carryin' like that. Why you bring them up in here?"

"Girl, one of them showed me his packages. He said he would give us our shit first. All they want is some head, Neesh. That's all. A blowjob. Come on. You game?"

"Reds, I'm tellin' you, when them two walked in, I felt eerie."

"Kaneesha, I don't know what's going on wit' you, but you need to cut it out. Now, I don't have to spend my money tonight on my Scotty cause those two said they was willing to give up some of their rocks to us if we got their rocks off tonight. So, I'm goin' get mine. You can stay around if you want but I need to use this bedroom. So what you goin' do?"

We went back out to the living room and Reds told the guys that we would accept their offer. Reds was going to go first.

She told me that I could use her mother's room but I declined. She then suggested we just bring them both in the bedroom and do them at the same time.

Reds and I had small clientele. There were only four heavy distributers and major dealers that Reds and I dealt with sexually. Manny, Benny, Dean, and Calvin. And if I had to, I'd fuck with small time drug dealer Baggs. Reds was breaking our code by bringing in bag boys. This arrangement did not sit well with me. But Reds was my girl and she was already in their doing her thing.

I couldn't back out so I sat down in the kitchen and waited for her to get done. I snuck a peek at the remaining bag boy sitting on the couch. He was just at the six-foot mark approximately and he was a little on the heavy side. He was dark skinned and had deep-set eyes and his right one was very lazy. I heard him sniff and I adverted my attention to the door. I was thinking about how long it would take before Reds was finished when I heard him begin to speak.

"You do this thing all the time?" He asked in a deep husky voice.

"Do what?"

"Suck dick for crack." He boldly asked.

"It depends upon whose dick I'm suckin'."

"What that mean?"

"Just what I said."

"What some mutherfuckas got special dick?"

"Yes." I affirmed looking intently at him. I didn't like this mutherfucka at all.

"So do I fit into your special category?" he asked smiling, rubbing his dick while talking to me.

"No, you don't!" I snapped back. His smiled disappeared from his face and he stopped rubbing his dick.

"Yo, what the fuck that posta mean?" He said, giving me a disgruntled look.

"It means that you are not in my special category. Look, I don't know you and I ain't sure why my girl even brought y'all down here. She wanted to do this, not me."

"Yo, what you mean you don't wanna do this? He said a little too loudly. "I ain't come out here for nothin'. Somebody suckin' my dick tonight."

I was definitely not about to suck his dick for any amount of rock or money.

"Well it ain't gonna be me." I said. "What's your name anyway?"

"Crack-hoe bitches don't get to pick. They just suck dicks. What'cha need to know my name fo'? I don't want to know yours. All I want is for you to suck my dick like you promised."

"I didn't promise you shit. So we ain't got no deal." I said clearly.

"Fuck you then, you crack-ass hoe! Fuck you! Tell my boy when he's done squirting his cum all over your bitch ass girlfriend's face that I'm in the car waitin' for him." He shouted.

"I ain't tellin' him shit. When that little mutherfucka comes out here, he'll see for himself that your ass is gone."

"Whatever, you nasty ass bitch!" He continued to yell as he stood up.

"Leave now nigga or I'ma call Five-O!" I raised the phone so he could see me getting ready to push the magical numbers. He sucked his teeth and opened the door and was gone.

Whew... I exhaled. I ran and locked the door. I sat down at the table to collect myself. That nigga scared the shit outta me. I couldn't wait for Reds to bring her ass out of that damn bedroom so I could lay her ass out. I looked at the kitchen clock. They had been in there now for twenty minutes. If that nigga didn't bust a nut within the next five minutes, then I was going back there and snatch his dick out of Reds' mouth and squeeze that nut out myself. It must have been his night to bust because exactly five minutes later, they came out of the bedroom. After Reds' bag boy left, I laid into her.

"Reds, man, that boy was crazy. Why you break code like that?" I needed to know.

"What code?"

"We said neva to fuck wit' the runners and bag boys. 'Cause they don't know how to act and to be honest, Reds, that nigga looked like he wanted to do some unethical shit to me. When I told him I didn't want to do him, girl the look in his eyes was enough to make me wish I was packing my Defender." I said.

"Girl, the defender is gone and you're being paranoid. That boy didn't want nothin' but his dick sucked. You probably hurt his feelings when you turned him down. Come on, Neesh, let's get beamed. Fuck him. He gone."

"Promise me that you ain't breakin' the code no more Reds." She put up her pinky finger.

"Pinky swear!" she said. I linked my pinky with hers.

She apologized for bringing them down and Reds showed me the package. It was ready rock. I hated ready rock cause sometimes it could be ivory soap or some other foreign substance that some dealers used to sell to customers to get over. This time the ready rock was legit. Although, it did have a different taste than the rocks we cooked up. Reds told me that ammonia was probably used as the agent instead of baking soda.

I don't care what it was. We blasted all her shit. When we were done, I went back to the hole. My cold, lonely, abandoned apartment. Tomorrow was Saturday and the night of the party. I was going to look pretty. Tomorrow, I would stop getting high. I was going to find some way to get myself clean. Manny said he would help me and I was going to hold him to his word. If I kept my end of the bargain, hopefully he would his. I had a new outlook about Manny. I was beginning to like him in lovingly way. I was feeling better about my life and myself. I fell asleep thinking about the party, Manny, and a change in my life.

Chapter Thirty-Three

"Did they make the connection? Good. That's fucking good! I want them to stay on their asses. When you get them to the location send the word." Dubbs closed his phone and looked out the motel window. The first part of his plan was working.

At a local strip club, "Blazing", one of the best dancers in the spot was commanding the stage.

"Yeah, that's right, baby, make that phat ass clap!" Kelly said tossing a handful of dollar bills on Blazing.

She was on her hands and knees with her perfectly, flawless round ass pointed at the table of young thugs who were cheering her on. Blazing did several splits, rolls and then went into a handstand on the pole like she was a dancehall queen. She worked every part of the stage. When she was done with her act, the men's table had rained two hundred dollars on her. Kelly's phone vibrated on his side and he snatched it open.

"Yeah!" he shouted into the phone. "Tell him to sit tight! We already seen the bitches and we 'bout to pull them in. We'll be in touch. I'm out!" He looked across the table at his partner.

"Yo, you know we got a job to finish. I'ma drown my yak and then we gonna bounce so I can give you the rest of the details."

"Okay man." his partner replied.

Kelly downed the Remy Martin Louie the 13th and tapped his other partner, who wasn't leaving with them, on the shoulder.

"We 'bout to bounce. We'll catch y'all later." Kelly said to everyone.

They all gave each other dap. Kelly and his partner rolled out leaving four others at the table. The group of young dealers continued to sit around drinking Hennessey, Louie the 13th and talking shit when someone mentioned Stone's name.

"Son, I heard Stone beat down that boy Jarvis that stole that package. Heard he put a hurtin' on him." Said T-boz.

"Word?" Someone said.

"Well, ya'll know Dubbs and Cappy right?" T-boz asked everyone at the table. They nodded their heads yes in unison.

"Man, I heard Stone got into Dubbs shit during a drop with Cappy." T-Boz continued. "And he told Cappy he never wanted to do business with Dubbs around. Cappy ended up cutting Dubbs off."

"You talkin' bout Dubbs from Annapolis?" someone asked.

"Yeah, mutherfucka! Ain't that what the fuck I just say?! But it turns out the package that Jarvis got punished for was a set up by Dubbs. He was tryin' to make Stone's fort weak by breaking down his crew. He was hurtin' for money when Cappy cut him off," T Boz affirmed.

"Well Stone's boys are slippin' then. How the fuck Dubbs infiltrate his area to get at the package?" Another dealer said.

"Yeah, I feel you on the sleep shit but personally I would have bust a cap in Stone's ass had it been me. I would have laid his ass in the cut! He fuckin' wit a nigga's livelihood by tellin' Cappy to cut him off," Another dealer said.

"Dawg, you must be high as fuck! You can't get near Stone. Shit if you see Stone it's a fuckin' miracle. That nigga like Casper the mutherfuckin' ghost. His shit be on lock. So best believe that package was flipped by one of Stone's own in Dubbs name. Somebody turned mole up in his camp son!" T-Boz said.

The young dealers continued to talk and wait for the other dancers.

"I'm goin' to light one." T-Boz said. He went outside and was surprised to see Kelly and his partner standing in the front talking.

"Thought y'all was gone man!" T-Boz said.

"We 'bout to bounce in a minute." Kelly said.

T-Boz took out his Newports and lit one. He leaned against the wall for support. He had one too many shots of Louie the 13th. He wasn't listening to anything in particular until he heard the names of several people fall from Kelly's lips.

T-Boz acted like he was drunker than he was and staggered over to where Kelly and his partner were talking. They didn't pay T Boz any mind. They continued on with their conversation. T-Boz lit another cigarette so he could go on listening to Kelly's conversation. When Kelly was done talking, he turned to T-Boz and told him he was out. At first Kelly was worried he'd gotten caught ear hustling but that wasn't the case.

Kelly and his partner left the front of the strip club. T-Boz flicked the half smoked cigarette as he watched his friends drive away. T-Boz was also friends with someone else and he knew the people that Kelly mentioned in his conversation. He opened up his phone and placed a call to Tok.

Chapter Thirty-Four

Saturday! The day of the party! The day that I would put on my new clothes, find a new attitude and be aspired to move into a new life. Tonight I was not smoking anything with anybody no matter what the offer was. Tonight, I was going out with my best friend Reds. Tonight we both were gonna look hot and sexy. Tonight would be a night that I would never forget.

The minute Reds' mother left for work, I dipped straight to Reds house. I pressed and curled my hair. I was still old fashioned that way. I took a long hot bath and pampered myself with scented lotion and the perfume to match that I found in Reds' mother's room.

"Come on, the cab will be here soon! Neesh, you been puttin' on makeup for almost a hour. Let me see what you look like already! Come the hell on!" Reds hollered through the bathroom door.

I slowly opened the door and stepped out. Reds' mouth dropped open as she put her hand over it and whispered something I couldn't make out.

"Well, stop gawkin' at me like I'm fuckin' retarded. How do I look?" I asked her as I twirled around.

"Kaneesha, girl, you're hot! You're so pretty when you are all dressed up!" She said.

"You don't do to bad yourself." I said running my hand over Reds' pretty long hair.

"Look at us. We too hot mamma jammas!" I said and gave my girl a high five.

"Reds, that outfit is slammin' on you and that color is crazy!" I said admiring her.

Reds had on a metallic blue denim pantsuit. It shimmered when she moved. Reds accessorized with some dainty silver heels and silver jewelry. I had on white, one of my favorite colors. I chose baggie pants, a simple V-neck top with a gold belt, gold accessories and gold and white shoes. I even bought the matching clutch purse. This would ensure that I didn't bring my purple bag tonight. I reached out and took Reds' hand.

"Reds, listen, I need to talk to you right quick." I said.

"What's wrong?" She asked with concern.

"Nothin's wrong, Reds. But tonight, I don't wanna get high. I don't care who comes at me—I'm not gettin' high. Now, I'm not sayin' that you can't—that's your choice. But me, Reds, I wanna stop smokin' this shit. So tonight I'm startin' a new story."

Reds looked at me for a moment.

"Ahhh, Neesha. I'm proud of you. Okay, if you don't wanna smoke, that's cool wit' me. You know I ain't got no problem wit' it. Just don't rain on my parade." she said laughing.

"Girl, you know I ain't never gonna do that."

Reds' telephone rang. The cab was outside waiting for us. We both squealed like little girls and grabbed our coats and headed out. We were on our way to the club and then to the after party.

The club was packed as usual. It felt good to be out among the partygoers. Reds and I got mad looks as we walked through the club. Reds still filled out her jeans nicely because she was retaining baby fat. I had lost a lot of weight, so I wasn't filling out anything but my face was still pretty and I felt glamorous. I didn't care about any man up in here anyway. I was there to get a couple of drinks and a couple of dances if nothing else. Right now, my focus was on how I was going to get clean and stay the fuck off of crack.

We found a table in the corner and sat down. Reds stated she would go get the drinks. I knew that she was trying to catch attention from any drug dealer that might be in the club tonight. She sauntered up to the bar to order our drinks. I took the opportunity to scan the room. Yeah, there were some major ballers in the joint tonight. Several men made eye contact but I was not interested.. All I wanted was Reds to bring me that drink. She came back with the drinks in hand and a wide smile across her face.

"Girl, there some fine ass men up in here!" She said looking around. "Shit, that one guy over there at the bar said he would take care of our drinks for the rest of the night." "Tell me you didn't." I whined.

"Didn't what?" Reds laughed.

"You know what the hell I'm talkin' 'bout Reds. Just don't be makin' no plans for me. We had that conversation before we left remember?" I reminded her.

"Yeah, Neesh, chill—I ain't hookin' you up with nobody. Shit. You turnin' into a miss goodie two shoes all ready." Reds joked.

"Reds, I'm not turnin' into a miss goodie two shoes nothin'. I just need to get my life straight. And my..." I stopped talking and looked behind Reds' shoulder.

She looked at me and then snapped her head around. There stood the two bag boys from last night. They had come up to our table. The one Reds was with spoke to her. The one that I kicked the fuck out looked like he was still pissed about me not doing him. Reds' friend was whispering in her ear. The other one continued to mean-mug me. I picked up my drink and held it in my hand. If a nigga wanted to get stupid, I was going to slap him in the face with my glass. Reds looked over at me.

"Neesha, this is Kelly." She pointed to him and then pointed at the mean muggin' dude.

"That's Mumps." she said.

I nodded my head at Kelly and rolled my eyes at Mumps. Kelly went to pull out a chair and I stopped him.

"I ain't tryin' to be mean or nothin' like that, but me and my girl came to enjoy ourselves by ourselves." I said looking him straight in the eye.

"What? A nigga can't chill with y'all?" Kelley asked.

"You can chill with Reds but not at this table."

"It's cool. I feel you, Ma, you don't want me cock blockin'—I got you." He said standing up straight, grinning.

"Yeah, somethin' like that. Whatever." I said rolling my eyes at him.

Kelly leaned down in Reds' ear and said something else to her. She had that stupid smile on her face like the fucking Joker from Batman. When he finished whispering he stood up and tapped Mumps on the arm. They left the table and walked into the crowd.

"Reds, don't say shit! I already done told you that I wasn't feelin' them two mutherfuckas. Especially that fuckin' Mumps. He looked like one big-ass mump. That nigga ugly as shit. I'm glad I didn't suck that dick. And how they think they was just gonna park their black asses at our table without bein' invited? I don't want no one thinkin' I was wit' either one of them mutherfuckas! And further more, you just pinky swore that you wasn't breakin' the code no more."

"Neesha, chill the fuck out! What the hell's wrong wit' your ass? I ain't breakin' no code. Okay? Now come on, let's toast."

We held up our glasses, made a toast and took a long hearty swing of our drinks.

"Oh shit, that's our song girl." Reds cackled with laughter. I fell out laughing too.

"Yeah that's our song 'aight." I said.

The DJ was spinning the old school classic by Rob Base called, "It Take Two." Our favorite verse was the first one—"I wanna rock right now!"

We danced and drank and had more fun than we had in such a long time. Reds was making rounds and getting numbers. I resigned to laying low and enjoying the moment. I was looking in my clutch for my lipstick when I heard a voice in my ear.

"You look beautiful." I didn't even have to turn around.

"Thank you." I replied back.

Manny came from behind me and sat down at the table. He gazed at me long and hard. I actually enjoyed him looking.

"I knew the old Kaneesha was still in there. I'm glad to see her back. Now, if you put back on about twenty pounds, you would be the old Kaneesha for real. But you still look very good. I like your hair. Shit, I didn't know you had that much hair." He said with a warm smile.

"Yeah, I got hair." I smiled back at him.

"Well I'm glad you came. I saw Reds prancin' around. Shit, before she got on the pipe, Reds ran these men in circles around here. I see she's tryin' to see if she still got it." Manny said shaking his head and laughing. "She'll never change. Anyway, here's the address to the after party." He handed me a small piece of paper.

"I wanna see you and Reds there. Look, I ain't tryin' to get in your business, but you both need to stay the fuck away from Kelly and Mumps. I seen them two niggas over here. Kaneesha, they bad news. You hear me? They bad news. Ya'll don't need to be wit' the likes of them. Y'all ain't that desperate are you?" Manny asked.

"No, as a matter of fact, I told Reds tonight that I wanted to quit this shit and get myself together. I ain't even smokin'. I'm just havin' a couple of drinks and callin' it a night."

"Well, 'aight, Kaneesha. I'm glad to hear that. And I meant what I said, you get clean, and I'll do my best to help you out." Manny reminded me.

"Okay. I'm givin' it my best."

"That's all that anyone can do." Manny said rising up from the chair.

"Listen, tell Reds don't do nothin with them boys!" Manny stated again.

"I will. And Manny?" I stopped him.

"Yeah?"

"Thanks for the shopping spree." I said blushing. "It made me feel special."

"You cool peoples, Neesha. I ain't have no problem hookin' you up." He winked at me and walked over to another table.

I saw Benny sitting there. Benny looked up and tried to make eye contact but I quickly adverted my eyes to the bar where Reds was talking and hanging all over Kelly like he was the last man standing. She came back to the table with him. He pulled out the chair and sat down. I didn't stop him this time. It was almost time to go anyway and I didn't see his ugly side kick anywhere. Maybe his ass went home.

About fifteen minutes later, the lights came on indicating the party was over. I need to go the restroom and I need to talk to Reds about the after party. She was so busy grinning in Kelly's face that I didn't want to say anything about Manny in front of him.

"Reds, lets go to the bathroom before we leave." I said motioning her to follow me.

"Right behind you."

She turned to Kelly and told him not to go anywhere.

Hell no, Reds ain't going nowhere with him. We're going to the after party where Manny will be and that's that. I thought.

In the bathroom, I confronted her as she stood in front of the mirror, looking at herself.

"Reds, Manny gave me the address to the after party. All we need to do is catch a hack outside. But listen, he also said to stay the hell away from Kelly and Mumps. He said they bad news."

"Girl, ain't nothin' wrong wit' Kelly. And Manny need to mind his business. He just mad cause Kelly and Mumps be in his territory sometime. Kelly already told me that Manny don't like him or Mumps or they crew for that matter."

"I don't know, Reds. Manny was serious about what he said 'bout them two. Personally, I'ma adhere to his warnin'. You should do the same, Reds." I pleaded to her. She seemed zoned out. "Reds, you hear me talkin' to you?"

"Yeah, Kaneesha, I hear that shit you talkin'. Look, Kelly and I are goin' to take a detour before we go to the after party. I needs me a hit and Kelly said he needs a little somethin' too." She giggled.

The drinks she had been consuming all night must have caught up with her because her speech sounded slurred.

"No, Reds. We goin' to get a hack (a person giving rides in his own car for cash), or a cab, and go to the after party. Manny said he'll be waitin' on us." I let her know.

"I heard you the first fifty times, Neesh. But I'm goin' to get me a package to take home for later tonight. It ain't gonna take me no more than twenty minutes to do Kelly and then we out. Shit, Kelly gotta car. He can take us to the after party. That way we can keep our money." She said holding onto the sink for support.

"Reds, why you gotta be so crazy for this dude? What is it about him?"

"I don't know, Neesh. Maybe it's nice to have somebody who likes me for me...like you have Manny." She said falling over a little.

I laughed at Reds. Very seldom was she drunk.

"What's so funny, Neesh?" Reds slurred.

"Your drunk ass. I don't get a chance to see you like this too much so I'm takin' full advantage of it now."

"What the fuck ever!" She giggled again. "Are you with me? I don't want to do this alone."

I stared at her in silence, still wanting to go with my gut.

"Neesh, you know I don't go no where without you," she persisted, "so do you got my back on this or not? We just gonna go to the motel real quick. You can even stay in the car. It won't take long, you know that. Come on, Neesh. Please!" Reds pouted her lips and batted her eyes.

I knew that my ass should not have given in but I did for my girl. She hugged me and we walked out the bathroom and across the empty dance floor to the front of the door. I caught Manny watching us even though he was engaged in another conversation. I read his eyes. Silently, he was telling me, "Do like I told you to do and leave them two alone." I pushed Reds in her back.

"Why you pushing me?" She said.

"Cause Manny is straight up watchin' every move we make. So if you want me to sneak off with you and Kelly, I suggest you get your ass in motion now."

"Damn you act like Manny your man or somethin'. Is there some shit goin' on that you ain't tellin' a bitch?"

"No. Keep walkin'." I said pushing her some more.

We got out to the parking lot and Kelly pulled up in a beat up Blazer. Just from the looks of the truck, I knew that Reds didn't have no business bringing them bag boys to her house to begin with. They weren't rockin' nothing like Manny, Benny, or even Dubbs for that matter. We got in the truck and headed to a motel. Reds and Kelly were talking nonstop. I sat in the back seat, wondering what my move would be to get myself clean. I sat up and tapped Kelly on the shoulder.

"Where your boy?" I asked.

"Why you tryin' to put him on?" he asked grinning.

"Hell no! I just wondered where he was that's all."

Kelly looked at me in the rearview mirror and sucked his teeth. "He's out."

I stared back at him. I didn't wanna ask him what that meant because I didn't care, just as long as Mumps wasn't anywhere near me. Kelly looked back to the road and he and Reds continued their chatter from the front seat. I sat back in my seat.

We pulled up at a motel. It damn sure wasn't like the ones that our regular ballers would take us to occasionally. This was a dump. I should have told Reds right then and there to fuck this shit and let's go, but she wouldn't have listened anyway. We were somewhere way out cause it took us almost forty-five minutes to get there. I looked around for any landmark and to see if anything looked familiar but that was wasted energy.

Kelly got out the truck and Reds followed and she told me wait. She and Kelly were talking outside the truck. A few minutes later I saw him go into the motel. Reds got back in the truck with me.

"This the deal. You can stay out here for a minute. I'ma go in there and handle my business and we'll be done and be gone. He's goin' to take us to the after party. Okay?"

"Reds, are you sure 'bout this shit? I really don't want you to do this. Why don't you just let it go tonight? Shit, we got some money. I'll give you mine and you can buy a package or get one from Manny." I pleaded.

"Girl, we here now. I ain't 'bout to tell that nigga that he brought me all the way out here and that I ain't gonna suck his dick. Girl, that shit right there could set a nigga off. No, Kaneesha. I already gave him my word so let me go handle my shit. Lock the door and chill for minute. I promise I'll be back in under a half."

With that, she opened the door and ran into the motel. I let out a long sigh and sat back in the seat. Shit, did the nigga at least leave the keys? Shit it's cold in this raggedy fucka. I sat back up and looked at the ignition. Hell no, that mutherfucka took the damn keys. Now my ass is probably gonna freeze to death out here waiting for Reds . I pulled my coat tighter around me and snuggled up in the corner of the truck. I closed my eyes and tried to relax.

I was thinking about my son and Jarvis. If I see that nigga right now, I'll cut his wrists open. Sorry son-of-a-bitch. That nigga just don't... An uneasy feeling came over me and suddenly I opened my eyes and screamed. Standing outside the truck was Mumps. I reached up and immediately hit the lock on the door. It didn't budge. What the fuck? Don't tell me this fucka is broke. I tried the lock it again only to have the same results. The lock didn't budge. Mumps put his hand on the handle and I scooted to the opposite side of the truck. He opened the door and got in. I tried to get out the left side but the back door was dented in on that side and wouldn't open. My ass was stuck. Mumps closed the door behind him.

"What do you want, Mumps?" I said. I was shaking in my mutherfucking shoes.

"I want what you said was so special for everyone else 'cept me. I want you to suck my dick, bitch, like I know your crack-ass can."

"Just leave me the hell alone, Mumps. I ain't botherin' you.

I don't do crack no more. So ain't no reason for me to be suckin' your dick."

Mumps burst out into a sinister laugh.

"What you mean you ain't doin' crack no mo'? It don't matter anyway, you owe me from last night. You made a deal with me and Kelly and I'm here to collect on my shit!"

"I said I ain't..." *Smack. Smack.*

Mumps had slapped me in the face twice. I tried to run up between the seats to the front of the truck but he grabbed me and pulled me back.

"Bitch, get out! We goin' in the motel so you can show me how good you suck dick."

Mumps grabbed a handful of my hair and pulled me out as he and I both slid out the backseat of the truck. I tried to kick him but he yanked my hair so hard I thought he snapped my neck. My eyes had begun to water from his pulling my hair. Was I about to be raped again? Was I that bad of a person to warrant this happening to me twice?

I kept trying to pry his hands out of my hair but it wasn't working. I screamed for him to stop when he punched me in the mouth and told me to shut the fuck up. I started to scream again until he brought out the amo...a nine millimeter with a silencer attached. I didn't part my fucking lips after I saw that. We walked up to the door that Reds went into. Mumps knocked three times and then knocked twice. The door flew open and Kelly was standing inside smiling.

"So I see you found the bitch, Mumps. I bet she'll give you some head now." He laughed.

I looked around for Reds but I didn't see her. I didn't hear her. I called out her name.

"Reds. Reds!" I shouted.

"Bitch, you better shut the fuck up and stop all that noise before I blast your ass!" Mumps said.

I looked back at him with terror in my eyes and in my heart but I found my voice.

"Where's Reds? Is she okay?" I asked, fearful of his

answer. "I just wanna know she's okay."

Mumps was waving his gun as he talked. "That bitch's fine. She back there suckin' dick like a good little crack hoe, but your stank ass think you all that. What was that shit you told me last night? Oh yeah, my dick don't fit into the special category. Well, my dick is special tonight. So you need to suck it bitch." He yanked me down onto the floor still gripping my hair.

My body shivered but I wouldn't do it. I just couldn't.

"What the fuck you waitin' on? Get my dick out and start suckin'. And you better do me right. Cause if you don't, I'ma beat that ass!" he yelled.

Mumps released my hair. He had the gun in his right hand, cocked up on his shoulder while his left hand was on his hip. With shaking hands, I undid his belt buckle and unzipped his pants. They fell to the floor.

"Open your bloody mouth bitch." I didn't open it.

He tried forcing his dick between my clenched teeth. When he couldn't get it in he struck me again in the head and I screamed out in pain, and fell over.

"Come on, girl. Make my dick stand to attention. I know you got it in you." He laughed.

I picked up his limp dick and put it in my mouth. I wanted to bite that motherfucker but he had that gun.

He must have read my mind and he said, "Bitch, don't bite my shit. If you do, I'll take your skull off. You hear me?"

I looked up at him and nodded my head.

"Good, now show me what the fuck them other mutherfuckas be talkin' 'bout when they refer to you and your girl in there." Mumps said.

I began to give Mumps a blowjob and he started to get hard. He started pushing his dick into my mouth with a force that was making me gag. The more I tried to pull away, the stronger he forced his dick in my mouth and down my throat. I was gagging beyond control and I couldn't breath. I hit Mumps on his thigh trying to get away and he got mad and hit me with the butt of the gun. The force of him striking me caused me to clamp down on his dick.

"Ahhhh!!! What the fuck you doin' bitch?! I just told you not to bite me!" Mumps began to beat me in the face with the gun and his hand.

I began to scream when he kicked me in the stomach. I doubled over in pain on the floor and I pleaded with him to stop. Mumps stood over me for a moment.

"Bitch, get up! Get up!" He commanded and pulled me by my hair again. The closet door opened and I was terrified as a figure came out and walked towards me. He walked over to where I was laying on the floor.

"So you still playin' that hard to get game? Huh? Now you don't wanna suck Mumps dick?! You must fuckin' really think your skank ass is special then, huh?" Dubbs said.

"Yeah, that's what the bitch told me last night. That she only sucks *special* dick Dubbs." Mumps said kicking me in the back.

"Is that so?" Dubbs laughed. "'Cause I heard you suck Stone and Baggs' dicks all the time."

I couldn't believe Dubbs was standing over top of me again. Where was Reds? Dubbs knelt down beside me.

"This is how it's gonna go, Reds is first and then I'ma come back and me and my boy here want a performance of a lifetime. Watch her." He told Mumps. "I got unfinished business waitin' for me in the other room."

Dubbs got up and headed to the bedroom. I heard Reds scream and then I heard silence. My heart quickened as the thought of Reds being dead crossed my mind. I wanted to run to the bedroom to get her but Mumps had his nine pointed directly at my head.

"Move and I will blast you!" He warned.

I laid on the floor whimpering softly. Not too long after, Dubbs returned with Reds. They threw her down on the floor beside me. Her face was bruised and swollen.

"Damn, this is sweet. I got both bitches where I want 'em. Kelly, I thank y'all for roundin' these two up for me. I told you them bitches couldn't resist crack. That's all you had to do was wave that shit in front of they stupid asses and boom," he paused clapping his hands, "you got 'em! Look at 'em. I bet you wish your dumb asses didn't smoke that shit now? Don't you?" Dubbs asked.

"Kelly said you give good dick service, Reds." Dubbs continued running the entire show. "Is that right? He said he had you on your knees slurpin' his shit like a softy ice cream cone. Damn! Just thinkin' 'bout that makes my dick hard. I wanna see if Kelly was tellin' the truth."

"Snatch the bitch up, Kelly and plant her ass right here so she can suck me off." Dubbs commanded.

Kelly pulled Reds up and stood her in front of Dubbs. He poked her in the back with his gun. Reds dropped to her knees in front of Dubbs. He had his dick out ready for her. He grabbed Reds' head and forcefully brought it to his crotch.

"Open your mouth and suck!" He demanded.

Reds put Dubb's dick in her mouth and began to suck him. She sobbed during the entire ordeal and so did I.

"Please leave her alone," I begged seeing her body weaken. "Please."

"Ah, that's it...That's it...Yeah, that's good." Dubbs said ignoring me.

Mumps and Kelly looked at each other. I guess they were surprised at how much he was enjoying it in front of everybody. Kelly was standing over top of Reds with his gun pointed to her head.

Kelly downed the rest of his beer and said, "Shit I want some of that too!" He pulled out his dick. He moved around to the front of Reds, posted the gun to her skull. "Suck me too, bitch." Reds was now giving Dubbs and Kelly head at the same time.

I saw Kelly look over at Dubbs dick and knew another man was turning him on. I also could see the tears falling from Reds' face. Mumps watched Reds but kept his glock aimed at me.

"Kelly, help Reds come up out them clothes." Dubbs said.

"No, Dubbs! Please I'm suckin' your dick like you asked me do! Please don't do this to me!" Reds begged.

Dubbs reached around and snatched a handful of Reds' hair and pulled her head back.

"Shut the fuck up! Kelly get them clothes!"

Kelly put his dick back in his pants and snatched Reds' top from the bottom and tried to get it over her head. Reds fought with Kelly to retain her clothing but when Dubbs reached in and punched Reds in the mouth, she didn't resist anymore. Kelly removed her top and then snatched her bra off. Reds was on her knees topless.

"Take off them jeans bitch. You know what the fuck to do!" Dubbs continued.

Reds removed her jeans. All that was left was her thong. Kelly reached around and tore it from her waist. Dubbs pushed her down on the floor and Kelly stood over her with his gun while Dubbs positioned himself between Reds' legs. She immediately began bucking her legs in an attempt to get him away. But Dubbs slapped her across the face. And when Reds fought back, Dubbs slapped her again. Kelly kneeled down and put his gun to her head.

"If you put them hands up again, I'ma pistol whip your ass! Now let Dubbs get what the fuck he came to get." Kelly said.

He seemed to be getting off on what Dubbs was doing. And I could tell by the look in his eyes, he wanted his approval.

"Dubbs, stop it!" I yelled. "Stop it! Why are you doin' this?!" I screamed.

"Shut that bitch down!" Dubbs said.

Mumps sat on my back and pushed his gun harder into the base of my skull.

"Don't say shit else or they'll be pickin' up your brains off this carpet." Mumps threatened.

I put my head down to the side and cried. God, how could this be happening? Kelly had grabbed Reds arms and pinned them down. Dubbs was still in between Reds' legs and took the barrel of his gun and ran it up and down her clitoris. I saw the scratches on it and knew it was my gun, my Defender.

"Yeah, you like this don't you?" He mused.

Dubbs took the barrel of his gun and mercilessly shoved it up into Reds vagina. She let out a wail and Kelly slapped her again telling her to shut the fuck up. Dubbs moved his gun in and out of Reds like a dildo.

"Yeah, fuck this gun, baby!" Dubbs panted.

Then he forcefully pushed it further into Reds making her cry out again. When he was done, he snatched it out and forced himself into Reds. As he raped her, he slapped her in the face several times while calling her names and telling her she was a worthless crack whore. When he was done, Kelly, who Reds had caught feelings for, raped her next.

All the while Mumps was sitting on my back waiting for his chance at Reds. When Kelly was done, it was Mumps' turn. I could hear my best friend whimpering as she was being assaulted gang style. When Mumps got up to rape Reds, Kelly sat on my back to hold me down. Reds was bleeding from her nose and mouth and she had bruises in between her legs and around her neck. She also had bite marks on her breasts from their attacks.

Reds was slapped around so much she lingered in and out of consciousness. When they had their fill of Reds, they focused on me. They left her laying there beaten and bruised and she appeared to be out cold.

"I want that bitch so bad my dick won't go down until I get that pretty little thing. I got a special dick for her." Mumps said.

"Yeah, I had that shit myself. She wouldn't give it to me so I had to take it! Go on.

"Ummm, that's finger lickin' good." Mumps said.

Mumps mounted me and pushed his dick in me with a brut force. I don't know how Reds got up unnoticed but she ran and jumped on Mumps' back screaming at the top of her lungs. She was digging her fingernails into his face as hard as she could.

Mumps was spinning around with her on his back but couldn't shake her. Kelly ran over and snatched Reds off of Mumps.

When Mumps turned, he raised his gun and let off two shots. Reds went limp in Kelly's arms. I saw blood begin to seep from Reds' chest and I ran toward her.

"Reds...don't die! Please."

"I...I...I'm sorry." Blood spilled out of her body.

"This isn't your fault."

"I w...was...pregnant by Jarvis. I...I'm sorry. But...I always lo...loved you."

With that she fought for her last breath, and died.

I was hurt by Reds' death and her admission of being pregnant by Jarvis. To be honest a part of me felt it all along when she got pregnant the second time. I didn't blame her or maybe I didn't care. All that mattered is that I had lost my best friend.

Right then, I made it my business to fight. I turned around preparing to go out battling for my life. But the moment I was about to lunge at them, the door to the motel room burst open. Red dots were everywhere.

Sounds of guns firing with silencers attached, filled the room. I managed to crawl in a corner while the shooting continued. After less than a minute, the shooting stopped. But I was too scared to lift my head. I looked around the bullet-riddled room. I couldn't take it anymore so I just screamed.

I figured we had been rescued and that maybe there was still time to save my best friend.

"Reds, wake up! Please don't leave me, Reds! I love you, Reds. Come on, Reds!" I continued to cry.

Her body didn't move. Her head lay to the side and her eyes were wide open. I picked up one of her arms and put it around my shoulder. I needed to get my best friend up and out the door. She needed to go to the hospital. She needed immediate attention. Yeah, the hospital would know what to do. They can fix her up. Reds will be just fine. I just need to get my baby up.

I began to pull at Reds' body. She was dead weight. I laid my head on her chest and cried hysterically. I lifted my face and body up off of Reds' chest and my white shirt and cheek were now stained with Reds' deep red blood. Then I heard his voice and felt myself being lifted to my feet.

"Get up baby! Come on!" Jarvis said.

"Jarvis?!" I cried

He looked good and I could tell he was clean. I wanted to be clean too. I wanted a normal life. And for some reason, I wasn't angry with him for getting Reds pregnant. It didn't matter, after tonight, I was moving on with my life and he was no longer apart of it.

"Here put your pants back on." Jarvis said handing them to me.

"Put his ass right here!" Jarvis demanded pointing to the chair.

Tok snatched Dubbs up and threw him in the chair. Dubbs mouth was duct taped as well as his hands and his feet to the chair. I was so into Reds, that I hadn't realized what was happening behind me. Mumps and Kelly lay dead while Dubbs had been capture.

Tok waved his hand and he and two of the Replacement Killa's left out the room. Stone walked in carrying a bag. Dubb's eyes almost popped out of his head. He was so scared that he pissed on himself. Stone surveyed the room. When he saw Reds lying on the floor dead, he put his hand to his face and shook his head.

"Get someting to cover her up wit!" He turned to Jarvis and said.

Jarvis went to the back of the motel room and returned with the bedspread. He covered Reds up and I fell down on my knees and cried some more. Jarvis and Stone watched me in agony. Stone walked over to Dubbs taped to the chair.

"You took five tings of mine. My product, Reds, Kaneesha's virtue, my partnership with Jarvis and my gun." He picked up the gun. "Thanks, now I can dispose of this properly. It has

Luchi's body on it, compliments of me"

My mouth dropped. That's why he wanted the gun back. He killed Luchi with it!

So now dem will take from you!" Stone continued. He then looked at me and pointed to Dubbs.

"Kaneesha, I promised you, Dubbs!" Stone handed me a machete that he withdrew from the bag he was carrying. Then he took out an ice pick.

"Jarvis, remember the story I told you once about the ironing board?" Stone asked.

Jarvis nodded his head and went into the closet and snatched down the ironing board. He put it on the bed. Stone nodded his head to Jarvis and Jarvis cut the tape from around Dubb's feet. He then snatched Dubbs up out the chair and pushed him over to the ironing board.

Dubbs tried to resist but Jarvis rabbit punched Dubbs in the kidney causing his knees to buckle. Stone assisted Jarvis. They taped Dubbs up to the ironing board in a spread eagle fashion. The board was then titled on the bed for leverage. Dubbs tried to rock the board and was met with a blow to the head from the blackjack baton that Stone had at his side. Dubbs head rolled to the side.

"Put dees on." Stone said handing Jarvis and me gloves and plastic ponchos.

He put on gloves as well. He then reached back in his bag and took out a whole clove of garlic, stuck the ice pick through it and rubbed it up and down on the ice pick. Dubbs was sweating profusely and tears were running down his face. Muffled sounds could be heard coming from behind the duct tape. His eyes were the only thing that could communicate his fear.

"You are one sicko. You know that, Dubbs? You know what we do to bloodclots like you back home? We punish dem. I shoulda had you killed a long time ago! You are only alive this long because Kaneesha and poor Reds wanted me to save your pussyclot ass for 'dem. Now my Reds is dead! You made me beat Jarvis within an inch of his life because *you* stole my package and set him up. And then you raped Kaneesha!" Dubbs was frantically shaking his head no.

"Are you tellin' me that you didn't do those tings?" Stone asked.

Dubbs nodded his head yes and Jarvis punched Dubbs in the face.

"We don't have time to play wit' dis pussyclot!" Stone said.

He stepped in and in rapid succession, stabbed Dubbs all over with the ice pick covered in the juice from the garlic clove. When Stones was done, he stepped back.

"You didn't even feel that did you? The garlic numbs the wound upon entry. Internal bleeding will happen slowly. Your insides will fill with blood and then you will feel the pain. Your own blood will kill you!" Stone laughed.

"Kaneesha, take that machete and take from him what he used to hurt you wit!" Stone ordered.

I walked up to Dubbs and looked at the pathetic piece of shit crying in front of me. His eyes were pleading for mercy. I looked down on the floor and saw Kelly and Mumps and remembered what they had done to Reds. I looked over at my best friend lying under the cover dead. I reached down and and grabbed Dubbs' dick that remained out since before the shoot out. I brought the machete up into the air and in one swift motion like a slave cutting sugar cane; I brought it down onto him. I held Dubbs' dick in my hands and brought it up to his face for him to see it then I dropped it on the floor in front of him. Muffled screaming could be heard from behind the duct tape. I looked to Jarvis.

"Jarvis, come get you some!" Jarvis took the machete and cut off both of Dubb's hands.

"You won't touch no body else motherfucker!" Jarvis spat in Dubbs face.

Stone picked up the hands and put them on the floor in front of him with his severed dick.

"Let this serve as a reminder of what the fuck you did, for the minutes you have left! Come!" Stone said to us.

Jarvis and I walked out with Stone. The Replacement Killa's were sent back in to clean up the room. Tok was on a special detail. He wanted to see Dubbs die his slow death. He would stay in room and wait for death to come and take Dubbs. Then he would dispose of the body himself.

Six months later

"Hysear, put my mixed Dancehall CD in." I said backing up out of my father's driveway.

"Dang, mom, you listened to this already. I want to hear the new Sean Paul!" He challenged.

I chuckled as he switched CD's in the changer.

"Open the sun roof, mom and turn up the music." He continued. "You can't be ballin' in the Range and not have the sun roof open and the music kickin'."

"What do you know about ballin'?"

"You need to make sure you ballin' in school with them grades, boy!" I chastised.

"Aww, mom, my grades are excellent and you know that!"

I laughed.

"Yep, you are one smart cookie!" I said.

Hysear laughed as we floated down the street in the double Black Range Rover.

I ended up being one of the lucky ones. I survived the rapes; the lowest point in my life and most of all, crack. Life changed for everybody actually.

Stone took Jarvis under his wing and made him his lieutenant over a section of his territory. Jarvis was now pulling in the type of paper that he always wanted and more. He was making a name for himself in the drug game and with the protection and guidance of Stone, Jarvis was destined to take over Stone's throne one day.

But for me, I could be nothing more than a friend to Jarvis even though he wanted different. I couldn't forget his abandonment or him having sex with my best friend. Later, he told me about the night him and Reds had sex, which resulted in her pregnancy. And just like I thought, crack was the contributing factor. They got so high one night that sex, was the next level to go to. And in a weird sort of way, it made me feel better to know that afterwards, Reds vowed to never let it happen again. And it never did.

Me? Well, I discovered that some men do keep their promises. I pulled up in front of my house and got out. I carefully waddled to my door. Hysear took the key from me and opened it. He's such a gentleman.

"Surprise!" A house full of people yelled at me.

I gripped my belly as fear rushed through my body. Hysear was grinning all hard and it took me a minute to be joyous.

"Hey, Baby. Did we surprise you or what?" Manny asked.

"Hell yeah, ya'll must want me to have this baby right now!" I replied.

Manny and my son ushered me in the house to join my surprise baby shower. I stayed clean and like the man I knew he was, Manny kept his promise to help me. I'm not going to lie; I never saw Manny and me together for the long run. And now, I can't see us apart.

Manny and I were due to have a little girl in a few months and we decided to name her Reds. I guess there is such a thing as living happily ever after.

The End!

NO ONE ON THE SHELVES
HAS SWAGGER LIKE US
POISON
PITBULLS IN A SKIRT
EYONE Williams
PITBULLS IN A SKIRT 2
YEAR
T. STYLES
CARTEL PUBLICATIONS
WWW.THECARTELPUBLICATIONS.COM

CARTEL PUBLICATIONS TITLES